"You're enjoying this a little too much."

"Vivi, I enjoy you. All of you. Flaws and all."

"Well, I don't know if I like you noticing my flaws this early in our..." She frowned. "Is it a relationship already?"

"Well, since it was only two days ago that you've agreed to explore what's happening with us, I think it's a little too soon to define it like that."

"Oh."

She sounded disappointed, and it made his heart race just a little. "But I'm definitely interested in moving in that direction."

Vivi smiled and scooted closer to his side. "Is the working part of our dinner date over now?"

Brian looked into her deep brown eyes and nodded. "I'd say it is."

"Good." She leaned in as if to kiss him but then turned away and picked up the menu. "Because I'm starving."

He could see that a relationship with Vivi would keep him on his toes.

Dear Reader,

Have you ever had one of those years when nothing seemed to go right? It was just one thing after another, after another, after... Well, you get the idea. Or do you have a bad year every few years? For me, it's every six years or so it seems. I first noticed it back in 2014. That was the year I got divorced and then later diagnosed with cancer. I realized then that my dad had died six years before that in 2008. And there seemed to be a pattern of five good years followed by a year that wasn't, going back for most of my life. And we all know what happened in 2020. The good news is that those bad years taught me some valuable lessons and made me stronger.

In *When Love Comes Calling*, Vivian Carmack is convinced that she's been cursed by a year of bad luck every seven years. And this upcoming unlucky year, she's determined to keep her head down and not risk anything. Which, of course, is when she meets the perfect guy. She has to decide if she should risk her heart or play it safe.

I hope that your year is full of blessings.

Syndi

HEARTWARMING

When Love Comes Calling

Syndi Powell

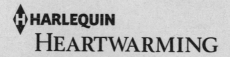

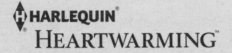

HARLEQUIN®
HEARTWARMING™

ISBN-13: 978-1-335-47543-5

Recycling programs for this product may not exist in your area.

When Love Comes Calling

Harlequin Enterprises ULC
22 Adelaide St. West, 41st Floor
Toronto, Ontario M5H 4E3, Canada
www.Harlequin.com

Printed in U.S.A.

Syndi Powell started writing stories when she was young and has made it a lifelong pursuit. She's been reading Harlequin romance novels since she was in her teens and is thrilled to be on the Harlequin team. She loves to connect with readers on Twitter, @syndipowell, or on her Facebook author page, Facebook.com/syndipowellauthor.

Books by Syndi Powell

Harlequin Heartwarming

Matchmaker at Work

A Merry Christmas Date
The Bad Boy's Redemption
A Hero for the Holidays
Soldier of Her Heart
Their Forever Home

Hope Center Stories

Finding Her Family
Healing Hearts
Afraid to Lose Her

Visit the Author Profile page
at Harlequin.com for more titles.

I dedicate this book in memory of
Russell D'Hondt, my stepfather and
brainstorming buddy. I always enjoyed sitting
around the dinner table and discussing the
plot of my latest book with him. He saw ideas
and solutions in ways that I never could. This is
the first book I've written without being able to
bounce ideas off of him, and it's not the same.
You are sorely missed and always loved.

Rest in peace.

CHAPTER ONE

THE LAST THING Vivian Carmack wanted to do was to celebrate the beginning of the coming year. And yet, here she was, attending a New Year's Eve party, squeezed into a borrowed taffeta gown, hair arranged in an updo, feet pinched into high heels and waiting in a long line to order a drink from the bustling bartenders.

Revelers in a much better mood than hers filled the Thora community center, dancing to the deejay's music blasting from the large speakers at the front of the room. Others congregated around the appetizer table or, like her, stood in line for the bar.

Vivi glanced around at the partygoers and asked herself for the hundredth time why she had agreed to accompany her best friend, Cecily, to a party when she would rather spend the evening in bed with the covers over her head. But one glimpse of the smile on her friend's face confirmed it. If anyone needed a night out, it was Cec. Her friend had reason to be home in bed with the covers pulled over her head, but she'd chosen to be out for a night of fun. She'd even loaned Vivi the ruby-red dress and shoes since the invitation to accompany her to the party had come at such short notice.

Vivi leaned in close to Cec to be heard over the pulsating music. "This is definitely different from my original plan of sitting home and eating ice cream by myself while I watched the ball drop in Times Square. Thank you for inviting me."

"I was hardly going to bring Tom, was I?"

Cecily's husband had announced he wanted a divorce from the greatest woman in the world only the day after Christmas. Claimed that he had fallen out of love with Vivi's best friend. Cec sighed. "Besides, I thought we agreed we wouldn't talk about the jerk tonight."

"We won't. Last time. Promise?"

Cec nudged her elbow into Vivi's side. "And you might try smiling more. We're supposed to be having fun."

"I don't feel much like partying tonight, but I'm trying."

"Forget the curse."

Vivi held up one finger. "If we're not talking about the jerk, we're definitely not discussing the curse."

They made it to the front of the line and Cec ordered several shots of tequila. Vivi raised her voice so her friend could hear her. "I'm driving tonight. I don't want any tequila."

"Who said any of them were for you?" Cec winked at the bartender as she placed a bill on the counter for the drinks. "I ordered you a glass of pop."

Vivi accepted the drink, then led her friend to a near empty table at the edge of the room away from the dancers. Cec placed the tray of drinks down and grabbed two of the shot glasses. She drank them both and picked up another. Vivi stayed her arm. "Don't you think you should slow down? We have a little more than an hour left until midnight."

Cecily frowned and shook off Vivi's hand. "I'm fine. Besides, you already said you're the one driving. Not me." She picked up the shot and drank it quickly, making a face before sucking on a lime wedge.

Vivi handed Cec her own drink. "Here. You should switch to something softer."

"Spoilsport. Just because you want to avoid the coming year doesn't mean we all do."

"I'm not the only one avoiding something, Cec."

Cecily took a sip of the pop before placing the sweating glass on the table. "One thing we aren't going to avoid tonight is the music. Let's go."

Vivi glanced at the crowded dance floor and shook her head. "I'm not in the mood."

"Liar. Besides teaching, dancing is your favorite thing in the whole world." Cecily held out a hand to her. "Come on. Let's show these people how it's done."

Vivi sighed but followed her friend. The deejay put on a fast song that had been popular when she and Cec were in college. Cecily raised her hands in the air and shouted into Vivi's ear, "I love this song!"

Vivi smiled and gave herself over to the melody, closing her eyes and letting her body follow the fast rhythm of the drums. She twirled around, lifting her arms into the air only to be stopped by another body bumping into hers. She started to fall, but strong hands grasped her by the bare shoulders and kept her upright. She opened her eyes to find herself staring into a stranger's gaze. "Sorry. It's a bit congested out here on the dance floor."

As if to emphasize her point, someone crashed into her and sent her body directly into the stranger's arms once again. His hands clutched at her waist and brought her upright. She leaned in to shout over the music, "Sorry, again."

His hazel eyes crinkled in the corners as he smiled. "I'm not sorry." His hands linked around her waist, and he danced with her for a moment. "You've got some good moves."

"But you don't like to follow my lead, do you?" she asked as she danced to the right when he twisted in the opposite direction.

"I'm not known for following directions very well. Probably why I always lost playing Simon Says or Red Light, Green Light."

Vivi felt herself grin at his words. "So, you're not into playing any childish games?"

"Not if winning means following any direction but my own." He smiled back at her, and she could feel her lips mirror his expression. He stepped closer. "My name is Brian. What's yours?"

"Vivian."

"That's an unusual name."

"I'm an unusual woman." She pointed behind her and turned her head to find Cec watching them with interest. "I should get back to my friend."

His face fell. "Don't tell me that you have a boyfriend."

Vivi chuckled at the sound of disappointment in his voice but didn't answer his question. Better to leave things on a mysterious note. "Maybe I'll bump into you later."

She gave a quick wave and moved through the crush of bodies to where Cecily had drifted. Her friend looked over Vivi's shoulder into the crowd. "Who's that guy you were dancing with?"

"His name is Brian. He knocked into me."

"He's cute."

Vivi turned to find him still standing and watching her while other dancers moved around him. She turned back to Cecily who seemed to be waiting for her reaction. She shrugged in response. He was cute in a guy-next-door kind of way, but he wasn't her type. Not even close. "Maybe he is."

The song ended, and a slower one began. She and Cec left the dance floor and returned to the table where they'd left their drinks. Cecily toyed with one of the empty shot glasses, then glanced around the crowd as she took a seat. "There seems to be more people here than last year, don't you think?"

"They didn't have the party last year because of everything going on, remember? But maybe that's why there's more people here this year. Everyone missed it and wanted to be a part of it coming back."

"You're probably right."

"I usually am."

Cec didn't return her grin but narrowed her eyes at her. "However, you're not right about this curse thing. When are you going to face it?"

"I thought we agreed. No talking about the jerk or the curse tonight." Vivi looked around the room. "We're here to have fun. Not talk about things that are better left unsaid."

"You can't let this thing keep you from living the next year of your life, Vivi."

Vivi huffed and rested her chin on her hand.

"You don't get it, Cec. I have always had a really bad year every seven years. That's this year. So, my plan is to keep my head down and survive whatever it is that life is about to throw at me. No risks. No changes. I'm all about keeping the status quo. And maybe, I'll get through it unscathed."

"Doesn't sound like a very good year to me."

"You were there for the last two times I had a cursed year, so you know I'm right." She shook her head and tried to shrug off the worries about what the coming twelve months could bring. "I can't go through that again. I won't."

"All I'm saying is that you might miss out on some of the good stuff because you're so worried about the bad that *might* happen." Cec looked around the room. "Like that cute guy who can't seem to take his eyes off of you."

Vivian turned to find Brian watching them from the other side of the room. He grinned and gave a small wave. She couldn't help but smile and wave back. Then she turned to Cecily and gave a shrug. "I'm not willing to risk it, not for him or anything else."

BRIAN REDMOND STUDIED the room, noting the number of attendees as well as the steady flow of beverages served from the bar and trays of hors d'oeuvres carted from the kitchen to the buffet table by an army of servers. A successful party, he'd say. And one that had been long overdue after last year's cancellation.

His younger sister, Jamie, walked toward him, snagging an antipasto skewer from a tray and nibbling on it as she approached. "You have to get me the recipe for that shrimp dip they're serving."

"What makes you think I have access to that?"

Jamie gave him a look that he knew well, one that meant he had better comply with her request or she'd nag him until he did. "You're the one who set up this party, so get me the recipe."

"Maybe the caterer doesn't share her recipes."

"Then use your supposed charm on her and get it anyway." Jamie nibbled some more, then narrowed her eyes at him. "Who do you keep looking at?"

Brian glanced away from Vivian's table. "What? Who? Where?"

"Maybe the better question is why do you keep looking at her?" Jamie followed the direction of his gaze. "She's pretty. Who is she?"

Vivian was more than pretty. From her glowing amber skin to the high cheekbones to the sweet mouth that seemed to smile back at him whenever he smiled at her, she was the entire package. "I don't really know. We literally bumped into each other on the dance floor." He found his eyes once again looking for Vivian. Meeting her had been an unexpected bonus tonight. Perhaps this was his reward for reviving the town's New Year's Eve party. "All I know is that her name is Vivian, and she looks smashing in red."

Jamie gave a short nod. "Give me a half hour, and I can find out the scoop about her."

She started to walk away, but Brian reached out to stop her. "I don't want you snooping around. You might scare her off. Make me out to be a stalker or something."

"It'll be fine. I can be discreet." He looked at her until she winced. "It won't be like the last time. She won't even realize I'm grilling her. Promise."

"Leave her alone, and keep the cop stuff for your job. I'll do my own investigating."

"Which means you won't take a risk and ask her out."

He waved off her objection. "That's the old me. We're on the edge of a new year. This is my chance to be brave. Bold. To go after what I want and take some chances."

"You have until the end of the night to get her number."

"And if I don't?"

She gave him a smile that made his insides tremble. "Then it's my turn."

THE MORE ALCOHOL Cecily drank, the more quiet and sullen she became. Trying to head off a dip into misery, Vivi went to the appetizers to get her friend a plate of nibbles. Maybe eating something would absorb the excess alcohol and revive her friend's earlier good mood. She placed a spoonful of shrimp dip on her plate when a voice said, "My sister claims that dip will solve all your worries."

She raised her eyes to meet hazel ones. "You, again."

"It's Brian. Remember?" He took one of the plates from her. "Looks like you could use a little help."

"Thanks."

They moved down the buffet, and she placed various foods on both plates. He murmured his assent when she added a few meatballs to the plates, then asked, "So what is it that you do, Unusual Vivian?"

She frowned at his words but then recalled her earlier comment from the dance floor. "I'm just an ordinary teacher."

"What do you teach?"

"American history at the high school."

Brian grimaced as she placed a couple puff pastries on the plate he held. "I can't say that was my best subject. Or favorite one, for that matter." He pointed to the antipasto skewers. "Try a couple of those."

She placed a few on each plate. "You never had me as a teacher, then. I try to make history come alive for my students."

"And how do you do that?"

"Role playing. Reading diaries and letters from the time period. Putting them into the mindset of the historical figure." Now she sounded like a braggart. And for what purpose? She'd told Cecily she wasn't going to do anything new this year, and that included getting to know this guy. Or trying to impress him. "Maybe I'm exaggerating my prowess as a teacher."

He looked at her. "Somehow, I don't think you are. I can tell that you're passionate about what you do, and that already makes you a great teacher."

She stared at him for a moment, then cleared her throat. It would be so easy to indulge her curiosity. Which is probably why she asked him, "What is it that you do, Brian? What are you passionate about?"

"I'm the community resource manager for the town. I have a passion for bringing together citizens and businesses for mutual benefit. Whether it's finding jobs or getting help to those who need it or holding events like this one." He glanced around the ballroom. "Bringing back a much beloved party for Thora. Hiring the right people and putting them together to help others."

"We have a resource manager? I didn't think our community was big enough."

"Our mayor created the position this past year and hired me to fill it." He dropped a few veggies on each plate. "Don't tell anyone, but I haven't been in town that long, so I'm still trying to figure out my role in it."

"I had a feeling that you weren't from around here. Where did you grow up?"

He gave a shrug. "Here and there. I was a military brat, so we moved a lot. Even around the world."

She sighed. "Except for the few years I went away to school, I've lived here my whole life. I grew up about ten miles away."

"You never wanted to leave?"

This time she was the one to lift her shoulders up and down. "I never considered it. You planning on staying around here for a while?"

He inched closer. "It's looking more attractive to me by the minute."

He was standing so close she could smell his cologne. A clean scent that made her tingle. She moved away. Distance would be better between them because then she couldn't do what she was considering. Wouldn't even entertain the possibility of what her heart proposed. She needed to maintain her status quo, which meant not getting interested in this guy. She needed to construct a wall around her heart to prevent any chance of him wiggling his way inside. Because she knew what would happen if he did. The trouble. The heartbreak. The tears and pain.

"I'd love to get to know you more. Maybe over dinner next week?"

Her heart did a little dance at the invitation, but her brain must have short-circuited because she couldn't find the right words to refuse him. Couldn't form the word "no" with her lips. Instead, she kept staring at him. Gave all of thirty seconds to contemplate what it would be like to accept his request. How easy would it be to see if this chemistry that sizzled between them could lead to something?

Then reason returned and she shook her head. "I don't think that's a good idea."

"Right. You'll probably be busy getting back into a routine with school starting up. Maybe the week after?"

"No." She took the other plate of food from his hands. "But thank you for your assistance at the buffet."

She started to walk away, but he pursued her. "How about your phone number, then? For when you change your mind?"

She stopped and turned. It would be so easy to give in. To take a chance. He was only asking her out for dinner, after all. One night couldn't hurt, could it? But she shook her head again. "You're tempting, but trust me. I won't."

Then she left him and didn't look back but continued to the table where Cecily sat. Her friend looked up at her as she approached. "Do you mind if we go home now?"

"Why don't you eat a little something first?"

Cec rose to her feet and pushed the plate of appetizers away from her. "I'm not hungry."

"But it's almost midnight. Don't you want to stay for the countdown to the new year?"

"I don't care what time it is. I just want to go home." She paused for a moment before her shoulders slumped forward. "Well, to your place since I can't go home, can I?"

Cec's previous ebullient mood had obviously fled, so Vivi nodded and rubbed her arm. "I'll get our coats."

It started to snow as they left the community center and walked toward Vivi's Jeep. The muffled sounds of the party crowd counting down to midnight drifted in the air as Vivi helped her friend get into the passenger seat before coming around the car and opening her own door. She slid into the driver's seat and glanced over at Cec. "Are you going to be okay?"

Cec shook her head through the tears that coursed down her cheeks. "None of this is okay."

"It will get better eventually. Things can only go up from here, right?" Vivi started the car before putting the gear in Reverse. She checked behind her before backing out of the parking spot. The accelerator pedal seemed to stick, and the reverse was faster than she intended. She stomped on the brake to stop their progress and winced as the crunch of backing into the car behind her echoed.

Happy New Year, indeed.

She got out of the Jeep and went to the dark SUV. Didn't seem to be major damage to the other car, but a glance at the rear end of hers made her grimace. Her brake light had been smashed, and the left side of the bumper crumpled. This was going to be an expensive mistake.

She checked the passenger side of the car to make sure Cecily was okay, then returned to the hall to find out whose SUV she had backed into. Of course, the first person she ran into once she entered the community center had to be Brian.

"Trouble?"

"I don't suppose you know the owner of a dark SUV with the license plate HWK122, do you?"

He frowned and headed to the door. Great. Of all the cars she could have backed into, it had to be Brian's. Proof that the curse was already at work in the new year. She followed him outside to find him checking out the damage where the two cars had made contact. "Lucky for me there is minimal damage to my car." He gave a low whistle. "Sorry about yours though."

"Of all the cars in this parking lot, why did I have to hit your SUV?"

"Maybe it was fate. Looks like you'll be giving me your phone number after all."

CHAPTER TWO

BRIAN ENJOYED SEEING the shock on Vivian's face. Maybe this year was going to turn out to be interesting after all. He held out his cell phone to her. "Why don't you plug in your phone number while I retrieve my insurance information from my car?"

Vivian sputtered but accepted the phone. She didn't look at him as she entered the phone number. "This is only because of the dumb accident."

He put a hand up to his chest. "Ouch. That kinda hurt."

"I'm not looking for a date right now." She handed the phone back to him. "No offense."

Maybe he'd misinterpreted her interest in him. He'd flirted with her, and she had thrown it back as good as he gave. Could he hope for a shot to change her mind? "I assure you that I won't use your phone number except for insurance purposes."

They exchanged insurance information,

and he opened the door of her car and peered inside. Held up his hand to wave at her passenger. "Are you okay?"

The woman nodded glumly before blowing her nose. "Thank you. We're fine."

Brian nodded, then held out his hand to Vivian to help her inside. His hand tingled where her palm met his, further proof that something good was happening. "I know that this doesn't seem to be a great start for the new year, but you never know. Good things could come out of this."

Vivian gave him a quick nod, then closed the door. Their interaction had been short and not entirely sweet, but it was enough to convince Brian that he'd just met a woman he'd like to know more. A lot more.

Once he returned to the community center, he found his sister on the dance floor. He waved her over once the song ended. "You're off the hook. I got her number." He waved his cell phone in the air.

Jamie raised her eyebrows at his announcement. "I'm impressed. I figured you'd let her slip through your fingers."

"Oh, I did, but then she backed into my car."

His sister laughed and shook her head. "Only happens to you."

"You know, maybe this is the sign I've been waiting for."

"To get a new car?"

"To get a new life." The holidays had left him feeling as if he'd been going through the motions the past year. Staying uninvolved. Untouchable. And completely bored. "I can't keep doing what I've been doing."

"The problem is you're not doing anything. You work even on the weekends when you don't have to."

"Exactly. I get out of bed. Go to work. Come home and have dinner. Go to bed and repeat the same thing the next day."

"You're existing. Not living."

He snapped his fingers. "So maybe this is my year to do something big. To risk it all for a great payoff. To finally put roots down here and find a life that has lasting power."

"Like this woman?"

Brian thought of Vivian and shrugged. "Meeting her is just the push I needed to show me that I can't keep going like I was. I want more. This can't be all there is, right?"

"You're a little young to be having a midlife

crisis." She put her arm around his shoulders. "You're having one of those new year, new me moments. I hope it lasts longer than tonight. You deserve to have a bigger life."

Brian nodded. "It's more than that. Can't you see? I need something more than what I have."

"And what is it that you want?"

He glanced around the room. "I've got to make the rounds before we wind things up here. Give me a half hour and then we can leave, yeah?"

STILL IN HER PAJAMAS, Vivi rested her head against the back of her sofa, a cooling mug of coffee in her hand as she stared at the blank television hanging on her wall. She hadn't turned it on so she wouldn't disturb Cecily sleeping in the guest room next door. Better to let her rest. Who knows what this new year would bring her friend?

That brought her own troubles to mind. The new year had started less than ten hours ago, and she had already had her first catastrophe. What more would the next three hundred and sixty-four days bring? She grimaced. In fact, since this was a leap year, she'd get to enjoy the pleasure of an extra day of pain.

"What time is it?"

Vivi turned to find her friend standing by the sofa and rubbing her forehead. "Need some aspirin?" Vivi asked.

"Yes, after a big cup of coffee." She winced. "Or three."

Vivi rose from the couch and walked to the attached kitchen to pour her friend a cup as well as freshen her own. She handed the mug to Cecily who had followed her to the counter. "How did you sleep?"

"Did I sleep? It seems like all I did was toss and turn." Cecily added sugar to her mug, then stirred it. "Tom called my cell and left a voicemail just after midnight."

Great. Just how her friend didn't need to start her year. "What did the jerk say?"

Cec shrugged. "I haven't listened to the message yet. Not sure I want to." She blew on the mug and lowered it. "Does that make me a coward?"

"No, that makes you a human being." Vivi put a hand on her shoulder. "Is there anything I can do to help you?"

Cec muttered, "No," and took her coffee

to the table to sit down. She placed the mug in front of her, then reached out to touch the edge of the lace runner that ran the length of the table. "I hate to ask this, but do you mind if I stay a few more days with you?"

Vivi joined her at the table. "Take all the time you need. A few more weeks if you have to. In fact, you are more than welcome to move in with me permanently if that will help."

"My mom says I shouldn't have left the house because that gives Tom leverage to keep it in the divorce. That I should have forced him to be the one to move out."

"I think she might be right on this one, Cec. You should have made him be the one to leave."

"What you don't understand is that I didn't want to be where there would be so many reminders of Tom. It would be like living in a house full of his broken promises. And since he owned it before we got married, I doubt I'd get it anyways." She rested her chin on her fist. "I keep trying to replay the last few years to figure out where I went wrong."

"This is not on you. This is all Tom."

"I just wish I understood where his change

of heart was coming from. How could he just fall out of love?" Cec sighed and rose to her feet. "I think I need a shower. Maybe wash all these negative feelings down the drain so I can restart January on a happier note." She started to walk away but turned back to face Vivi. "Thank you for being a good friend."

"Whatever I can do, just ask."

Vivi watched her friend leave the kitchen. Enough of this. Maybe Cec was right. She'd take a shower later to wash all these negative thoughts down the drain. She needed to start the new year with a new attitude.

LATER, VIVI HANDED Cec a glass of wine, then poured herself one. She glanced around the kitchen of her friend Mel, who owned the bookstore in downtown Thora. When her friend had called with an invite for her and Cec to attend a game night, Vivi figured it would be a good way to distract Cec and get to spend time with some more adults before she returned to teaching her students.

Mel's best friend, Shelby, entered the kitchen and placed a platter of mini burritos on the counter. "You've got to try these. My sister is a genius with food."

Vivi took one and bit it, then glanced at Cec who nodded. "These are *really* good."

Shelby grinned. "Told ya." She snagged a few and left to return to the living room.

Cec leaned in to grab more of the delectable treats, then followed Shelby. Vivi did the same.

In the living room, a large table with twelve chairs around it had been set up, the other furniture pushed to the borders of the room. A stack of board games sat on top of the mantel of the fireplace. The doorbell rang, and Mel's husband, Jack, left to answer it. He soon ushered in a familiar face. Brian's eyes seemed to focus on Vivian's before he turned to Jack and handed him his jacket. He crossed the room and approached her. "Well, hi there, Vivian."

She gave a nod. "I didn't realize you knew Mel and Jack."

"Actually, it was Josh who invited me. He thought I could use an evening out after all my work on the party last night."

"It was fabulous. You did a great job."

He gave a short nod. "Thank you. It was worth all the stress of planning, then."

"So what will your next party be?"

"Not a party, but several projects around the city. I'm looking to get one of the parks converted to barrier-free and more inclusive."

Vivian smiled. "We could use a park like that."

"My thoughts exactly."

"Did you come alone tonight?"

She shook her head. "I brought my friend Cec who you met last night."

"Right. I did. She was the passenger in your car." He cocked his head to one side. "Are you guys okay? No residual effects from the fender bender?"

"We're fine. You?"

"Good."

She looked at him, then glanced over her shoulder. "I should get back to Cec."

"It's good to see you, Vivian."

She nodded and left him. When she reached Cecily's side, her friend whistled. "He hasn't taken his eyes off of you since he entered the room."

Vivian looked back to find that he was watching her, a smile playing around his lips. "What do you think that was about?"

"I think he likes you." Cec took a sip of her wine. "And I think he'd like to get to know you better, if you'd give him a chance."

"I really wish I had met him at a different time. I think it would be fun getting to know him better, too."

Cec raised a brow. "I wouldn't count him out just yet. There's nothing wrong with spending time with him."

Vivi was about to protest when Shelby whistled loudly, catching everyone's attention. "Now that everybody's here, we can get started. Make sure you have some food and something to drink because once the games start, it's going to be nonstop fun."

Vivi noted that Cec was smirking. "Sounds like she's as competitive as you."

"That's not a bad thing."

"Says Miss Take No Prisoners. Remind me again why we didn't have any reindeer games at the teachers' Christmas party this year?"

"That was hardly my fault. If Neil can't handle losing at charades, I can't be blamed for that."

"True. But I bet it was *how* our team won that he was more upset about. How many people would know all those Swedish film titles? I mean, besides you." Cec grinned at Vivi. "Do you mind getting our seats? I'm going to grab more appetizers before the first game starts."

She raced off, and Vivi claimed two spots at the table. Brian approached and eyed the empty chair on the other side of her. "Is this one free?"

She smiled. "It's all yours."

Brian returned the smile. "Good. I was hoping to snag a spot close to you."

As he sat down, she could smell the scent of his aftershave. Pine, maybe. A little citrus? Whatever the particular notes, it was fresh and clean, and memorable. Yet, she tried to ignore the tingles it gave her.

Cec sat down, her plate towering with appetizers. "I figured we could share."

"Good idea," Vivi replied.

After the first board game of Chutes and Ladders, Cec and Vivi had taken a slight lead in the points. Vivi gave her partner a high five. "That's what I'm talking about."

"We'll take a ten-minute breather before the next game begins. And to change things up a bit, we'll be switching partners," Shelby announced. "Also, I should warn you. I'm an expert at removing the pieces without triggering the buzzer in Operation, so you might want to choose me for the next game."

Brian leaned over to Vivi. "Congratulations on winning the first round. I have to admit that I haven't played that game since I was in elementary school. Who knew a slide would ruin my game?"

"That's the point of it. You're either rising up fast or make a misstep and find yourself sliding to the bottom."

"Sounds like you're commenting about more than just the game."

"Aren't board games a microcosm of the real world? You win some. You lose some. It happens."

"What would you think about being my partner for the next game, then?"

She paused. Playing one game with him wouldn't hurt anything, she supposed. "You're on."

"I've got steady hands, so I could take the lead on this next game, if that's all right with you?"

Vivi nodded in agreement, knowing they could use that competitive edge. "Deal."

Brian watched Vivi as she pulled a card from the top of the stack, then crowed as it brought her team's piece to the end of the game board straight to the gingerbread house. "That makes four wins for me tonight."

Though he sat across the table from her, he exchanged big beaming smiles with Vivi. He liked observing her as she played the different games that evening. Very competitive, she wouldn't let anything, or anyone, distract her from victory. For some reason, that made him want to see her win even more.

Shelby stood with her clipboard, looking authoritative. "With that last win, it means Vivian has won game night." She took a trophy and a couple of small, wrapped gifts from the mantel and handed them to the victorious Vivi. "And just so no one goes home empty-handed…" She passed out wrapped gifts to everyone around the table.

With the prizes distributed, the party seemed to be winding down. Brian caught up with Vivi. "How about I take the winner out for a drink after this?" he suggested.

Vivi raised a brow. "You're asking me out?"

He tapped at his watch. "It's still early."

"I'd love to," she blurted. But then she pursed her lips and shook her head. "I mean, uh, no. I don't think so."

He noted she seemed to be debating her final answer. "It doesn't have to be a drink. We could have coffee instead, if you prefer."

Her mouth opened then closed several times. Then she sighed. "Thank you for the invitation, but no. I can't."

"We could go another night if you'd prefer?"

Vivi looked at him, and he could sense a war going on inside of her. *Say yes*, he thought. *Please, say yes.*

Finally, she said in a soft, low voice, "This is a really bad time for me. If it was any other year."

He frowned at her words. "I don't understand. What do you mean?"

"I…"

Cec walked up behind Vivi and handed her her coat. "Hey, Simon needs to leave, but your car is blocking him in. Do you mind moving it?"

Vivi paused, her gaze still on Brian for a moment before she faced Cec and nodded. "Sure thing."

After she left, Brian felt as if he'd missed out on what might have been a special moment with Vivi.

THE DIN OF her students' conversations reached her ears before Vivian walked into the classroom. She grasped her thermal cup tighter and went to the front of the room, then placed it and her canvas messenger bag on top of the desk.

One of her students, Michael, called out to her. "Hey, Miss Carmack, did you watch that last episode? Was it killer or what?"

Vivian smiled at his words. "I certainly didn't see that twist coming when I first read the book."

"And now we have to wait a whole year to find out what happened to the captain." Michael groaned and took a seat. "And don't tell me to read the books. I don't like it being spoiled before the series airs."

"Even if the books are better than the show?"

Michael looked at her as if she'd told him the sky was green. "There's no way that's possible, bruh. My imagination can't compare to the show."

"You'd be surprised. Your mind can create all sorts of details you'd never thought possible."

The first bell rang, and the rest of her students claimed their seats. She took a deep breath and looked over her audience. "I don't need to tell you what the new semester means, especially if you're friends with one of my previous seniors. It's time for the annual History Snapshot assignment. You'll choose a famous day and research to find out every detail possible." She took the instruction packets from her bag and counted out seven before handing them to the student in the first row to take one and pass the others back, then she repeated the process four more times. "I want you to dive deep into a single historical event from the 1940s to the present, like Pearl Harbor or the moon landing."

A hand shot up in the back of the classroom. "Will there be extra credit?"

"Yes, Ethan, there will." She took her own packet and opened to the second page. "With your research, I want you to discover the major players, the timeline and the impact of that one event. You'll get to know the library very well, but I encourage you to check on-line sources as well. Just be sure to verify those sources."

She surveyed the sea of faces and tried to tamp down her disappointment. They looked bored rather than excited by the prospect of deep diving into history. "You'll need to start by writing a one-page proposal stating what historical event you will be exploring. This assignment is a major part of your over-all grade, so I hope you will take this project to heart. Any questions?"

Seeing no hands raised, she retrieved the textbook they were using. "Let's review what we were studying before the Christmas break. Who can tell me what was the effect of western expansion of the United States on Congress?"

Later in the teachers' break room, Vivi complained to Cec about her class. "I swear that senioritis begins sooner every year. Those kids act like they are only tolerating my lessons instead of being engaged."

Cec looked up from the pop quizzes she'd been grading. "Were you any different at seventeen? Or were you already counting down the days left of high school and planning what your first year at college would be like?"

Vivi contemplated the cucumber at the end of her fork. "I guess you're right. But I'd hoped that my honors students would be interested in the snapshot project. Last year's class didn't act like this."

"That was a group of exceptional kids."

"Nothing says that this year's class couldn't be, too." She sighed and placed her fork on the table. "Maybe I'm the one who needs to be different this year. Scrap what I usually do and find something else that will capture their attention."

"Unless you're going to start acting out historic moments and posting them on a social media app, good luck with that." Cec made more marks on the quizzes but then stopped to look up at Vivi. "Uh-oh. You've got that look in your eye."

Vivi raised an eyebrow. "Look? What look?"

"The one that says you're going to throw out your lesson plans and do something completely off the wall."

"Now is not the time for that. Status quo, remember? But I'll admit it's tempting. I want my students to be engaged with the world. Not watching life happen to other people on their cell phones." She used a napkin to wipe her hands. "No, it's better if I stick with what I know. My seniors will find their groove. They always do."

But she couldn't ignore the germ of an idea that had been planted.

BRIAN PUSHED THE stack of papers he'd been meaning to file to the other corner of his desk. He'd get to them eventually. Filing rarely made it to the top of his to-do list, but based on the growing stack of documents, it might be sooner than expected. Hopefully, his assistant, Mallory, could help him with it later.

The door to his office opened, and the mayor, Josh Riley, strode in and took a seat in front of his desk. "Ready for some lunch?"

Brian glanced at the clutter surrounding him. "Remind me again why I agreed to leave my private practice and become your paper pusher."

"Because you needed something to excite you again."

"Ah." Brian waggled his finger. "Yes, I

believe you convinced me that I craved the excitement of public service. Any idea when that is supposed to start?"

"You should be feeling at least a little bit excited. The New Year's Eve party turned out to be a major success."

"That was a group effort. And thank you again for recommending Laurel's catering services. Guests couldn't say enough good things about her food. Although I think we will change to a band rather than a deejay for next year."

Josh nodded, then leaned back in the chair. "Already planning the next one? I like that."

"Unless you find a replacement party planner."

"Why should I? You excel at bringing the right people together to create a successful event."

Brian mirrored Josh's move and sat back in his chair. "Call me suspicious but I get the feeling that you didn't come here just to take me to lunch and compliment my planning skills."

Josh gave a short nod. "You're right. There's something else I want to discuss, but I'm starving. Let's talk about it over a couple of burgers."

A few minutes later, the owner of the nearby diner greeted Josh as they entered the busy place. "Your usual table, Mr. Mayor?"

"Thanks, Danny."

They followed the owner through a maze of tables to a back corner booth. Dan put menus on the table, but Josh handed them back to him. "We're not going to need them today. Cheeseburgers and fries for the both of us."

Danny nodded and left to put their order in. Josh stared across the table at Brian, then put his arms across the back of the seat. "I have another project that I'd like you to head up."

"Just get right down to it, huh?"

"We're both direct, so I don't see a reason to pussyfoot around. Do you?"

Brian looked up as Danny brought two glasses of water to their table. He took a sip of his before turning his attention to the mayor. "What kind of project?"

Josh leaned forward over the table. "Local history printed in a booklet ready in time to coincide with our library's fundraising event in July."

"You've already got the text, then?"

"Not yet, but if you agree to this idea today, you could have submissions in a couple of weeks, and the booklet ready to sell in time for the fundraiser."

Brian shook his head. "I think a local history project is a great idea, but you're cutting it too close. We should have had these items written and edited by now. Shortages and supply chain issues being what they are, we need about eight months to get a booklet published and available by July."

"Well, you'll have less time than that. Can you do it?"

Brian fiddled with the silverware on top of the napkin in front of him. "You're asking for the impossible. And you know it."

"What I know is that I was approached by an upstanding citizen who had a great idea of recording the stories of the older generation before they were lost." Josh looked sad for a moment. "My wife's great aunt has been sick, and Shelby is afraid that she won't survive it this time. All her stories could be gone in a moment if we don't re-cord them now."

"So, this is Shelby's idea."

"Actually, it came from an American his-tory teacher at the high school. You remem-ber Vivian Carmack from game night, right?"

"Vivian came up with this?" If she was involved in the project, they'd have to meet. Have to talk, and maybe he'd have a shot to win her over. Brian tried to hide his excite-ment. "Fine. We'll work on this together. But we'll have to move that deadline up in order to get the project ready for publica-tion in time."

"Fine. Whatever you say... Romeo."

BRIAN WASN'T SURPRISED to find Vivian star-ing at him later that afternoon. She was currently standing in his office doorway, looking a little peeved. He gave her his best smile. "Vivian, it's a pleasure to see you again."

"Yeah, uh, yes. Right. It's nice to see you, as well. So, I've heard through the grapevine that you want to work with me and my stu-dents on our history project. How come?"

Brian stood and motioned to the chair in

front of his desk. "Why don't you take a seat, and we can discuss the logistics of your proposal? It's really great. Perfect for the community. You spoke to the mayor about it and he spoke to me. I can explain."

Vivian entered the room. She strode to the chair and stood behind it, her hands resting on the back. "Please continue."

"There's more to this project than your students collecting stories. As you envisioned, this project has the possibility to grow in scope, and the resources my office has to offer would be invaluable to you." He went to the coffee bar and held up a mug. "Can I get you something to drink? I've got coffee, tea, hot chocolate."

"I'm fine, thank you. But I'm still confused. Why do *you* want to be involved? Don't you have an assistant or two who'd be willing?"

"I'm happy to do it. I like digging in, getting my hands dirty, so to speak." He held up his hands to show her and wiggled his fingers. "These blustery January afternoons make me long for something warm to drink. Are you sure I can't get you something?"

"I'm good."

Brian gave a quick nod and put a hot chocolate pod into the machine, then pressed the button to start. He sat on the edge of the credenza while he waited for his drink, his ankles crossed as well as his arms. "It's an inspired idea, by the way. Bringing history alive for your students while also preserving the times with recollections of older residents for later generations to come."

The machine sputtered to an end, so he retrieved his full mug and returned to his desk, taking a seat behind it. "And I'm looking forward to working with you."

Vivian took a deep breath. "Brian, I know that you think you can help with this project, but we're fine, I'm fine, doing this on my own."

"Then why did you go to the mayor with your proposal?"

She opened her mouth, then frowned. He watched her struggling to find the right answer. "My office can not only arrange and organize the access you'll need to more of the town's oldest citizens for their stories, but we'll put up the initial funds to see the booklet is published in time for the library fundraiser in July." He leaned across the desk toward her. "This is your project, Vivi, a hundred percent. But I know I can contribute in a good way."

She muttered something under her breath. Brian couldn't quite hear the words but thought maybe she'd said something about seven. *Seven o'clock? Seven chapters?*

Vivian finally took a seat and slipped off her coat. Her expression a little worried. "I could use a hot tea. With honey, if you have it."

Brian hoped his smile was reassuring. "Of course."

VIVI RUBBED HER right temple where the headache had formed when Mayor Josh had called her to tell her the proposal had been approved and that Brian would be involved. She had to admit that the thought of spending time with Brian fascinated her. He enticed her simply by existing. What would he do to her if they worked side by side for the next six months? She rubbed her forehead harder. It was why she'd hightailed it over to his office right away, thinking she could dissuade him.

But he'd made such good points. How

could she say no to his involvement when her students and the library were now count-ing on the best booklet possible?

Admittedly, Vivi knew she could easily slip into a friendship with the man, and then it could develop into something more. She had to figure out how she was going to fight her attraction to him because this couldn't happen. Not this year.

"Your tea?"

Vivi opened her eyes and took the offered mug from him. "Since I had the idea for this project, it has gotten more involved than I planned. The mayor was talking about print-ing and fundraising, and my head is swim-ming because I don't know anything about any of that."

"But I do. That's why this should work out. You'll handle the students and the story collection. I'll handle the logistics for the publication." He took his seat again. "In order for us to get the material to a printer on schedule, we'll have to crunch the time-line a bit. Trust me. You need me."

That's what she was afraid of. Sure, she wanted him, but what if it turned out that she needed him? Really needed him. As in needing, needing him. Wait, they were discussing the project, right? Her students' bright, shining faces flashed in her mind. She took a sip of her tea and thought that maybe she could handle her attraction to him by focusing on the booklet.

"Vivian…"

She looked up at him. "Only my mom calls me Vivian. It's Vivi."

"Vivi, what I need from you is a step-by-step description of what you need from me, as well as a timeline you think the students will need for each stage of the project. But, to be honest, I'm guessing the text has to be handed in to my office by the end of March."

March? "That's only a little more than two months. And the kids have a ten-page paper to do to accompany what they've recorded."

"If we want the booklet published in time…"

Vivi realized he was right again. "Okay. End of March it is." She cupped her hands around the warm mug. He'd been right about enjoying warm drinks on such a cold day. "I can get you what you need by—"

"I need it by tomorrow night if possible. Please. There's no time to waste."

She'd have to spend the rest of the evening typing up her ideas and email it to him tomorrow morning before her first class. Of course, she hadn't planned on throwing out a big portion of her next lesson plan to go over this new idea of hers. She stood and handed him the half-empty mug. "I'd better go now so I can have my part ready by tomorrow."

He looked into her eyes, and she found herself looking back. "I really am looking forward to working on this with you, Vivi."

She gave a short nod since she didn't think she could find the right words to say what she was feeling. This could be the beginning of something wonderful.

Or the worst mistake of her life.

CHAPTER THREE

BRIAN HANDED VIVI a wide ceramic mug topped with a mound of pink whipped cream, then motioned to an empty table near the front of the coffee shop. They each took a seat, and Vivi had a sip of her hot drink, closing her eyes. *Bliss.* She opened them to find Brian looking at her. "It's good?"

"Better than good." She set the mug on the table. "When you said to meet you at the new coffee shop on Floral, this isn't what I pictured." She glanced around the small booth, noting the posters of oversize cupcakes and cups of steaming coffee on the freshly painted walls. "I didn't even know there was a place like this in Thora. When did this open?"

"The building was sitting empty for months, and I convinced the city council to allow small business owners to use it as a pop-up shop. The idea is part of the town's new initiative to support small businesses.

So far, it's mostly been rented out for eateries and cozy shops like this one." He gave his coffee a stir. "Even though it's only a temporary setup, it gives business owners a chance to get their foot in the door, so to speak, and try out new ideas without a large time or financial commitment first. We've divided this space up into several different sections to have more than one owner here at a time. Have you gone to the yarn booth? The variety of colors she has displayed is amazing."

"I'm not crafty, but it sounds cool."

"Of course, not all types of businesses work out. We had someone try to open a rock store."

Vivi was skeptical. "Rocks?"

"He would charge customers to paint rocks in customized designs. Turns out not many people were interested in paying someone else to paint a rock." He took a sip of his coffee. "But it was an interesting concept for a store. At least he didn't lose much money, having given it a shot here."

Vivi agreed and enjoyed another taste of the sweet chocolatey liquid in her cup. Realizing how comfortable she felt, and how much she was enjoying being with Brian, she set the drink aside and quickly reached for her planner. "So, we're here to discuss the booklet, not Thora businesses, right?"

"I've read over your proposal and made a few changes." Brian pulled several pages out of his briefcase and handed them to her. "You'll notice them marked in red."

She frowned as she took the pages and flipped through them. "Changes?"

"More like suggestions. But the bottom line is that I'm putting the full support of my office behind this project. Whatever you need, just ask. I checked with a friend who owns a publishing company. In order for us to have the booklet printed in time, the completed stories will have to be submitted by mid-March."

She flipped to the last page and scanned his "suggestions." "So, my students will need to start interviewing their senior citizens immediately."

"I've contacted Christopher Fox, who is the director at the seniors' assisted living complex, to get a list of willing participants for the project. He'll have it ready by Friday, but your kids will need to hit the ground running to get these interviews finished in time."

"Right."

He then handed her a business card. "This is another friend who is a freelance editor to help you shape the stories. She's waiting for your call."

Vivi placed the card on the table. "You've been busy."

"I need to stay busy since we don't have a lot of time."

AFTER TWENTY MINUTES, they had a timeline detailed with the specific points listed where they would check in with each other. "So, I'll be talking to you in about a week to see where your class is at."

They both stared at each other until they reached for their mugs at the same time, their fingers touching briefly. Vivi jumped when some of her cocoa sloshed over the lip of the mug. Brian took a few paper napkins from the metal dispenser in the middle of the table and sopped up the mess. Vivi ducked her head. "Sorry. I don't know what came over me."

"It's okay." He handed her a napkin and

pointed at her lip. "You've got a little…
cream…right…" He reached for another
napkin and dabbed the corner of her mouth.
"There."

"Thanks."

They looked at each other some more before Vivi blushed and glanced away. Brian
thought he could stay there all night looking at Vivi. He tried to find something besides the project to talk about to keep their
time together going. "Man, the weather
has been brutal this month, hasn't it?" He
winced. He'd picked the weather? She probably thought that he was boring.

Instead, she nodded vigorously. "Right?
These cold temperatures are vicious. I'm debating buying a second coat to put over the
other one."

"At least we're not getting the piles of
snow that they are up north. Although, when
we lived in Germany, I loved going on snow
hikes."

Vivi put her chin in her hand. "You said
you grew up in different countries. Where
besides Germany did you live?"

"We were in Belgium for a few months

until my dad got transferred to Italy. I think that was my favorite place."

Vivi sighed. "I love Italian food. Tell me it's as amazing as I imagine."

He grinned back at her. "Better." He paused to look at her. "Tell me what it was like to grow up near here."

"That's nowhere close to as exciting as living in Italy."

"So why don't you go for a visit?"

She looked down at her mug. "Someday."

She raised her eyes, then gasped and pointed to the clock on the wall. "I didn't realize it was so late. I need to get home." She shot to her feet and started pulling on her coat.

Brian stood and pulled on his jacket as well, then helped her when her hair got caught in the collar of her coat. She grabbed her pages. "I'll be in touch."

"Well, until then… Enjoy the rest of your evening."

AFTER SHE LEFT, he placed their used mugs to the left of the register where a large tub waited. He gave a nod to the woman running the register. "Have a good night, Malva."

"You, too, Mr. Redmond. Thanks again."

By the time he reached his house, the sky had darkened. Seemed like all he did was live and work in the dark. He left before the sun was up in the morning and returned after the sun had set. Short days of winter, yes. But his life seemed to be stuck in a rut. Get up. Eat breakfast, then go to work. Work, then have lunch and work some more. Come home to eat dinner, watch a little television, then off to bed only to repeat the pattern the next day. And the next. And the next. Then weekends were full of finishing up on projects from work, supporting different charity events in town or an occasional evening out with friends. Only to return to Monday and the same old routine.

There had to be more to life than existing in between bouts of work, right? He set his keys on the kitchen counter, then opened the freezer door. Nothing appealed there, and it had been a while since he'd gone to the grocery store. He should have bought a pizza on the way home. Instead, he pulled up the app on his cell phone and ordered one for delivery.

He seated himself on the sofa in the living room and turned on the television. He settled on a news station but jumped when his phone rang. Caller ID showed his sister's name. "Hey, James."

"Have you asked her out yet?"

"Who?"

His sister chuckled. "Unusual Vivian, of course."

"Heard from Mom lately?"

"Nice change of subject, which means either you haven't got the guts or you did, and she turned you down flat."

"I shouldn't be surprised that you know me so well. And she did say maybe." Besides being his sister, Jamie was also his best friend. That's why he confided in her even though he knew she could and would tease him mercilessly. But in the end, he also knew she would love and protect him at all costs, as he would her. They were there for each other, no matter what.

Jamie gave a low whistle. "I guess your supposed charm has its limits."

"Did you need something, or did you call just to annoy me?"

Jamie laughed. "I'm multifaceted, so I'm

doing both at the same time. I'm gifted that way." She paused. "I need a favor."

"Of course, you do. And you always come to big brother. What is it?"

"Do you know anyone who's an expert on getting rid of a raccoon that's taken over a wood-burning stove? And not just the mama raccoon, but her babies as well."

"I suggested you should seal up the chimney when you bought the house."

"Help me first. You can lecture me later."

"How do you know it's a raccoon?"

"I opened the stove to lay a fire, and she hissed at me."

Only his sister. "And you closed her inside, right? You didn't let her out to have free rein of your house?"

"I'm not that nice."

He mentally ran through his list of acquaintances until he landed on a name. "Let me give my buddy Shawn a call. If he can't take care of your raccoon problem, then he knows someone who can."

THE SOUND OF groaning from her seniors didn't deter Vivi from laying out the new plan for their final project. "I can tell from your enthusiastic protests that I haven't sold you on this idea yet, but this is an important way of preserving parts of our local history."

"Who cares about what happened in Thora a hundred years ago?"

Vivi observed Madison, one of her best students, doodle in her notebook as she waited for an answer to her question. "Great question, Maddy. Does someone know why?"

Ethan popped his hand in the air. "Those who ignore history will repeat it."

"Actually, the quote is 'those that fail to learn from history are doomed to repeat it.'" She looked around the room at the uninterested faces. "Anyone know who said those words?" Her students reached for their phones. "Without googling it?" They looked up at her. "Winston Churchill gets credit for it from a speech he gave to the British House of Commons after World War Two. I'll give anyone extra credit if you can discover who he paraphrased it from originally. But Ethan is right. We learn history so that we don't repeat the mistakes of the past. Why else?"

"To keep memories alive after someone has died."

She nodded at Ava. "Another good point.

Anyone else?" The room was silent. "Why would I push you to write down the stories of people you don't know? Why would I care? Why do I think you should?" She walked around the desk and sat on the edge. No hands in the air, but her class seemed to be waiting for her to answer. "Why do I bother teaching history instead of…American lit or physics?"

"You like dead stuff?" Noah asked.

"I do like old things, although I prefer to call them *vintage* or *classic*." She surveyed the classroom. "I like to find connections to other people who are not like me." She picked up the list of senior citizens who had volunteered to be a part of the project. "People like Sarah Duffy, who was born in Thora when World War Two began and saw it grow from a small town into the busy suburb it is today. Or Gladys Pierce, who lost her first husband and a brother to Vietnam. Or Stanley Korman, who served as Thora's mayor for twelve years during the recession of the eighties."

She stood and walked the aisles between the students' desks. "They were each like you once. About to graduate high school and enter the real world. They each had dreams and goals. They got jobs and had families. Let their stories open your eyes to the possibilities out there. Let them teach you the lessons they learned. And record their memories so that we don't forget."

She held up the list of senior citizens. "I've assigned you each someone to interview. You'll have two weeks to record their stories. And then we'll find a way to shape those into a book. Any questions?"

No hands, but at least her students looked a little more engaged than they had when she first proposed the project. "Great. Let's get started."

Cecily entered the room after the bell rang for the end of class. She nodded to a few of her students, then walked to the front of the classroom. She waited until she and Vivi were alone. "I need a night out. Interested?"

"How's your grandfather?" Cecily had gotten a call recently that her grandfather had fallen at home and had been hospitalized.

"They're still running tests. I need something fun to do tonight in order to distract me."

Since it was Friday, they wouldn't need

to curtail their activities early. Vivi looked at her friend. "What do you have in mind?"

"Remember the roller rink? They're having an eighties party tonight."

Vivi wrinkled her nose. "Roller skating? The last time I tried that I was a decade younger and barely escaped without spraining both my ankles."

"There's no movie I want to see in theaters right now, so that's out." Cec looked thoughtful for a moment. "But there is a trivia night at the pub."

Vivi considered this. The last time she'd gone to trivia night, she had cleaned up and gone home with several hundred dollars' worth of gift cards to shops and businesses. She could really use a win about now, and so could her friend. "That sounds like a great plan. Between the two of us and our vast knowledge of random facts, we should be unbeatable."

BRIAN FOLLOWED HIS SISTER into the pub and felt his eyebrows raise at the large, noisy crowd that had gathered that wintry evening. He leaned in close to Jamie. "Are they giving away the alcohol tonight or what?"

She didn't answer but gave him a smile that made him think she was up to something. He followed her to a table where several of her female friends sat, sipping on drinks. Jamie pushed him forward. "Hey, girls. You remember my brother, Brian."

Two of the women got up and approached them. He narrowed his eyes at his sister but made the muscles in his face relax as he faced the women and gave them a nod. "Jenna. Leslie." He turned to a third woman and said, "I don't think we've met."

She looked him up and down, then shrugged and held out her hand. "Elena."

They shook hands, and she quickly removed hers from his. He pointed to the bar behind him. "I'll go get some drinks. Anyone need a refill?" He took orders, then turned to Jamie. "Care to help me, dear sister?"

He turned on his heel and headed to the bar. Jamie joined him and leaned on the bar while they waited to get the bartender's attention. "Don't kill me. It's not worth the jail time."

"So, which one are you trying to set me

up with? You already tried and failed with Leslie."

"Wait a minute. I didn't fail with Leslie because you didn't go out with her."

He turned to look at her. "We never went out because I never asked her. Because I'm not interested."

"Because you never gave her a chance. Which is a real shame because she's a great woman. Financially independent. Smart. Beautiful." Jamie glanced behind them at the table they'd left. "You'd be lucky to date any of them, though."

"I don't need you to keep fixing me up with your friends."

"Maybe I wouldn't need to if you actually went out on occasion instead of sitting at home every weekend."

"I don't sit. Sometimes I walk on the treadmill while I watch television." He gave her a wink and nudged her side.

The bartender approached them, and Brian ordered the drinks and handed her his credit card. He turned back to Jamie. "I'll have one drink with you and your friends, then I'll make an excuse to leave. Got it?"

"Fine. We already have a full team for the

trivia contest anyways. But you might want to think about doing more than just saying you want to change your life. You actually have to make an effort at some point." She took two of the drinks the bartender placed in front of them. "You get the rest of the drinks and join us. But think about what I said."

He watched her leave, knowing she was right. He admitted that something had to change because he couldn't keep going the way he was. He led a charmed life, but he was bored. He needed something more, even if he wasn't sure what that something was.

The bartender placed the last of the drinks on the bar, then slid a receipt over to Brian for his signature. He left a hefty tip and pushed the three glasses together to get a grasp on them. When he turned, he bumped into another patron, sloshing one of the drinks over his fingers and on to her pristine white blouse. He looked into the startled eyes of Vivi. "Oh, no." He turned and placed the drinks on the bar, then grabbed a stash of napkins to wipe the wet splotch on her shirt. "I am so sorry."

She grabbed the napkins from his hand to finish sopping up the liquor. "I've got this."

He dropped his hand and shook his head. "It was an accident."

"We seem to be prone to getting into them together, don't we?" she asked and placed the damp paper napkins on the bar. "But a wet blouse is minor compared to a crumpled bumper."

He winced and handed her another napkin. "And a lot cheaper."

She nodded, laughing. "It's fine. This is my year to get bumped into, I guess. I should have known it was going to be busy here tonight with the trivia contest and all, so it's not your fault. I should have been watching where I was going."

She looked good. She had her dark hair pulled back into a ponytail, and he wondered what it would be like to release it and slip his fingers through it. And her lips had a glossy sheen that made him wonder if they tasted as good as they looked. Realizing he was staring at her, he shook his head. "I better get back to my table with these drinks."

"Good luck in the trivia contest. I'm pretty unbeatable."

"Then maybe I should be on your team because there's a lot of useless knowledge that I store in my brain."

Where had those words come from? But he knew that spending the evening sitting at Vivi's table would be enjoyable.

Vivi eyed the crowd, then the group of drinks he'd been carrying. "You must be here with somebody or are all those drinks for you?"

He pointed to the table where Jamie waited. "One's mine, but the rest are for my sister and her friends."

"Won't they miss you if you join our team?"

He didn't think they'd mind. Besides, hadn't his sister been pushing him to spend time with Unusual Vivian? "Hardly. Their team is already full." He leaned in closer to her so he could be heard. "Would it be okay if I drop off their drinks and join you at your table?" He looked around the room. "Unless you're here with someone."

"My friend Cec is with me. But we could use another member for our team."

"Then it must be good luck that I bumped into you."

VIVI FOUND HERSELF smiling back at Brian and wanting him to join her team. Only because she wanted to win, of course. And three people would fare better than two. Bad luck had made him spill his drink on her, but maybe they could eke out a victory and turn that luck into something good. She pointed at a table across the room. "We're sitting over there. I hope you'll join us."

And she meant it. Which was silly and foolish because she had to remind herself that this was a really bad time for her to get to know someone she might actually like.

He nodded at her before leaving. She watched him go for a moment, then returned to her table. Cec frowned at her blouse. "What did you do? You weren't gone that long."

"Ran into someone. Literally." She plucked the damp cotton from her chest. "I found our waitress and updated our order to add sour cream and guac to the nachos."

"Perfect."

"And I invited someone to join our team for trivia." She glanced across the table at Cec, hoping she'd done the right thing. She hadn't considered that her friend might not want Brian to be included. "It's Brian from the New Year's Eve party. Did I mess up?"

Cec shook her head. "I don't mind. Maybe he knows about sports better than the two of us. Tom was always great at that category for our team." She winced and closed her eyes. "Last time I mention him tonight. Promise."

Vivi took a seat next to her friend and placed a hand on her arm. "It's okay to talk about him, Cec. He was a part of your life for a long time."

"Well, he doesn't want to be anymore, so I need to get over it. Over him." She grabbed her sweet tea and took a long sip, then gave Vivi a smile that looked forced. "I'm not going to cry tonight. Or think about him. Or any of that. But I am going to freshen up in the ladies' room."

Vivi scooted her chair in so that Cec could get around her. Maybe bringing a guy to join them was a really bad idea. Cec didn't need the reminder of her suddenly single status. Maybe she'd make an excuse so Brian would stay with his sister and her friends.

As if thinking his name would make him appear, he stood by her side and placed his beer on the table. A shorter woman that had the same dark blond hair and hazel eyes stood next to him. "Vivi, I'd like you to meet my sister, Jamie. She didn't believe me when I said you had asked me to join your trivia team."

Jamie smiled at her brightly and thrust out her hand. "Brian has been talking about you nonstop since New Year's Eve. It's so good to finally meet you."

Vivi shook the woman's hand but turned to look at Brian. "Nonstop, huh?"

He made a face at his sister before giving a shrug and a laugh. "She's exaggerating. Little sisters tend to do that."

Jamie rolled her eyes. "Please. It's Vivi this and Vivi that. He told me that you're both working on a local history project together."

They chatted for a few minutes before Cec returned from the bathroom with red-rimmed eyes, but a smile on her face. "Do we have a full team?" she asked.

Jamie shook her head. "I'm just here to make sure that my brother wasn't lying about finding someone else to sit with. So, thank you for taking him off our hands. Our team was already full as it is." She gave

Brian a little shove. "I have to get back to my friends, but it was nice to meet you both."

Then she was gone, leaving almost as fast as she'd shown up. Brian gave another shrug. "So that's Jamie. I guess you can tell that she's the outgoing sibling. Which I guess helps make her a good cop. She's not afraid to jump into a situation to help if needed."

Vivi eyed him. "I wouldn't say that you're shy."

"At least not when it matters."

He gave her a look that she could feel down to her toes. The crowd in the bar seemed to fade for a moment until she remembered Cec and stood so that she could take her spot at the back of the table. Brian sat down across from Vivi as the waitress arrived with the platter of nachos and two plates. She looked at the new third party at the table. "I'll bring another plate for you guys. Can I get you anything else to eat before the game starts?"

Brian looked at Vivi, then Cec. "Their loaded potato skins are to die for. You ladies want to share some?"

"And another sweet tea, please," Cec said, holding up her almost empty drink. "Double lemon wedges this time."

The waitress left, and the three fell silent, sipping their drinks and people watching. Vivi glanced at a nearby table and groaned. "Ugh, I wish he wasn't here tonight."

"Who? Tom?" Cec popped her head up, searching the room.

"No. Jasper."

Brian winced at the name. "An old boy-friend?"

Cec laughed at that a little too loudly. "He wishes."

Vivi looked across the table at Brian to explain. "He thinks he knows everything. And he's the one we will have to beat if we want to take home the big prize tonight." She glanced at Jasper's table to see who was on his team. "And he's got Sheila with him. This might not be as easy as I thought."

"But now you've got me." Vivi turned back to look at Brian who gave her a wink. "I don't intend on going home a loser."

Cec scooted a little closer to him. "I doubt you ever have. No wonder Vivi likes you."

His smile grew wider. "She does, huh?"

Vivi held up a hand. "Now, wait a minute. I never said I liked him."

"Actually, your exact words were he might

have had a chance with you if only you had met him at a different time."

Vivi placed some nachos on a plate and handed it to Cecily. "House specialty. They're really good."

Cec followed her sip of tea by dunking a tortilla chip in some guacamole. She sighed. "I do love their nachos."

Brian looked across the table at Vivi and smiled. She found herself smiling back and wondering why she kept him at arm's length. Because Cec had been right. If it was any other time, she might have pursued something with him. But this year meant she couldn't. It came down to bad timing.

The music stopped, and Vivi dropped those thoughts, clapping her hands to get her team focused. "Okay, this is it. We have to win tonight."

Brian nodded. "Don't worry. We will."

BRIAN GLANCED AT the table where Jasper and Sheila sat with their two teammates, whispering and laughing. He narrowed his eyes at them and then felt someone pat his hand. He turned to look at Cec. "Don't let them get in your head. We only have the final round left, and we can't afford to lose any more points to them."

It seemed like they had taken an early lead in the first round but had lost it in the second as Jasper and his team sprinted past them. In the last category of the third round, it was going to come down to the final two questions. They needed to win tonight. And for more reasons than just because he was trying to impress Vivi.

He took a deep breath. "Do we know what the last category is going to be?"

Vivi shook her head and glanced behind her at Jasper. "As long as it's not gardening and horticulture, we still have a chance."

"Gardening?"

"Jasper owns a landscaping company." She huffed. "And he's a walking encyclopedia of all things green."

"Got it."

The trivia host rang a bell. "We're down to three teams for our final category, which will be...US geography."

Vivi groaned and put her head on the table. "Why did it have to be that?"

Brian grinned. "Oh, we've got this."

She lifted her head, and even Cec smiled at him. "You know geography?"

"I used to read the atlas for fun."

Vivi returned his grin. "You're right that we've got this. I'm so glad I invited you to join us."

The host cleared her throat. "First question for ten points: Which two lakes are connected by the Niagara Falls?"

Brian shot his hand in the air seconds before Sheila from Jasper's table. The host nodded at him. "Lake Erie and Lake Ontario."

"That is…" The host consulted her notes. "Correct."

Vivi applauded then gave him a high five. She turned and pointed at the other table. "Take that, Jasper." Wow, where did that come from? Was she taking this too seriously?

The team at the other table frowned at them as the host asked, "For an extra five points, Brian, what is the height of Niagara Falls?"

Brian frowned. Height, height, height. He knew this. He tapped his forehead, trying to retrieve the information from his brain. Vivi peered at him from across the table, and Cec put her hand on his arm. "Come on, Brian. You can do it."

He took a deep breath. "One hundred and…" He squinted his eyes as if he could see the page of the atlas in the distance. "Uh…one hundred and sixty feet."

The host winced. "Close. One hundred and sixty-seven feet."

The people at Jasper's table clapped as Vivi groaned and dropped her head back. "It should be close enough. You were within ten feet."

"Last question is worth twenty-five points and will decide the game." The host paused, taking her time and increasing the tension. "Where would you find the Graveyard of the Atlantic?"

Vivi stared at Brian. "What in the world is that?"

He gave a shrug as he tried to recall. "I don't know. I don't think I've ever heard of that before."

Cec groaned. "Come on, Brian." She peered over at Jasper's table where they were leaning in and whispering to each other. "I don't think Jasper knows either, so that's good, right?"

"Five more seconds," the host announced. "The Graveyard of the Atlantic...where would we find it?"

Brian shook his head. "I'm sorry, ladies. I don't know this one."

"Let's take a guess before time runs out. What do we have to lose?" Vivi asked.

She raised her hand, and when the host called on her, she pointed at Brian. He took a deep breath. "The Florida Keys."

"That is...wrong."

Jasper's hand shot up. "The Outer Banks?"

"That is...correct."

Jasper's team broke into shouts and applause while the rest of the pub seemed to groan. Vivi moaned. "It's not fair. We should have had that one in the second round about John Quincy Adams. My hand was up well before Sheila's."

Brian sighed. "I'm sorry, ladies. I really thought we were going to take that one."

Vivi patted his arm, then settled her hand on the spot. "It's okay. We can't win them all."

Cecily snorted and stirred the watery slush at the bottom of her glass. "Are you kidding me? You don't play if you know you can't win." She gasped and reached under the table. "There's no need to kick me. I speak the truth."

Brian raised his eyebrows at this. "So, you're competitive. I should have known from the board game party."

Vivi gave a shrug. "Perhaps a little." Then she turned and glared at Cecily. "Not that there's anything wrong with that."

Brian settled back into the seat and realized he was grinning at her. "I'm finally starting to learn more about you. And I'm enjoying it."

"It's not exactly putting me in a flattering light though, is it?"

"I'd rather have reality than something that turns out too good to be true." He leaned in and rested an elbow on the table, his hand holding up his cheek. "So, tell me more about your flaws, Vivi. I'm fascinated."

"Fascinated to know that I can be cut-throat?"

He couldn't keep the admiration out of his voice. "Cutthroat is a fierce description. Maybe not one I would have given you, but…interesting."

"I can be interesting."

"You already are. That's why I'd like to find out more."

"You'll have plenty of time while we work on the booklet." She smiled and sipped her drink. "There are so many details to sort through."

"I think you're on to something. We've mostly been emailing each other back and forth. But maybe we should have more one-on-one meetings?"

Jasper stopped at their table and held out a hand to Vivi. "No hard feelings, Carmack?"

Vivi gave him a cutting look but shook his hand. "Why would there be?"

Jasper chuckled and acknowledged Cecily and Brian. "Better luck next time."

Vivi rolled her eyes as he left. "I've never liked the guy."

Cec slugged her shoulder gently. "Yes, that's obvious. But good to see you could be the better person."

Vivi laughed at her friend's teasing.

"I can understand being relentless when it counts. That's how I am when it comes to helping someone in the community. I do everything I can to find the resources they need. Whether it's grant money or the right contact. Or... Sorry. I told you I could be relentless."

Vivi smiled. "Actually, I think it's cute. And it's helping me get to know you a little more."

"What else do I need to know about you?"

Vivi looked around the pub, then gave an exaggerated yawn and stretch and tapped the watch on her delicate wrist. "Wow, is that the time? It's getting pretty late, don't you think, Cecily?"

"Just answer the man. I need to go make a quick call to my mom and check on Pops before we leave anyways." She waited for Vivi to get up and move so that she could come around the table. "Be right back."

Brian stood as she left, then took the seat next to Vivi. "Is there something wrong with me?"

Vivi startled at his words. "No, uh, not at all. What are you talking about?"

"It seems that you don't want to spend time with me unless we're discussing the project. So that must mean there's something about me that you don't like?" He glanced down at the shirt he wore. "Is it this shirt? My smile?"

"It's not you."

Brian groaned. "It must be me, and to be honest, my curiosity has got the better of me. I feel like I have to ask."

Vivi flicked her gaze toward the bar, likely hoping to see her friend returning. But Cecily wasn't anywhere in sight. Vivi focused on him again. "Fine. It is you. Does that make you feel better?"

He frowned at her. He'd been nice. Kind. Funny. He hadn't been that bad of a dancer when they had first met, had he? "You're not being honest with me, and I wish you could tell me what's wrong."

Vivi stood and put on her winter coat, though Cecily hadn't yet returned. Brian helped her into it, then held the lapels as he looked into her eyes. "I'm a nice guy. If you want, I can give you my mother's phone number. She'll vouch for me."

"I get it. And if I'm being honest, I want to say yes, I'd be saying yes, yes, yes, in fact. You're the nicest guy I've met in a long time, but…it's just…stuff with me. This is a really bad time for me."

"When would be a better time?"

"Next year."

Brian was so confused. "What's wrong with this year?"

Vivi looked into his eyes, then glanced over his shoulder. "Ready, Cec?"

Brian turned and helped Cecily with her coat as well, but by the time he went to wish Vivi good-night, she had already left. Cecily shrugged. "It's not you. You're lovely. It's all her misguided…" She stopped and patted him on the shoulder. "Never mind. It would take too long to explain it. Have a good night."

He gave her a nod. "You, too. Sorry we didn't win."

"Maybe next time."

She walked on, followed the route Vivi had taken to the front of the pub. Brian was soon joined by Jamie, who had watched the two women leave. "You've really got a talent for ticking people off, don't you? Two of them at once?"

"I didn't tick anyone off." He took a seat at the empty table and picked up his beer that had an inch left at the bottom of the glass. He finished it, then pushed the chair across from him so that Jamie would take a seat. "Are you ready to leave yet?"

Jamie sat down. "You guys almost won the trivia contest." She glanced over her shoulder. "I wish you would have. The winning team would not stop bragging about how they creamed you guys. Is that why your teammates left?"

"I don't understand why she won't even consider going out with me."

"Is there someone else?"

"Nope. According to her friend, she's misguided. About what, I don't know. Which means I don't know how to convince her to give me a chance."

Jamie cocked her head to the side. "I could find out for you. I know people."

"So do I, but I think it would be better if Vivi told me herself. I would certainly feel better if she did."

"And if she doesn't?"

"Then I guess I'll never find out why she let a good thing pass her by," he joked.

Jamie chuckled. "You? A good thing?"

"What? You don't think I'm a catch? Isn't that the reason why you keep trying to set me up with all your friends?" When she didn't answer, he snapped his fingers and pointed at her. "Got you there."

"Speaking of my friends, we're talking about hitting up another bar before we call it a night, so you don't have to drive me home. Unless, of course, you want to join us."

"Wow, look at the time. I should probably get home and to bed."

VIVI USED THE side of her fist to wipe the steam from the mirror before running a pick through her hair. She stared at her reflection, then shook her head. Why couldn't she give Brian a chance? Because she didn't want her heart to get broken. That's all that this year would bring. Heartache and pain. And she wanted to do whatever she could to avoid it.

Once she was in her pajamas, she joined Cecily out on the sofa in front of the television. Cecily used the remote to turn down the volume on the show she had been watching. "What's with the sad face?"

Vivi reached up to touch her cheeks. "I'm not sad."

Cec gave a shrug. "That's not what it looks like to me." She pulled one of the sofa pillows on to her lap so that Vivi could take a seat next to her. "You want to give Brian a chance. You know you do."

"It's not going to happen."

"Why not? He paid for our dinner and our drinks even though we insisted he didn't have to. And I saw the tip he left for the waitress, so he's not only nice but generous, too."

Vivi had also noted that, but it wasn't enough for her to forget why this was the worst time of her life to meet him. "It doesn't matter."

Her friend rolled her eyes and settled farther into the couch pillows. "When are you going to realize that ninety-nine percent of what you worry about never happens?"

"But it's the one percent that does that really hurts."

"Life isn't always rainbows and unicorns, Vivi. You only have to look at mine to see that. But does that stop me from moving on?" She paused and looked down at the fringe of the pillow that she rubbed between her fingers. "I got the official notification from the court today. Tom's filed for divorce."

Vivi leaned toward her and grabbed her hand away from the fringe. "What a mistake he's making by letting you go. He doesn't know a good thing when he has it. Divorce?"

"According to my lawyer, because we don't have children, it should be fairly quick and simple. I'll be single again before the summer break begins." She gave a chuckle that sounded hollow. "I guess I'm lucky that all our talk about having a family was only that. Talk." She put her face in her hands. "But you know what? I won't let this stop me from living. I'm going to move on. Because I have to. He doesn't love me anymore."

"Tom's a jerk."

Cecily looked up at her. "It doesn't matter if he is because I know that I'm strong enough to handle this. And whatever is going on with my grandfather, I'll deal with that, too. Just because life is hard right now doesn't mean that I stop living. Or do whatever I can to possibly avoid more pain. I'm looking to the future."

Vivi knew that part of what Cec said was true. You couldn't completely avoid pain no matter what. But she could steer clear of situations that would only make her heart ache. She didn't want to contradict Cec when her friend needed her to be just as strong as she was. Instead, she put her arms around Cec and hugged her tightly. "Whatever you need from me, just ask."

"So you keep telling me. But right now, I need to think about things other than Tom or Pops." She grabbed the remote and turned up the volume on the reality show. "Did you see what the designer did in the kitchen with black and yellow subway tiles? What in the world was she thinking?"

CHAPTER FOUR

VIVI'S FIFTH-HOUR sophomore American history class filed out as soon as the bell rang, and she sank into her desk chair. They'd been having a roundtable discussion about Sacajawea leading Lewis and Clark to the west, really getting into the role of the Native American guide. The kids had been enthusiastic about someone so young—as young as them—having such an important part to play in a pivotal moment in history.

Since sixth hour was her planning hour, she stuffed her grade book and scheduler into her messenger bag and hefted it onto her shoulder. She wanted to visit the school library to double-check on a book she'd asked them to order before Christmas break.

She paused at the door when she spotted one of her students, Devonte, still sitting at his desk, his head down. "Class is over, Devonte."

He raised his eyes to hers, then glanced around the room. "Oh. Sorry."

He rose to his feet and stuffed a book into his backpack. Slinging it over one shoulder, he started to exit the classroom but then turned back to face her. He looked as if he intended to ask her something, but he shook his head and started to walk away.

She followed after him. "Something on your mind, Devonte? You haven't been your usual self lately and seem distracted. And I'm getting concerned, since you're not handing in your assignments on time."

He turned back to look at her. "No, ma'am. I'm fine."

"Is everything okay at home?" He didn't answer but glanced away. She leaned in closer and lowered her voice. "Is there something I can do?"

He frowned. "Nothing anyone can do."

"Why don't you tell me what's going on first? Then we'll figure this out together. What do you say?"

"I say I'm going to be late for my next class."

Devonte bolted and she chastised herself

for not handling that better. She'd look for another opportunity to try soon.

After confirming with the school librarian that her requested book would be in before the week was out, Vivi settled herself at an empty table in the teachers' lounge. She noticed one of her fellow teachers at another table. "Hey, Mark, you have Devonte Miller in chemistry, don't you?"

Mark glanced up from the stack of papers he'd been reviewing and took a few seconds to register her presence. He blinked several times, then nodded. "First hour, yes."

"Has he seemed okay to you since we got back from Christmas break?"

Mark paused but then shrugged. "Nothing unusual. Why?"

"Maybe it's my overactive imagination, but he hasn't been his usual self lately. I wondered if he'd talked to you about it."

"If he talked to any of his teachers, it would be Sandy in the English department. I can ask her, if you'd like."

Vivi nodded. Of course, she should have thought of Sandy herself. "That's okay. I'll check with her."

Mark went back to his papers.

Vivi took out her own stack of papers she needed to grade, but her mind kept drifting to Devonte. He looked as if he hadn't been sleeping well lately, if the dark circles under his eyes were any indication. Dark circles and a frown etched on his face. She couldn't let go of the feeling that something was wrong with him.

"What are you going to do? Keep asking him until he tells you what's going on?" Cec asked her as they prepared dinner together later that night.

She was right. As Devonte's teacher, she was limited on what she could do. Vivi drained the pasta in a bright yellow colander then rinsed the noodles under the faucet before sliding them into a large ceramic bowl. Cecily poured the tomato sauce over the noodles, and Vivi tossed the spaghetti until everything mixed together.

She carried the bowl to the kitchen table, then took a seat. Cec followed her with a bowl of salad. They filled their plates as Vivi considered her options. "I can't let it go, though. Something is going on with him. What if he's in some kind of trouble?"

Cec filled her plate with spaghetti, then passed the pasta fork to Vivi. "I have his little sister, Tiffany, in my second-hour class. Now that you mention it, she's been really quiet the last couple of weeks. She didn't do as well as she usually does on our last test, either."

"See? I think we should find out if we can help them."

"If they're not sharing any information, what else can we do?" Cec twirled spaghetti onto her fork. "I think we should keep an eye on them and approach the counselor if it gets worse."

"Or I could call his parents and ask."

Cec sighed as she sprinkled parmesan cheese over her pasta. "Do you remember what happened the last time you called a student's parent about her behavior in class?"

"She got pulled out of the school because her father thought I was interfering." Vivi tapped her fork on the edge of her plate. "But I knew that Rhonda had something going on that she needed help with."

"Well, she was pregnant. That's a lot for a fifteen-year-old."

Vivi agreed. "It was. I'm glad she eventually got the care and advice she needed. Even if her father disagreed with me getting involved. The fact is that she needed someone to step in and help her."

"You think Devonte needs that sort of help?"

"I do." He'd said that no one could help, but what if she could? Didn't she have a responsibility to see if there was something she could do for him?

"You're not going to drop this, are you?"

Vivi poked at the pasta on her plate. "I can't."

Cec smiled and reached over to take her hand. "I'll do what I can to help you, then."

VIVI HAD BEEN on Brian's mind since he'd competed with her at the pub's trivia night the past weekend. He stirred his cup of coffee and found himself smiling at the memory of her flushed expression after every correct answer. It made her look even cuter than he had thought before. He glanced at her name on his phone, and he toyed with sending her a text.

Hey there.

No. Too generic.

Dear Vivian.

He wrinkled his nose and erased the letters. He glanced out the window and tried to come up with something witty that would finally convince her to give him a chance.

What are you up to?

He let out a moan and started to erase it when someone knocked on his open office door. Jamie stood there. "You need a break. Take me to lunch."

"Can't. I'm busy."

She glanced around his empty office and cocked her head to one side. "You look like you're really slammed. Besides, you forget that I'm friends with your assistant. I know your schedule. So, come on. Let's go. I'm craving Mexican."

A chicken burrito did sound pretty good. But he wanted to get this message off to Vivi before he chickened out. He pointed to his phone. "I'm trying to figure out how to convince Vivi to go out with me."

"Let me see what you have so far." Jamie held out her hand, and he placed the phone into her open palm. She cringed at the words he had typed and erased them before typing something else. She must have sent the text because a swooping sound emitted from his phone. He stared at her as she handed him back the phone. He read what she'd sent.

Dinner tonight?

It was direct. To the point. Maybe that would work. He paused to see if Vivi would respond, but there was no notification that she'd read it yet. "I'll take you out to lunch if she actually agrees to dinner."

Jamie folded her arms and took a seat across the desk from him. "That doesn't help me feed my hunger now."

"Maybe you should pack a lunch instead of depending on your older brother to take you out."

"That's boring." She slapped her hands on the arms of her chair and rose to her feet. "But because you're such a terrific big brother, you're going to feed me despite not hearing back from her yet."

He looked at her, then agreed. Maybe he could get some advice from her over a bowl of warm tortilla chips about how best to talk to Vivi. He grabbed his jacket and followed his sister out the door.

At the local Mexican restaurant, they found an empty booth near a window that overlooked the parking lot. Jamie still had her coat on as she dipped a chip into salsa and chewed it as she took her coat off and placed it next to her on the bench. "Any response yet?"

Brian pulled his phone from his coat pocket and shook his head. "Did you really think that would work?"

"I didn't. But it did get you to take me to lunch." She took another chip and drowned it in salsa. When the server approached their table, she asked, "Do you still have that spicy ranch dip? We could use a bowl."

The server nodded and left to retrieve it for them.

Brian glanced at the menu. "Is there something wrong with me?"

"Besides the usual, no." Jamie smiled at him. "You know I'm teasing. You're the best big brother I could ask for. You're practically perfect."

"Then why won't she go out with me?"

Jamie considered him as she nibbled on a chip, then thanked the server who brought a bowl of the spicy ranch. "We'll both have the chicken burrito special with rice, not beans."

When the server left with their order, Brian scoffed. "What if I wanted something different for lunch today?"

"Please. It's your go-to dish here. When haven't you ordered the chicken burrito?"

Brian considered this. "Maybe that's why she's not interested in me or my so-called charms. I'm too predictable."

"About your menu choices, yes. But I don't think that's why she's not interested." She leaned toward him. "Are you finally willing to let me do my thing and find out what's going on?"

His sister had the reputation of sniffing out the truth about things that might have gone unnoticed, which is also what made her a good cop. But she was also relentless and had been known to stalk a few people to get answers. Was he willing to risk completely alienating Vivi? Wouldn't it be better to just let nature take its course? He put his head in his hands. "I can figure this out on my own."

"Are you sure? Because I'm more than happy to help you."

He raised his eyes to meet hers. "I need to do it myself. But I'll keep my options open if things don't get better."

HER FIFTH-HOUR students hunched over their books, silently reading, as Vivi watched over them. Devonte in particular. His eyes seemed to be reading the text, but it was like his mind was a million miles away. The bell rang, and she stood. "Finish chapter twelve tonight, and we'll discuss Teddy Roosevelt tomorrow." She paused. "Devonte, can you stay behind for a moment?"

The other students rose to their feet and gathered their belongings before leaving the room. Devonte stood, watching them leave, not facing her until she walked up the aisle toward him. He focused on her at her approach. "Ms. Carmack—"

"Do you want to tell me what's going on?"

He glanced away and shook his head. "No, ma'am."

She figured he'd say that. "I'm sorry, Devonte, but I'll have to call your mother after school today. With your low score on the pop quiz yesterday and the late assignments, your grades are slipping. Your mother needs to be involved."

He looked at her, his eyes wide. "No, ma'am. You don't want to do that."

"Why not?"

"My mom, she's..." His mouth moved as if he wanted to say more but didn't have the words. Finally, he said, "She can't answer the phone."

"Of course, she can. Why wouldn't she be able to?"

"She's in the hospital, ma'am. She's not home."

Vivi took a seat at the desk closest to his. "The hospital? Will she be okay?"

Devonte's expression was full of panic. "Car accident. It's pretty bad."

Vivi had heard there had been a bad accident before the new year, but she hadn't put it together that it had been Devonte's mom. She put a hand on his. "I'm so sorry. What can I do to help?"

"Like I said, nothing anyone can do."

"Do you need meals? I'm always cooking extra, and I can deliver food to your house."

Devonte glanced at the door. "My auntie is living with us until my mom gets released. She cooks."

"There's got to be something you need. Because if everything was okay, you wouldn't have those dark circles under your eyes."

Devonte slumped at his desk as if everything that had been holding him up had suddenly fled. "She's going to be in a wheelchair, and our place isn't exactly made for that."

"What about your dad? Can he help out?"

Devonte frowned. "I take care of my family. Not him."

This kid thought he was in an impossible situation by himself, but Vivi knew that he wasn't alone. She walked to her desk and grabbed her cell phone from her messenger bag. She noticed she had a waiting text but ignored it to scroll through her contacts until she found the community support coordinator's name. She walked back to Devonte. "Can you get your phone out? I have some information for you. This is the phone number of someone who can maybe help you.

His name is Brian Redmond, and he works at city hall. He does all sorts of things to support the town and the people who live here."

Devonte got out his phone but only stared at it. "I don't need another social worker."

"He's not a social worker. But I bet he does know people who can get your place made wheelchair accessible. He probably knows every grant or type of funding available, or an organization that does this kind of work. And that's just the start." She pushed at the phone in his hand and after another moment he relented. He copied the info into his cell. "Should I let him know to be waiting for your call?"

The warning bell rang, and Devonte got to his feet. "I gotta get to class."

Vivi returned to her desk and wrote a quick note. "This will excuse your tardiness." She handed him the note. "You don't have to do this alone, you know."

Devonte shot her a look that she couldn't interpret and left the classroom. She walked to the door and watched him hustle down the hallway, his shoulders hunched, and his head hung low. She only hoped that she'd done the right thing by referring him to Brian.

She grabbed her phone once again to check the text. Dinner tonight? Her chest warmed. She hovered over the message, debating. On the one hand, Cec would be visiting her grandfather in the hospital. Making dinner for one was a very lonely prospect. And dinner with Brian could be interesting.

On the other hand, she worried about encouraging this attraction to Brian. And she needed to keep to her plan. Head down. Get through the year unscathed. She could be with him when they worked on the project but seeing him outside of that seemed to be inviting trouble.

She typed, "Sorry, not available. But thanks for the invitation."

Even though every part of her told her that was a mistake.

BRIAN STOOD FROM behind his desk and glanced around the room to see if the task force members had reached an understanding. "Listen, folks. This isn't that hard to decide. Either we go forward with the renovation of the park to make it more accessible and safer, or we shut it down."

The mayor rubbed his top lip, but it didn't

squelch his smile. "You're absolutely right, Brian. If we are committed to making public spaces accessible to all, then there really is no choice." Josh turned to observe the town council member who had originally asked for the meeting to address funding concerns. "Wouldn't you agree, Gail?"

She pursed her lips. "But the budget—"

"Will find a way to accommodate these changes," Brian said and passed a piece of paper across the desk to her. "If you take a look, I found a company that will do all the required fixes for less than what you had set aside for the original project. That leaves plenty for them to update the park with the needed ramps and soft turf."

Gail took the paper and looked it over, nodding. "You're right. Good work, Brian. You'll present this at the next meeting for the final vote?"

"That's the plan." He wanted to punch the air in victory but kept his professional composure. "I'll have concrete figures by then for your approval."

The council members seemed pleased by the outcome of the meeting as they put their coats on and left the office. Josh held out his hand for Brian to shake. "You really know how to handle the council members and their complaints. I might have to watch my back in the next election."

"I'm no politician, so you have nothing to worry about," Brian answered. "Now, about the citizen board's complaint about the planned detours for the road renovations on Main Street this spring."

Josh waved his hand. "We'll cover that in our next meeting, if that's okay with you. If you can find a way around the congested traffic issue, then I'll know you're a true threat." He stood. "The weekend is about to start. Do you have any plans?"

"We're supposed to get a few inches of snow tomorrow, so probably shoveling my walk and a few of the neighbors' walkways."

"That's nice of you."

"It's a way of tricking myself into getting a workout without noticing I'm exercising."

"And does that work?"

"Sometimes. Unfortunately, it also means the neighbors feel obligated to pay me back with food, which negates my physical exertions."

Josh laughed and walked to the office door.

"You know, Shelby has a few cousins who are single if you're looking for a date this weekend. I could set something up."

"While I appreciate the offer, Mr. Mayor, I have to decline."

"Come on, they aren't that bad."

"That might be true, but I have really bad luck when it comes to blind dates."

"You should compare horror stories with Mel from the bookstore. She's got quite a few of her own." Josh gave him a salute. "Enjoy your weekend."

He turned to leave and scooted out of the way of a young man who burst into Brian's office. "Are you Brian Redmond? I need to talk to you."

Brian quickly glanced at his planner but didn't see a meeting scheduled. "Did we have an appointment?"

The young man shook his head and approached the desk. "She didn't say I needed to make one."

"Who said? My assistant?"

"Ms. Carmack."

"Vivian told you to come see me?"

He gave a short nod. "She said you could help. I should have called first, but I'm worried and I didn't want to lose another minute. If you can't help my family out, I don't know what I'll do."

Brian motioned to the chair in front of his desk. "Why don't you take a seat and tell me what the issue is."

The young man introduced himself, explained how he knew Vivi, and laid out his story for Brian. His mom had been in a car accident that had confined her to a wheelchair at least for the next few months, if not longer. They lived in a second-floor apartment that didn't have an elevator, and the doctors would be releasing her soon but that left her nowhere to go. "And I can't exactly change our address in the next couple of days."

Brian pulled out a pad of paper and started writing down details and a few names. "Your mom is employed?"

"She can't work right now, but she was before the accident."

"Does she have insurance? Are they paying her on disability at least temporarily?"

"I don't know. I don't think so. She doesn't talk about stuff like that with me." The kid put his head in his hands. "Her boss did come by the hospital the other day, Mom said, but I don't think it went well. And rent is coming due soon, and I can't access her online banking to know if we have enough to pay it. And my auntie has to go back home and that leaves me and my sister alone and..." His shoulders started to shake.

Brian got up from behind the desk and took the seat beside Devonte. He put a hand on the kid's shoulder and gave it a squeeze. "Hey, we'll figure this out, okay?"

Devonte raised his eyes, which were wet. "How?"

"First of all, I'll contact her employer and see about short-term disability. Then I'll reach out to someone I know who might have a house rental..."

"We can't afford a house..."

Brian held up a hand. "Then I'll check into some state programs that will help your mom cover costs while she recovers from her accident." He paused and gave the boy another squeeze on the shoulder. "How are you doing personally? Are you okay?"

Devonte gave a one-shouldered shrug. "I guess."

"You said you have a sister?"

"Little sister. Tiffany."

Brian made a face. "Ugh. I have a little sister, too. Jamie. Is Tiffany a pain in the neck like mine is?"

"Worse."

Brian laughed at that.

"Well, Devonte, I can promise that I'll get you any help that you need, okay? You don't have to worry about what's going to happen with you or your mom."

The kid gave him a look that screamed skepticism with a tinge of wariness. "Why would you do that?"

"Because it's my job, it's why the town pays me. And it's also the right thing to do. I believe in this community, and we have to support one another, right? We all need someone we know we can depend on." Devonte gave him a slight smile. It was all the payment Brian needed.

They made plans to meet on Monday after school to discuss what Brian discovered. They shook hands at the office door. "I'll be sure to let Ms. Carmack know that you came to see me."

"Yeah, she's pretty cool. For a teacher, at least."

Brian tried to squelch his smile at the faint praise, then shut the door behind Devonte. It might be Friday, but he still had a few minutes to make a couple of calls to help the kid and his family. Because there was nothing on his schedule that was more important than that.

STANDING AT THE kitchen window with a cooling cup of coffee in her hand, Vivi stared at the backyard as more snow fell on the several inches that had been accumulating since the early morning hours. She leaned her head on the cool glass of the window. Good thing she had finished her errands during the week so she could stay warm and cozy inside her house this Saturday. She'd have to shovel the driveway and sidewalk later once the snow had stopped falling, but she could reward herself with some of the split pea soup she intended on making in her slow cooker.

Hopefully the snow would stop before the community theater performance later that night. It would be a shame for the weather to cancel it.

Her cell phone buzzed from the charging

station and took her attention away from the window. The caller ID said it was her mother. She took a deep breath before taking the phone off the charger and answering. "Hi, Mom."

"Have you seen the snow outside?"

"I was just watching it fall. It looks so pretty and peaceful."

"I hope this doesn't mean you'll be canceling dinner with me tomorrow night."

"Mom, I haven't missed a Sunday dinner with you in years."

"Good. Because I found a recipe I want us to try."

Vivi thought about their last attempt at trying a new recipe. "This one doesn't involve making a risotto, does it? Do you remember that time we tried it?"

"And how it turned out to be basically soupy rice? Oh, yes." Her mom, Connie, chuckled on the other end. "At least that's better than how my mom made rice when I was growing up. She'd put some in a pan, cover it with water then boil it until the water was gone. If it didn't all absorb, she'd drain the excess out. I didn't know that rice wasn't supposed to be crunchy until I was about ten."

"Grammy wasn't much of a cook, but she was one heck of a seamstress. She made all your clothes."

"And a lot of yours, too, until we lost her."

They fell silent, remembering the kind woman that Grammy had been.

Her mother broke the silence. "By the way, your auntie Cora called me last night. Have you heard about the new woman your father is now dating?"

"Um…"

She had in fact heard about her dad's new girlfriend from her father. She had talked to him at the family Christmas party for over an hour about the interesting new woman in his life. He had said he hoped they could all meet for dinner some night soon.

Before her parents divorced when she was fourteen, Vivi had looked up to him. He'd been her hero.

Oh, who was she kidding? He still was. So strong and confident. Maybe that explained why she was still single. No man seemed to measure up. Even Ray, her ex-fiancé, had seemed close, but never quite reached the same heights. "He seems to be happy with her." She paused. "Maybe it's time for you to date again."

"Who, me?" Connie laughed at the suggestion. "I told you before. I like my independence. Besides, I'm too old to be dating. It's fine for your father, but I'm too set in my ways."

"You're hardly old, Mom. What could it hurt to be open to the possibility?"

She laughed more but then it petered out. "I don't know. Maybe." She hesitated. "And maybe it's time for you to get back out there, too."

"Mom…"

"What? Can I help it if I'd like to see you find a nice guy?"

Vivi's thoughts turned to Brian. He seemed like a nice guy. And she wanted to get to know him better. But the thought of opening herself to that kind of hurt again made her pause. When she'd turned down his text invitation to dinner, she had spent most of the night regretting her decision. She had wanted to see him. Wanted to talk to him. Get to know him better. But doing that would only bring pain later.

Vivi quickly changed the subject. "Cec

might be coming with me for dinner tomorrow. Would that be okay?"

Her mother exhaled loudly. "That poor girl. I know the pain she's going through right now. Yes, bring her tomorrow. I'll make something comforting to cheer her up. Maybe a nice pot roast."

"Sounds good. Love you."

Vivi hung up from her mother and collapsed into a kitchen chair. She rested her head on her fist and returned her gaze to the backyard. Her mom had stayed single for twenty-one years after the divorce. Would Vivi turn out to be like her?

"Who was on the phone?" Vivi turned to find Cec at the counter making herself a mug of coffee. She brought it to the kitchen table and took a seat across from Vivi.

"My mom."

"What did she have to say?"

"You're invited to dinner tomorrow night. She plans to make pot roast for dinner to cheer you up."

"That is sweet. Maybe I will go with you after all, even though it's going to take more than a pot roast to cheer me up."

"She heard about my dad's new girlfriend.

And I suggested that maybe it was time for her to start dating again."

"Ah. I take it Connie wasn't happy with that suggestion."

Vivi shook her head. "She's been alone all these years. You'd think that she would have moved on by now. It's not like she's still in love with my dad."

"That's why I've got to move on from Tom. I don't want to be complaining about his latest fling twenty years from now and still wondering what might have been." Cec reached over and took her hand. "*And* I don't want you to be wondering what might have happened if you'd pursued something with this nice guy you met one New Year's Eve."

"I can't do it."

"You can, but you're choosing not to. There's a big difference." Cec shrugged. "I'm going to take my shower."

THE CURTAIN DESCENDED upon the stage after the actor's last line, and the lights turned on signaling that the fifteen-minute intermission had started. Brian stood and twisted to his right, trying to work out the kinks in his back. He'd spent most of the afternoon shoveling his driveway, along with the driveways of several of his neighbors. Later, he'd come over to the community theater to clear sidewalks before tonight's performance.

He turned and noticed Vivi staring at him from across the auditorium. He lifted his hand and gave a short wave. She nodded and said something to her friend Cec before walking over to him. "I didn't know you were into local theater," she said with a smile.

"I'm always trying to support our community."

She gestured to the crowd. "Good to see so many people came out for the show despite the nasty weather."

"I think people want Thora to succeed, and they show up no matter what. It's one of the reasons I opted to settle here when I moved from Pittsburgh." He gave a jerk of his head toward the stage. "What do you think so far?"

"It's funnier than I was expecting. And the woman playing the love interest is fantastic." She peered at him. "What do you think?"

He smiled at her. "I think you're right."

She pointed out a young teen standing

with a group of what looked like her peers. "You see the girl in the red coat over there? That's Victoria. She was interviewing her senior citizen at the complex and discovered that the older woman is related distantly to her grandmother. What a coincidence, not to mention connection. It seems our project isn't just a history assignment anymore, but something that's affecting people's lives in a good way. I'm pretty proud of my students."

"That would be a great story to add to the booklet. You should ask Victoria to write it up."

"And I heard from Michael, who found out that his grandfather served in the same unit as the husband of his interviewee. Connections are being made all over the place." Her eyes sparkled as she told him this. They fell silent, just looking at each other until she shrugged. "Well, I just wanted to update you on that. Enjoy the rest of the performance."

"What are you and Cecily doing after? Maybe we could grab a bite somewhere."

She looked behind her to where Cec stood talking to another couple. "I, um… I don't know."

"I'm asking the both of you to go with me,

so it's not like I'm asking you on a date, if that's what's making you hesitate."

"It's not that. Like I said, I'd love to accept, but…maybe another time. I appreciate you thinking of us, of me."

"I wish you could help me understand what I'm doing wrong."

Vivi stared at him, then reached down and grabbed his hand. "You don't know how much I want to say yes. But…"

Brian squeezed her hand. "It's okay."

"I'm not ready to share why just yet."

Brian nodded and let go of her hand. She walked away. He didn't know what else to do to convince Vivi that he was a good guy and that she should consider giving him a chance.

BRIAN WATCHED THE young man read over the papers he'd given him. "I hope you don't mind, but I called your mom's current landlord to find out if we could get you out of the lease. It's going to cost us, but it's doable. That would open your mom up to be able to sign a lease on that house. It's all on one floor and has got wide doors that will fit a wheelchair. Has metal hand bars in the bathroom to help your mom get in and out of the tub."

The kid still hadn't said anything but kept his eyes on the papers. Had Brian stepped too far? Meddled where he wasn't wanted? "And I've applied for a grant on your mom's behalf that will help her with bills until she is able to return to work. It won't cover everything, but that's where her short-term disability checks will help."

Devonte looked up at him, and Brian wasn't sure if the kid was going to thank him or yell at him. Finally, Brian tried to give him a smile. "Well, say something."

Devonte blinked, as if in shock. "So, what happens now?"

"I'll stop into the hospital and get signatures from your mom, then get moving on the paperwork. If everything moves quickly, and I think it will, we can have you moved into the new place by the time the hospital releases your mom."

Still the kid sat, not saying much as he gazed at Brian. "Why are you doing this?"

Brian looked at him and weighed what words to say. This was all part of his job, but Devonte's case had become something more. He felt for the kid who was taking all of this on his young shoulders. Instead of answering, he asked, "How old are you?"

Devonte's chin lifted a little. "Old enough."

For what, Brian didn't ask. "This is a lot for anyone to be taking on, especially for a person so young, and you shouldn't have to. That's when people like me can step in and give a hand. You should be allowed to not have to worry about adult stuff until you are one. Focus on school and just being a kid."

"I'm not a kid."

Brian let the comment pass, even though he figured Devonte couldn't be older than sixteen.

"Why do you care, though? I still don't get it."

Brian thought about the people he hadn't been able to help over the years. The ones who had come to his office when it was too late to do anything. Those who had been too proud to accept his assistance. The ones who didn't know how to ask. Brian's answer to Devonte's question was loaded with regrets, but with successes, too. Those he had gotten into better housing or a better job. Those who had been lifted out of a bad situation and started over somewhere new. "Growing up, there were times that I needed someone to help me out. I grew up in a military family, so we were tight, always looked after each other, and each other's families, too. I liked that, still do. So I made a promise that I would always help out others whenever I had the chance once I got older."

Brian hoped Devonte was listening. "I want to give you and your family a hand because I do care. It's why I do what I do."

Devonte stared at him for a moment, then gave a short nod as if it was answer enough.

DAYS LATER, Brian got a phone call from Vivi. "I don't know what you did, but thank you for helping out Devonte. It's like he's a different kid since he talked to you."

"It's my job."

"Something tells me that he wasn't just another part of your job, though. Am I right?"

Brian paused. Part of his job required discretion when it came to the details in the lives of those he helped. He also didn't think Devonte would want his teacher to know all that was going on unless he shared it with her himself. "Devonte is special."

"He is. Thank you for whatever you did."

Brian smiled at the warmth in her words. "Does that mean you would want to do something for me in order to thank me?"

There was quiet on the other end of the phone before she answered, "You know, you're right. I think I'll write a letter to the mayor recommending you get a raise."

He couldn't hide his disappointment. "I was thinking something more like dinner."

"Dinner is eaten, then forgotten. A raise is more impactful and long-lasting."

"You having dinner with me would be something I'd remember the rest of my life, Vivi."

"Oh."

She sounded surprised by his response. But it was the truth. Vivian was unique. A real individual. Someone not easily forgotten or overlooked. She could be the adventure of a lifetime if she would only give him a chance. "Think about having dinner with me. You might be surprised to discover that I'm a great date. Imagine if we were together—"

She laughed softly. "You once said that

your mother would vouch for you, so I'm going to need her phone number."

He remembered telling her that, but he'd never thought she'd take him up on his offer. "You're really going to call my mom to ask her for references?"

"Well, sure. You offered it to me once, so I thought it would still stand."

"And if I give you her number, does that mean you will go out to dinner with me?"

"As long as everything checks out, I'll consider the invitation."

"'Consider.' It's better than an outright rejection, I guess."

He gave her the number and repeated it once more to verify it. Vivi thanked him. "I'll let you know what she says."

"I'm free tonight, by the way."

"You seem awfully confident that she'll be singing your praises."

"I wouldn't be giving you her number if I wasn't."

BRIAN SMOOTHED HIS TIE down the front of his shirt, then looked across the table to peer at Vivi. "My mother obviously had some good things to say about me."

Vivi brought her gaze up from the menu to meet his eyes. "She did."

"Did she tell you about the time I won the county's eighth-grade spelling bee?"

She paused as if thinking it over. "She must have left that story out."

"I won a huge trophy and a brand-new dictionary. It was pretty impressive. I still have them both."

Vivi laughed. "She did tell me that you won a full scholarship to college. And that you wasted it on a degree in political science that you're not even using."

He winced at the familiar words from an argument he'd been having on repeat with his mother ever since he graduated. "You'd think she'd be over that by now. I think she had grand ideas of me becoming president one day."

"So why aren't you running for office? It seems like you have the right connections and skills for becoming something bigger in the community."

He glanced up at the waiter who came to take their order, glad for the reprieve. Once they ordered their meals, Brian asked, "So what was it that made you change your mind? Besides my obvious good looks and charm, of course. What did she say that convinced you?"

Vivi fiddled with the silverware, then placed the cloth napkin on her lap. He leaned forward. "Oh no. Did she tell you the story about my saving the dog that fell through the ice?"

She finally looked at him. "No, but I think I need to hear more about that one."

"Later. What did she say, then?"

"It wasn't one thing, Brian. It was all of it. She loves you."

"She's my mom. She's contractually required to."

Vivi smiled, and he was struck by how something so simple could steal his breath. He reached over and took her hand, rubbing his thumb across the palm. "Whatever it was, I'm glad you're giving me this chance."

She removed her hand from his grasp. "One chance. That's all this is."

"Then I'll have to make the most of it." He glanced around the restaurant and winced. "I guess I should have taken you somewhere nicer if this is my one shot."

"No, this is perfect. Like I told you before,

Italian food is my favorite. And I've been meaning to try this place since it opened last fall." As if to prove her point, she took a piece of the warm bread that the server had left on their table and dipped it into the shallow bowl of olive oil before popping it into her mouth. She closed her eyes and moaned softly. "Amazing."

Brian mirrored her movements but didn't eat the bread. "A buddy of mine knows the chef here."

"You seem to have a lot of friends."

"I have a lot of acquaintances."

"What's the difference?"

Brian gave a shrug. "Friends are there when you need a helping hand or an ear to listen.

"I've learned through the years that there are only a handful of people that I can depend on. My parents. My sister. And Josh has turned out to be one good friend that I can count on as well."

"Is that why you work so hard to help others? So that you can be someone that they can depend on? Like how you helped Devonte?" She reached across the table and took his hand in hers. "I can't tell you how much it means to me that you went above and beyond for him and his family. He hasn't said much, but I can tell that you made a difference."

"He's a good kid who needed a hand." He squeezed her hand then. "I'm glad you thought of me."

She slipped her hand from his, and an awkward silence fell between them before Brian took a deep breath and let it out. A smile grew on his face. "But that's not why we're here tonight. You didn't call me to discuss your student."

She shook her head. "I figured you deserved to know why I won't go out with you."

Brian cast a glance around the restaurant. "Yet, here we are. Out on a date."

"Fine. Why this will be the only date, then."

Brian winced. "It's because I'm too good-looking, isn't it? You can't handle being seen with such a handsome man."

"That's not it."

"It's because you discovered that public servants like community resource managers are grossly underpaid."

She shook her head. He bit his lip and

narrowed his eyes. "Then it must be that my great personality makes you jealous. You wonder how a man so good-looking and kind and generous can be so perfect for you."

At this, Vivi laughed, almost choking on the bread she'd been chewing. "You really have an overinflated sense of yourself, don't you?"

"Just trying to keep it light." He leaned forward. "Now, why don't you tell me the truth? What is it that has you so scared?"

She looked stricken by his words, and the smile faded from her face. "I'm not scared."

He cocked his head to one side and gave her a look to let her know he didn't believe her. She shook her head again. "The reason is not because I'm scared."

"Then what is it?"

She took a sip of her wine. "It's because I'm cursed."

CHAPTER FIVE

Vivi watched Brian's reaction to her words, but he didn't flinch or even blink in wonder. Instead, he shrugged. "I guess there could be worse things in a relationship."

"Worse than knowing that whatever relationship we might have is doomed to lead to heartbreak and tears?"

Brian held up a hand. "Vivi, this is our first date. I don't think we need to go down that road just yet, do you?"

"I know what's going to happen."

"How could you possibly know?"

"Because it's happened before. Every seven years, I have the worst luck, and my life sucks for that entire twelve months."

"So, this has happened before?"

She felt as if he was making fun of her, but the look on his face seemed to show that he was listening and trying to understand. "Yes. When I was seven, my grandmother died and then my best friend moved away. My parents divorced when I was fourteen."

"And when you were twenty-one?"

"I was in a skiing accident, which broke my pelvis and caused a lot of internal damage. And my first serious boyfriend cheated on me while I was recovering."

"Okay."

"Then when I was twenty-eight, my fiancé broke off our engagement a month before the wedding."

Brian winced. "That's a tough one."

"It just proves my point. Seven. Fourteen. Twenty-one. Twenty-eight."

"And now you're thirty-five?"

"In a few months, yes."

Brian held up his hands. "Well, there you go. You're in the safe zone until then. We can go out until your birthday without having to worry about it."

If only she could be that lucky. "Not quite. My luck is bad for the entire calendar year."

"Vivi…"

"Don't act like I don't know what I'm talking about. Experience has proven that this will be a bad year for me. And I can't drag you into it. I won't."

"Don't I have any say in that?"

"It's my curse, so it's my choice."

"You don't really think the universe is conspiring against you, do you?"

She had expected that he'd be skeptical about her confession, but she was surprised by this jump in logic. "Do you mean that spiritual forces are somehow orchestrating the events of my life? That I don't somehow have free will in all of this?" She waved off his suggestion. "Not at all. It's just bad luck to the extreme."

Brian nodded. "Good. Because I believe we make our own luck. And we can turn this so-called curse around."

"I'm not willing to play games with my life like that. It's too risky."

"Life is a risk."

"But I don't have to play along if I don't want to."

Brian paused. "This is getting a little too serious for a first date. Why don't we change the subject?"

"Fine. Because like I said, this will be our only date."

He plucked a piece of bread from the basket and dipped it into the oil. He gave her a

warm smile and said, "We'll see about that."
Then he took a bite.

She found herself smiling back at him.
"So, tell me why you became a community
resource manager. Seems like a rather ob-
scure career choice."

"I was always good at finding solutions to
problems when I was a kid no matter where
my dad was stationed. I organized softball
games, then found sponsors so we could
actually start a league. I started a newspa-
per delivery service with a few friends, and
we eventually took over distribution in my
end of town. Then after I graduated high
school, I went to Georgetown to get my poli
sci degree but discovered that while I was
great at organizing and fundraising, I didn't
have the stomach for politics, which is why
I don't run for office. So I changed tactics
and got my MBA at Pitt, where I met Josh,
the mayor. Although he obviously wasn't
mayor of Thora at that time. I don't even
think it was on his radar. Instead, he was a
businessman who had a desire to help kids
have the same chances he had, and I used
my skills to raise money and find mentors
for his first programs."

"And he convinced you to move to Michigan to help our little town?"

"Me and my sister, Jamie. We were a package deal for my move here."

Vivi rested her chin on her fist as she looked across the table at Brian. "She seems fun. I always wanted a sister."

"I'd be happy to let you have her."

He grinned in a goofy way and a flutter started in her chest. Thankfully for her heart, the server arrived with their meals. She focused on putting the perfect bite on her fork and placing it in her mouth. She closed her eyes at the spicy garlic marinara that surrounded the penne. *Perfection.*

Just like this evening was turning out to be. To keep her thoughts from heading too far in that direction, she cleared her throat and looked up at him. "So, what's Jamie like? I didn't get much of a chance to talk to her the other night."

"Too smart for her own good. Thinks she knows it all." His expression was sheepish. "And she's usually right. Enough about my sister. Why go into teaching? And don't say it was for the money because we both know that couldn't be true."

"Because I get paid to delve into the past and then share my discoveries with my students. Growing up, I always wanted to be Indiana Jones."

"You ever go on an archaeological dig?"

"When I was in college, sure. And I've always wanted to do another during my summer breaks. But…"

Brian waited for her to finish the sentence, then asked, "But what?"

"But there always seems to be something that keeps me in town. One year it was a health scare with my mom, but it turned out to be nothing, thankfully. Another year, my dad needed my help with getting his house ready to sell. Like I said, it's always something to keep me here in town."

"You said you always wanted a sister, but why can't your brother step in to help with your parents?"

"No brother, either. I'm a lonely only child."

"So why not go this summer?" He watched her, and she felt herself squirming under his scrutiny. "Let me guess. You're letting this curse keep you from going off on a dig to Mexico or somewhere."

"You don't know me as well as you think you do."

He raised one eyebrow at this. "Or do I? Maybe I have ways of reading your mind that you don't know anything about."

The expression on his face changed and it made her laugh. "Oh, *really*?" She tried to do a blank look and empty her mind of all thoughts. "What am I thinking right now?"

He peered at her, squinting his eyes and setting his mouth in a tight line. Then his eyes widened, and she could swear that he blushed. "Ms. Carmack, I'm surprised by your boldness. We're only just getting to know one another, after all." He placed a hand on his chest. "And I don't kiss on the first date."

Now it was Vivi who blushed. "I'm not the one with a lusty mind."

Brian gave a shrug. "Fine. What were you thinking?"

"That I haven't had a dinner with a man that I've enjoyed as much as this one."

Brian lifted his wineglass in a salute. "The feeling is mutual. I haven't enjoyed dinner like this with another man either."

Over dinner, Vivi discovered that Brian

really was as charming as he'd claimed. He was funny, smart and sweet, and by the end of the evening, she realized she could find herself in trouble by falling for him. But she was sticking to her plan. One date. Period.

He paid the server for their meals despite her protests, then left a generous tip. As they stood to leave, he held her coat so she could slip her arms through the sleeves. She could feel his warm breath on the back of her neck, and it sent shivers through her. *Get yourself together. This is only one date.*

He drove them back to her house, and the interior of the car was silent except for the soft sounds of the radio playing pop hits. He pulled into her driveway and turned off the ignition. He got out of the car, ran around to her side and opened her door for her. He extended his hand to assist her out of the car and held on to her hand for a moment longer than necessary, before letting his fingers slide from hers. "I'll walk you to your door."

They proceeded up the shoveled sidewalk to her front porch, and she fumbled with her purse to find her keys. She had placed the key into the lock and turned it when Brian put a hand on her shoulder and she turned to face him. She looked into his hazel eyes and wondered if he would kiss her. The moment stretched between them until he shook his head. "I told you. I don't kiss on the first date."

"What if it's our only date?" she asked him.

"About that." He glanced down at his feet, then back up at her. "The fire department is holding their annual chili cook-off and fundraiser next Saturday night. I was wondering if you'd like to go with me."

Hadn't he been listening to her? "No. I told you. This was only for tonight. Nothing has changed."

He took a step closer to her until their lips almost touched. "Everything changed tonight, Vivi. And I hope with a little bit of time and space maybe you'll see that, too."

She opened her lips, knowing that she only had to take a step forward until they would be kissing. But Brian dropped a quick kiss on her cheek, then stepped down off the porch. "I'll wait to leave until you get inside."

She turned back to the door, grateful to be able to hide her disappointment. With the door open, she turned and gave Brian a small wave. He returned it, then walked to his car. She watched him get in and drive away down the street.

When she closed the door and locked it, she discovered Cec on the couch. Cec lowered the volume on the television and patted the couch as she asked, "So how was dinner?"

"Completely wonderful. And the worst thing that could have happened."

BRIAN FLIPPED THROUGH the channels, but nothing on the television screen could erase this sense of unease in his chest. Dinner with Vivi had been enlightening. Now he knew why she had turned him down. But that didn't offer him any solutions. Luckily, he had a knack for finding answers where there didn't seem to be any. He only needed to approach it like one of his work projects.

But Vivi and a future with her meant a lot more than his job. Yes, he liked what he did for a living. He thrived on the feeling of accomplishment when he found a way forward for someone who thought a situation was hopeless. A relationship with Vivi might seem hopeless to her at the moment, but he knew they could really have something special. If only he could figure out how to convince her.

He settled on watching a hockey game, then picked up his phone. A text from Jamie asking how the date went.

Great until she turned me down for a second one.

Don't get too far ahead of yourself.

She's the one. I know it.

Bubbles appeared to indicate that she was typing but then disappeared. He waited for a moment before placing the phone down. He picked it up again to see if she had responded. Nothing.

He pulled up his email program and started weeding through the messages when his phone vibrated with an incoming call from Jamie. "She is the one, James. Don't try to argue with me."

"Did you tell her that tonight? Maybe that's why she refused a second date because you came on too strong."

"Maybe, but we had a real connection, you know?"

Jamie sighed. "I haven't had one of those in forever. So did you kiss her?"

"A gentleman never tells."

"Which means you didn't."

He thought about that moment on the porch with Vivi. He'd wanted to kiss her so badly. And she seemed like she would have welcomed it. But one kiss with her would never be enough. And if he couldn't figure out a way to show her that they should be together, curse or no curse, then it wouldn't matter. "I should look over the figures for the Hansen project."

"Brian, you're my big brother and I love you. But I refuse to let you do work on a Saturday night."

"I thought I could find a way to bring the developer to town without having to pay as much as he wants."

"Would you look at that? I gotta go."

He chuckled at her. "Fine. Maybe you can help me brainstorm ideas for it tomorrow over brunch."

"Tomorrow is Sunday."

"And your point?"

"You're hopeless." Jamie paused. "Vivi is just one woman. If she's not interested, maybe it's better if you move on."

He considered his sister's words after hanging up with her. Vivi was one woman, sure. But he knew that she was the only one for him. If only he could fan her interest in him to a flame that would leave her without any doubts.

Because Vivian Carmack was definitely interested. He'd bet his paycheck on it.

VIVI OBSERVED THE lobby of the seniors' assisted living home and found the manager's office. She walked up to the door and opened it. A receptionist looked up at her. "Ms. Carmack, right? Christopher is waiting for you inside."

Vivi took a deep breath and stepped inside. A tall man with dark hair stood and thrust out his hand. "It's nice to finally meet you in person, Vivian. Do you mind if we walk down to our kitchen? I've got a fire to put out before we discuss the reason for your visit."

"A fire?"

"Figurative, not literal. One of our head chefs is going to be on vacation for a few weeks. Doing a food tour of Italy. I can't wait to see what she makes for us when she's finally back. Anyway, the staffing change leaves us shorthanded." He gestured for her to go on ahead of him. "After you."

Vivi followed him and they walked down the hall to a set of double doors, then inside.

"I assure you that I didn't call you about a problem with any of your students. The residents have told me they've been great to have around the place."

She let out a breath, relieved. "Thanks. I had a vision of one of them getting into some sort of shenanigans and upsetting the residents."

Christopher raised an eyebrow at this. "Shenanigans? We have plenty of those here, but not any associated with your students." He paused and gave her a wink. "Yet."

He opened another set of double doors and waved to a woman in chef whites and hat. "Annabelle will be out until the end of this month. Where do we stand with the schedule?"

As they ironed out the details, Vivi let her mind wander back to Saturday night. She'd had trouble falling asleep after saying good-night to Brian, and every evening since. Why had Brian been so perfect? Why couldn't he have been rude or condescending or at least a tiny bit flawed? Instead, he'd been, well, charming. Handsome. And she was having a hard time trying to convince herself that a second date wouldn't hurt.

"Sorry about that. I wanted to get that squared away." He pointed toward the dining room. "Want a cup of hot coffee while we discuss why I called you? I might even be able to scrape up a few fresh-baked cookies left over from lunch."

They took a seat at one of the round tables that dotted the large dining room. Vivi fiddled with the spoon, stirring her coffee even though the cream and sugar had already blended into the drink. "If you've changed your mind about the project…"

Christopher set his coffee in front of him. "Hardly. The seniors are enjoying meeting the kids and talking about their lives. I wanted to see if there was a chance to expand the project."

Vivi stopped stirring her coffee and looked up at him. "Expand it?" Well, this was unexpected.

"As word about the project has spread through the place, I've had more seniors asking if they can be a part of it. In my office, I have a waiting list two pages long of residents who would like to participate next time."

"Next time? But we only have this one booklet planned."

Christopher set aside his cup of coffee and held up his hands. "That's just it. What if we make this an annual project for your students? Make it almost like a yearbook with pictures alongside the stories the kids write based on the experiences of their storytellers?"

Vivi liked the idea, but the execution of it made her head swim. "I don't know, Christopher. I had only planned on this year. And even that is giving me nightmares with all the logistics."

"It would give more students a chance to better their writing and research skills, and even learn editing and layout, as well as a focus on local history. So much gets lost as more and more of the older folks pass on."

He looked at her with an eager expression on his face. She didn't doubt that this was something he truly believed in. The question was how would they turn this into an annual project? Could she make this happen? "I'd have to talk to Brian about how we could continue it. If that's even a possibility."

"And the complex would be willing to contribute toward the cost of publication. Especially because we would offer copies for sale through our gift shop. All proceeds would still go to the library, of course." His eyes twinkled at her. "It's been a while since something has captured my residents' attention and enthusiasm as much as this. And I'd like to make it happen for them."

Vivi had to admit that overhearing her students talk about the stories they'd collected had brought back some of their drive and passion. She smiled and gave a nod. "Tell you what. I'll talk to Brian about it and get back to you later this week."

ON THE LAST Saturday of January, the Thora firehouse held their annual chili cook-off. The competition could be fierce between the competitors in the various categories, including hottest, most unusual combo and best overall. Last year, Vivi had attended with Tom and Cecily, who had fed the chili to each other while looking into each other's eyes. This year, Cec had insisted that she'd go with Vivi alone.

"If you get uncomfortable, we can leave whenever you want," Vivi reminded her friend as she paid for both of their admissions into the town's recreation center.

Cec unzipped her coat and slipped off her hat. "I'm already uncomfortable, but we're not leaving until I've tried all the chilis." She took the long strand of tickets from the cashier and entered the main hall, Vivi trailing her.

Vivi wasn't sure if she was impressed with Cec's determination to face her fears or wary of her false cheeriness. Long tables lined the walls displaying the chilis entered in the competition. A small bucket for tickets and a whiteboard describing the type of chili and its ingredients accompanied each offering. The firefighters stood in front of their chilis waiting to serve. Vivi clutched her tickets in one hand and glanced around the slowly filling room.

"Looking for someone?"

Vivi shook her head at Cec. "Like who?"

"Hmm, I don't know. Maybe a certain community resource manager who originally invited you here tonight?"

Maybe she had been thinking she might catch a glimpse of him. But only to see him. Maybe say hi. She couldn't risk more than that. "I'm here with you."

"Only because you're too scared to accept what he might be offering."

"And what might that be? Heartache and pain?"

"Or maybe a chance at something really great?"

Vivi stopped looking around the room to peer at Cec. "You can't know that."

"And you do?" Cec grabbed her hand. "Does this divorce hurt? Yes. Would I still marry Tom if I had a chance to go back?" She bit her lip and shrugged. "Probably. Because despite what's going on right now, I was happy. In love. And everything seemed possible."

Vivi squeezed Cec's hand. "You sound like you're in a good place. I can only wish to be half as strong as you are."

"Give me about five minutes and I'll be brooding again. Don't worry." She pointed to where they had set up a bar for the evening. "Ooh, look. I wonder if they have that cranberry spritzer like they had last year?"

Her friend headed toward the bar and nodded at Vivi to follow. At the same moment, someone bumped into Vivi from behind and she turned to find Brian, who was smiling broadly. "Imagine running into you here. I didn't think you were coming tonight."

"Brian." She looked into his hazel eyes and tried to remember why she had turned him down. Their one date had been fun. Amazing even. And that almost kiss on her front porch had kept her awake every night since last week. If a kiss that didn't happen could be that good, what would the real deal be like? "I'm here with Cecily."

He nodded and eyed her from head to toe. "You look good."

She glanced down at her sweater and jeans. This was good? Then she noticed what he was wearing. An oatmeal sweater, like hers. Dark vintage jeans, like she wore. And similar brown leather boots. "You must have gotten the memo about the dress code for tonight also."

Brian laughed at her words, and the sound

made her chest grow warm. "Too bad the rest of the town didn't. But I like your style." He waved a hand at his outfit. "Obviously."

"Well, look at the cute twins." Cec winked and handed Vivi her drink. "Some might say it was as if fate was trying to get the two of you together."

Vivi turned to shoot Cec a look, but Brian put an arm around Cec's shoulders. "I like how your friend thinks. What other wisdom do you have to share with us?"

"That if Vivi isn't careful, she's likely to lose a good guy before she's even had the chance to catch him."

Brian wiggled his eyebrows as he looked in Vivi's direction. "Definitely good advice. What do you think, Vivi?"

"I don't think you two take what I think seriously." Vivi wandered over to the first table that advertised a sweet and spicy chili. She put a ticket in the bucket and accepted a small cup of chili with a plastic spoon.

The fact that her best friend sided with Brian stung a little. Cecily was supposed to support her and her choices. And if Vivi chose to let Brian go, then she would be fine. Maybe a little sadder. Maybe she'd have some regrets. But she would be fine.

She took a spoonful of the chili and blew on it before putting it in her mouth. Chewing slowly, she could taste the heat of the chili peppers and something else. Was that cinnamon? Interesting. But not her favorite. She chased the bite with a sip of her juice.

"How is it?" Brian asked her as he put in a ticket and accepted a cup of chili.

"Different." She turned to look behind him. "Where did your new best friend Cecily go?"

"To be honest, it got awkward without you there. And she found one of your fellow teachers to talk to instead." He took a bite of the chili, then made a face and put the spoon back in the cup. "Why did you run away?"

"I didn't run. I walked."

"Still, you left. Why?"

"Because…"

"Was it the way we were talking, or what we said?"

She moved to the next table and placed a ticket in the bucket. This firefighter had made a green pork chili. Bold choice. She tasted a tiny bit and discovered she liked it.

Brian tasted his sample and then put in another ticket to get a second cup. "Wow, this is good."

"I know, right? Even though it's green. Wonder how he got it that color?" She tried another bite and closed her eyes, letting the spices dance on her tongue.

"Sometimes you have to try something to see if it's good or not. Even when you doubt it could be."

She opened her eyes to find Brian watching her. "I know you think I'm being silly about this whole curse thing."

"I don't think you're silly." He spoke with a serious tone, no more teasing, she realized. "Stubborn about it, yes. But not silly."

"I don't want to get hurt."

"And you think I do?" He placed both of his empty cups of chili on the table, then took hers out of her hand and placed it alongside his. He threaded his fingers through hers, and tugged her closer. She looked into his eyes and wondered again what she was doing. Why was she staying away from him? She'd missed him this last week. Had wanted to see him but knew that it would only make it harder for her to eventually stay away. Better to end it before it really had a chance to start.

Right?

With his other hand, Brian caressed her cheek. "Don't run off on me, Vivi. Give us a chance."

She let herself fall and ignored the tiny voice that reminded her of the consequences of pursuing anything with him. Maybe it was time to show this curse who was the one in control. She bit her lip, then nodded. "Okay."

Brian's head shot back at her word. "What did you say?"

"Fine. Let's give this a chance, whatever it is."

"You mean that?"

She smiled as she leaned in closer to him. "Every word."

They visited the rest of the tables, enjoying more chili, and later joined up with Cec and a group of teachers from the high school. Her best friend glanced at Vivi and Brian's joined hands and raised her eyebrows but didn't say a thing.

CHAPTER SIX

THE FOLLOWING MONDAY EVENING, Vivi handed Brian copies of the stories that her seniors had already collected. "You'll find some interesting reading in there."

He lifted the first page, read a few lines and nodded. "You're right. Oh, and there's one more bit of business before we can switch to date night."

"I can't wait. So, what's this last bit of business?" She held his gaze. "I'd like to get to the date portion of our evening a little quicker."

Brian smiled. "Me, too. It's good we're on the same side, or same page on this one."

"Brian. The last bit?"

"Oh, right." He picked up his cell phone and located the text he'd received from Arlene, the editor for the project. "I got a message saying that we need to start emailing the stories that we've already received. Arlene's hoping to edit them as we go along rather than all of them at one time. It will help her with our deadline."

Vivi took the stack of papers back to her side of the desk. "I can take care of that in the morning and scan these to her."

Brian put his hand over hers. "Why don't you let me?"

"Because this is my project."

"Which I'm helping with. Plus, you'll be busy teaching."

The shot of electricity from their fingers touching made him pause. He wondered if it was the same for her, considering she was silent, too. Another beat passed before Vivi finally spoke. "And you'll be busy with meetings and budgets. I can do this, Brian."

"But you don't have to. This is part of how I'm contributing to the project."

She slid the papers to her side of the desk. "These are my students, so my stories. End of discussion."

Better to choose his battles, and this was a minor skirmish. "You're right. You should take care of it."

Vivi opened her mouth as if to disagree,

then shut it and stared at him. "Did you just say I was right?"

"I can relinquish control when I have to." He grinned at her, teasing. "But it's nice to see that you can be as stubborn as I am. I just learned that you're not perfect."

"You're enjoying this a little too much."

"Vivi, I enjoy you. All of you. Flaws and all."

"Well, I don't know if I like you noticing my flaws this early in our..." She frowned. "Is it a relationship already?"

"Well, since you've only agreed to explore what's happening with us two days ago, it's a little too soon for us to define it like that."

"Oh."

She sounded disappointed, and it made his heart race just a little. "But I'm definitely interested in moving in that direction."

Vivi smiled and scooted forward. "Is the working part of our dinner date over now?"

He looked deeply into her dark brown eyes and nodded. "I'd say it is."

"Good." She leaned in as if to kiss him... but instead grabbed her coat. "I am curious about one thing. Why did you say I should dress in layers tonight? And bring a thicker winter coat?"

"You'll find out soon." He stood and retrieved his own coat and together they walked outside to his car. He then drove to Ted's Diner and parked in the carryout spot. "I'll be right back."

"Wait. We're not eating here?"

"Patience." Brian grinned at her, then hurried inside. He stopped at the pickup window and gave the cashier his name. He handed her his credit card, and she handed him several bags of food. The aroma was making him hungrier by the second. Laden with their dinner, he returned to the car. He placed the food in the back seat then got in on the driver's side. He turned to Vivi. "Miss me?"

"You're being awfully mysterious. Are we going back to your place with dinner?"

"Nope."

"Back to the office?"

"No. Something different. Something we'll remember. Trust me."

He drove to the central downtown area and parked. "Interested in a picnic?"

Vivi glanced out the window. "It's dark.

It's cold. And there's snow." She turned to look at him, must have seen the enthusiasm on his face, and said, "It is something I've never done before, so I guess we could give it a try."

"Great."

They got out of the car, and Brian retrieved their dinner, asking Vivi to carry it while he collected their other supplies from the back seat. "I ordered the daily specials for us. I'm sorry, I should have asked you what you like, but I kind of wanted all this to be a surprise. I hope that's okay?"

"No allergies for me, and I like most foods. I'm sure it'll be fine."

The park was well lit, and thankfully there wasn't too much snow on the ground. They walked to the nearest picnic table and Brian cleared the top with a gloved hand. Vivi placed the bag of food on the table and began to open it, while he put down one blanket on the bench for them to share, and handed her another to wrap herself in.

He also produced a trio of little battery-operated votive candles and switched them on, giving the space a pretty glow. "The stars are nice, but I thought we might need more light."

Next he produced a bottle of red wine and offered Vivi a glass, which she accepted readily. "This will warm me up," she said, raising the glass in a toast before taking a sip.

He joined her on the bench, sharing the blanket underneath them, and putting another around his shoulders.

Vivi leaned close to him and put an arm through his. "Thankfully, it's warmer tonight than it was earlier in the week."

"You're right. It's not too bad, is it?"

She opened her take-out container and picked up a plastic fork. "It's certainly memorable…"

"Oh, first, there's soup." Brian started to pull out the containers from the bag. "There's beef barley and chicken noodle."

"Ooh, beef barley, please."

He handed her the tub. "And I got us lasagna and cheesy garlic bread for the main course."

"Italian. My favorite."

As they ate, they shared body heat as well as stories and jokes, and whatever else came to mind. The hot soup was tasty and warmed them, and the spicy lasagna filled them up. Vivi pushed her container of lasagna away from her. "Ugh, I'm too full to finish. That was so good, though. Thank you."

"The nice thing about it being in a take-out container is that it's already set for you to bring home for lunch tomorrow."

"You're always thinking ahead."

He laughed and nudged her with his shoulder. "I do that a lot. Maybe that's why I'm good at my job."

"You're good at your job because you care about people and doing what it takes when they need it."

"Thank you. You're good at your job because you care about your students and getting them to open their eyes and minds to the world around them."

"I appreciate that."

He reached over and pushed a silky strand of hair away from her face. "So, what do you think of your first snow picnic?"

"I think it was different. You get points for creativity, but I'd prefer going on the next picnic when it's warmer."

He liked the direction of her thoughts.

Maybe there was a future for them. "It's a date, then. We'll go in the spring."

"Sounds good."

AFTER THEY GOT to a point where they couldn't feel their toes, they decided to pack up. Hand in hand, they walked over to his car. Once inside, he blasted the heat and steered them toward city hall to retrieve her Jeep.

The journey didn't take very long and soon she was standing beside her car. He joined her there. She looked into his eyes. It had been a good date. Like she had said, it was different. Fun. Even if her fingers still tingled from the cold. Or was that because she was tempted to touch his cheek?

She opened her door, and he stepped forward and asked, "When can I see you again?"

She mentally reviewed her schedule for the next few days. "How about Friday? They're having another eighties night at the roller rink. Cec and I had talked about going."

"Roller-skating?" He looked sheepish. "Actually, I have a fancy charity fundraiser for a friend that I promised to go to that night. I completely forgot." He raised a brow and had a speculative look in his eye. "Could you go with me?"

"A fancy fundraiser? That sounds…" *Boring. Fatal.* Like the worst idea for a date night ever. She noted the eagerness on his face, then nodded. "That sounds fantastic."

"Are you sure? It's going to be deadly boring. But I promised that I'd go to support this friend." He paused and took a step toward her. "It's a bad idea. Don't worry. I take back the invite. We'll do something else."

"But I want to go."

"Trust me. Even I don't want to go."

"But you promised you would. And if I know you even a little, you keep your word even if it's the hard thing to do." She leaned closer and put her mittened hands on his chest. "So, Friday night, then?"

He put his hands over hers. "I tell you what. If you go with me Friday night, I'll make it up to you on Saturday."

"Two date nights in a row? Do you really think that's smart with my curse and all? Maybe we should space them out a little more, just in case."

He grinned. "I'll risk it." He held her tight, then kissed her cheek. "Until Friday night."

Kind. Considerate. Funny. And oh so charming. What other great qualities did this man have? She couldn't wait to spend more time with him to find out.

FROM ACROSS HIS office desk, Jamie handed him the gloves he'd forgotten at her place. "What time are you picking me up on Friday night?" she asked.

"You're off the hook. I found a date for Paul's fundraiser."

Jamie's eyebrows rose at this announcement. "Really. Who lost a bet to you?"

"Ha ha." He took the gloves and waved them at her. "Vivi agreed to attend with me."

"And here I thought you were trying to impress her, not bore her to tears."

"Actually, she insisted on going with me."

Jamie eyed him for a moment. "Wait. The last I heard, she wasn't interested in you. What changed?"

He smiled and leaned back in his chair before attempting to put his feet up on the desk. Unfortunately, his chair almost tipped over and he had to lean forward so he wouldn't fall to the ground. "Obviously, my abundant attributes have finally won her over. Why are you so surprised?"

His sister narrowed her eyes at him. "How much did it cost you? A hundred, no, two hundred bucks?"

"You're impossible. Why do I put up with you?"

"Because I'm the best sister you ever had. And hey, as family, you can't get rid of me."

"Don't tempt me." He picked up a pen from the desk and tossed it at her. "But seriously, I really like this woman, James. What if taking her to the fundraiser screws it all up for me?"

"Oh please. You shine when you're schmoozing. She's going to be impressed like crazy by the way you work a crowd." She put a hand on his shoulder. "And let's be honest. If one bad night ruins it all for the two of you, then maybe she isn't the woman for you."

"Meeting Vivi, it was like fate. I told you that I wanted more for my life. Well, guess what? Vivi could be it."

"Have you told her this?"

"No." He paused, then glanced at his sister. "Do you think I should?"

She looked at him as if he had proposed something ludicrous. "Do you want to scare her off?"

"Of course not."

"Then you keep it to yourself." She put her hands on her hips. "It's a miracle that you get any dates at all. Well, besides the ones I set you up on." She gave him a smile. "And if things don't work out with Vivi, I met this woman at the grocery store who could be perfect for you."

He held up his hands. "Nope. Vivi is it for me."

"Fine. But I'll keep her number just in case." She buttoned her coat and started to leave his office. At the door, she turned back to face him. "You know, if this woman is willing to attend the snooze fest on Friday with you, maybe she is the one."

Brian nodded. He turned his gaze to the window and watched the snowflakes drifting down from the sky. Vivi was everything he could want. He just needed to prove that to her, curse or no curse.

VIVI WALKED OUT of her bedroom, the hem of the satin and crepe dress swishing along the wood floor. From the sofa in the living room, Cec looked up from the romance novel she had her nose buried in and whistled. "Wow. Look at you."

Vivi did a twirl, her hands lifted in the air. "Do you think it's too much?"

"For a fancy fundraiser? I think it's perfect. Besides, you're going to knock his socks off."

"Thanks. I'm not sure what I got myself into."

Cec placed a bookmark in her novel before dropping it next to her. "Hey, if you're feeling uncomfortable, it isn't too late to cancel. You could call him and tell him you have a headache and can't go. Then you could stay home with me, and we could watch home renovation shows together."

"I want to go." She bent down as she put her feet in the high heels and lifted the first back strap over her ankle. "What's so bad about going to a fundraiser? We went to the chili cook-off last week and had a blast."

"Because that emphasized the fun in fundraiser. I have a feeling this one is heavier on the funds part. Meaning rubber chicken. People in fancy clothes looking down their noses at each other. And dry speeches that put you to sleep."

"How many have you gone to in your life?"

Cec gave a shrug. "None, but I've seen enough of them on television shows and movies to know that I'm right."

"Even if you are, I'm actually looking forward to this one." And she really was eager for her evening with Brian. Even if they did serve rubber chicken and put her to sleep with boring speeches.

Cec smiled and reached for the remote control for the TV. "Because you're going with Brian and you really, really like him, right?"

Vivi's lips twitched, and she couldn't help the smile that bloomed on her face at the thought of Brian. "Maybe."

"Girl, please. It's obvious by the spark in your eyes that you're getting feelings for this guy."

Vivi took a seat next to Cec on the sofa. "I've tried not to. Really, I have. I don't know how he does it, but he gets past all my defenses somehow."

"And you like him."

She nodded. "I really do. Am I making a mistake?"

The doorbell rang, and Vivi shot to her feet. "He's here." She put a hand to her cheeks. "Um, could you answer the door? I'm not ready yet."

"Yes, you are."

"No, I just need a few moments to check on…stuff." Then she fled to the safety of the bathroom where she stared at her reflection in the mirror. Her makeup looked perfect. Her hair was twisted up and pinned into place. Her outside looked ready for the evening, but now her insides trembled at the thought of a fancy evening with Brian. Maybe Cec had been right, and she should have canceled. *Deep breath, Vivi. Just breathe low and slow.*

There was a soft knock on the bathroom door. "Your date is here, Vivi. You ready yet?"

She took one last glance in the bathroom mirror. She could do this. She could walk out and knock his socks off, then go and have an evening that she'd never forget.

Another deep breath. She put her hand on the doorknob and turned it. Cec gave her a thumbs-up as she went to find Brian, who was waiting for her in the living room. He smiled and stepped forward to meet her, taking her hands in his. "Wow. You look amazing," he said.

She took in the sight of his tux. James Bond had nothing on Brian. Especially with that smile on his face that had the power to enchant her. "So do you."

He released her hands, then held out his arm. "Our chariot awaits, milady."

Cec ran to the coat closet and pulled out a long wool cloak that mirrored the burgundy in Vivi's dress. "You'll freeze in that dress if you don't put this on."

"Thanks, Cec."

She reached out to take it, but Brian took it from Cecily's hands and placed it over Vivi's shoulders. He leaned in as he fastened the gold clasps. "Tonight, I'm a lucky man." Then he kissed her cheek before placing her hand at the crook of his arm and leading her out to his car.

"Have a great time, you two," Cec called out.

Inside the car, he turned up the heat and rubbed his hands before pulling out of the driveway. When he got to the end of her street, he glanced at her. "Thank you again for agreeing to go with me to this thing. In fact, my sister thanks you as well. If you hadn't gone tonight, she would have been in that seat."

"Is it really that bad?"

Brian gave a shrug. "Bad is a relative term. Is it a barrel of fun that you'll talk to your family about for years? No. Is it a nice evening with good food?" He paused. "Again, no. But it's a nice thing to do for a friend of mine, which I appreciate."

"What's the fundraiser for?"

"Paul is in charge of a summer camp for kids who have a parent or sibling with cancer. He doesn't charge the families a dime but depends on fundraising events like the dinner and auction tonight to cover the expenses."

"Sounds like a nice guy."

"I think you'll like him."

BRIAN NARROWED HIS EYES as Paul seemed to fawn all over Vivi. "You really outdid yourself finding her, Bri. Though she's obviously out of your league. Tell me your name, angel. And I'll add it to my own."

Vivi blushed but slipped her arm through Brian's. "Brian said you were a nice guy, but he didn't mention that you were so…"

"Suave? Sinfully handsome?"

Paul slipped his wheelchair next to Vivi, acing Brian out of his prime spot. He should have anticipated the move. "I said you were nice."

Paul made a face. "Is there any word that is less attractive than being called *nice*?"

Vivi smiled. "Brian told me about your charity. I think what you're doing is amazing."

"Amazing enough that you'll agree to dump him and spend your evening with me instead?"

Vivi chuckled. "Good try, but I'm afraid I'm already spoken for." She turned to Brian. "I'll be right back."

Brian watched her cross the ballroom, heading toward the restrooms and admired the view, before turning to find Paul enjoying the same. "Eyes back in your head, buddy."

"How in the world did you find a woman like that?"

"Bumped into her. Literally." Brian pulled

a seat away from one of the tables and sat down. His feet were sore in the stiff shoes he wore. "Did you get my message about the new grant program coming out of Lansing? It could boost your funds so that you could expand the camp like you've been talking about."

Paul waved off his words. "Can't we have a little fun tonight without you bringing business into it all the time?"

"Tonight is the best night to be talking about this. With the grant and the money you raise this evening, you could move up your expansion by at least two years."

Paul put a hand on Brian's arm. "Buddy, I know this is as important to you as it is to me. And I promise I will do my schmoozing with all the heavyweights to get the big dollars, but right now I'm more interested in catching up with you. So, is she someone special?"

Brian gave a nod, and Paul smacked him on the shoulder. "I knew it. The moment you two walked in, I could see it in your eyes when you looked at her. Is it serious?"

"Not yet."

"But you want it to be." Paul said it as if

it was fact, which it was. "So, what's the holdup? Are you still gun-shy? Or is she the one holding out?"

Brian glanced up as Vivi rejoined them and took the seat next to his. She slipped her hand in his and smiled at him before turning back to Paul. "Looks like a good turnout tonight."

"I should hope so. I think Brian invited half the state." A gentleman with a microphone approached Paul and leaned down to whisper in his ear. He nodded, then turned to Vivi and Brian. "Duty calls." He reached out and took Vivi's hand and kissed her knuckles. "I hope to get the chance to talk to you more later tonight."

When Paul left them, Vivi said to him, "What did he mean by inviting half the state? Did you organize this party?"

Brian gave a short shrug. "I serve on the board of his charity, so we all pitch in to make this his biggest event of the year. And he might have exaggerated my role a bit."

Vivi lifted one eyebrow and looked at him. "I don't think it was an exaggeration. You're being modest."

"It's nothing." True, he'd made the invitation list and followed up to make sure people were coming out for the event, but it was a minor thing compared to what others had done to make the evening successful. "Did you know there's a silent auction? Lots of great stuff to bid on."

"Nice change of subject."

He stood and held out his hand. She accepted it and got to her feet. In her heels, she stood several inches taller than him. No matter. He felt as if he was escorting royalty through the ballroom to the alcove where items were advertised and up for bid. They weaved through the many tables to see all of the different items. Vivi stopped at one table and put a hand to her heart. He peered at her. "Are you all right?"

She picked up the clipboard with the details and read the list of bids made, before paling and placing it back on the table. "I'm fine."

He glanced at the clipboard. "You're interested in tickets to a musical?"

"This isn't just a musical, but *the* musical. And these are the best seats in the house."

Brian lifted the clipboard and noted the amounts that had been bid. Obviously, there were quite a few in attendance who were interested in seeing the production. "What's the big deal about some guys singing on a stage?"

"They're founding fathers singing about the birth of our nation. Coming from nothing and creating a system of government that has survived two-and-a-half centuries. It's history coming to life onstage." She closed her eyes and put a hand to her forehead. "I've only been dreaming about seeing it live onstage since it came out."

"Then you should bid."

She chuckled and took a step back. "Way too rich for someone on a teacher's salary. But I can still dream about seeing it someday. Even if it is from a scat in the nosebleed section."

"I could take you."

She stopped. "I don't think it's your thing. You said it yourself. It's not a big deal to you."

"But it is a very big deal to you. Would you like to go with me?" He put her hand in the crook of his elbow.

"Yes," The word came out as if a whisper. "But they've been sold out for months."

"Well then, the next time they come to town, we'll go."

Vivi smiled and put her arm through his. "If we're together when they come back to town, then it's a date."

If? Was she still having doubts about them? Brian tried to ignore the burning feeling her words had put in his chest and moved forward to look at more auction items.

Vivi picked at the chicken on her plate and glanced at Brian, who she discovered was watching her. He leaned in close to her. "Don't worry. We'll make a run by a drive-thru or something on the way home. You don't have to eat that."

"It's not that it's bad, per se. It's just…" She put the tines into the white meat and wrinkled her nose.

"Rubber." He nodded. "I tried to talk Paul into going with the caterer that we had for the New Year's Eve party, but he'd already committed to this one. The same one he used last year. And the year before."

"If they're trying to raise money, why can't he serve better food?"

"Because the point about this evening isn't the food."

"Then what is the point?"

"Paul started the camp to help out kids like his brother. He watched how Mark lost heart as he went through cancer treatment."

Vivi was stunned at the will and determination it must have taken to create such a special place. She glanced over to where Paul sat at a table near the stage. Beside him sat a younger man with similar features. "Is his brother okay?"

"Now he is, yes. But Paul is always thinking about those around him, and less about himself. The camp encourages kids and gives them a safe space where they can just be themselves." Brian turned to look at Paul and Mark. "The two brothers have become partners in the camp. They're looking to expand since there's a huge waiting list for kids who want to attend but there's not enough space."

Someone tapped on a microphone near the front of the room, and Vivi turned to see Paul waving to the crowd. "I don't want to interrupt your dinners with a bunch of speeches about why we're here tonight.

About the good that we can do when you sponsor a child to attend the camp for two weeks this summer. You've heard all that before, plus you've read all the literature I've emailed you through the years." He motioned for a group of kids to join him on the stage. "I thought tonight we'd try something a little different. I'd like to introduce you to some of the children who have been attending the camp. Instead of simply thanking you, they've come up with the idea of singing it. Choir and coaching for singing are two of the most popular activities at the camp every year."

Paul gave a nod to Mark who sat at a piano behind the kids, who had organized themselves into small groups and faced the audience. A few bars of an inspiring song played on the piano, and the singing started. The kids seemed to wobble at first, but quickly found their groove. Vivi watched them, impressed, unable to stop the smile on her face.

By the end of the performance, she was one of the first to shoot to her feet, clapping so hard that the palms of her hands ached. Brian stood next to her, and she leaned into him. "They were wonderful. I'd give Paul all the money in my savings account if I could."

"Let's hope the rest of the audience agrees."

They took their seats again, and Brian took her hand in his as the kids started to sing a second song. Vivi looked over at him, but his gaze was on the children. A smile played around his lips, and he watched them with a look of fondness. She squeezed his hand. He glanced over at her, then chuckled as he reached up to wipe a tear from the corner of one eye. "Sorry. This song always gets to me."

She scooted her chair closer and put her arm through his. "Don't apologize for that. I think it's very sweet."

"Oh. Sweet. Exactly what every guy wants to hear when he's trying to impress a woman. You might as well call me *nice* and put me out of my misery."

"There's nothing wrong with sweet or nice, and you're plenty of both." She ran her hand over his arm. "Who are you, Brian Redmond? And why did I have to meet you now?"

If only they could have met next New

Year's Eve, then she wouldn't be wasting her time worrying about what was going to go wrong. Things were good now. Great even. But they couldn't last. There was still more than ten months of the year to go.

Brian reached up and pushed a stray strand of her hair behind her ear. "I met you when I was supposed to. Maybe I'm the one to help you end this curse business."

"But what if you're the one that only proves it?" She had whispered the words, but they seemed to ring loudly in her ears.

"I don't see how something that's one of the best things in my life could possibly go bad."

A woman at their table shushed at them and glared until Brian motioned for Vivi to follow him outside of the ballroom. They found a cozy corner, the dim lights creating shadows on the planes of Brian's face. He put a hand on her cheek and whispered, "Vivi, I know you're probably not ready to hear this, but I'm falling for you. Hard. And I don't want to talk any more about a curse."

"Brian…"

He leaned closer to her, and she reveled in his warmth. "This thing between us is powerful, more powerful than anything to maybe be wary of. And I'm going to prove it."

She wanted to believe him. Yearned for it. But she couldn't. Hadn't she thought the curse wouldn't affect her wedding because she loved Ray, and their love was stronger than the curse? But she'd been wrong. She'd ended up with a broken heart and a vow to never risk it again.

So why was she here? Why was she with this sweet man who she was falling for, despite her best defenses? Why was she staring at his mouth and wishing he'd stop talking and kiss her? And why couldn't she close the distance between them instead?

She screwed up her courage and pressed her mouth softly to his. A whisper of a kiss. A taste. A tease. She stepped back and waited to see if the roof would fall in or whether any other calamity might happen.

Instead, Brian followed her lead and deepened the kiss. He brought her body next to his, and she turned them around so that she could press him against the wall. His hands moved from her cheeks to push through her hair. She felt the pins that kept her updo in place loosen as his fingers pushed farther, anchoring her to him.

The squeal of the microphone brought Vivi's attention to their surroundings. No one was in the hallway except them, but someone could leave the ballroom at any point and discover them. She took a step away from Brian, and he followed her. "Wait. Don't stop."

She put a hand to his chest as if to keep him at a distance. "There's too many eyes here."

"But it was just getting good." He ran a finger across her bottom lip. "We could…" He glanced around the hall and pointed to the coatroom. "We could continue this in there."

"Brian…"

He sighed and nodded. "You're right. I don't know what I was thinking."

"But it was good."

"Better than good."

"Perfect." She leaned over and kissed his cheek. "We should get back to the event."

"All right, fine." Together they returned to the ballroom, where Paul had taken the microphone once again. Brian continued,

"But I definitely think we need to discuss this later." He looked at her hair and grimaced. "Maybe you should fix your hair in the restroom?"

Vivi put a hand to her loose locks and then felt her cheeks warm.

VIVI COLLAPSED ON the comfy sofa next to Cec and pulled pins out of her hair. Seconds later, she shook her head so that her hair flowed loosely around her shoulders. Cec looked her over. "So, how was it?"

"Amazing."

Cec frowned and stared at her. "You're kidding me, right? It was probably okay food and boring speeches. Maybe some dancing, but..." Her friend leaned in and narrowed her eyes. "He kissed you."

Vivi glanced at her, then blushed. "I didn't say that."

"It's written all over your face." Cec grinned and pulled her knees up on to the sofa. "It was that good, huh?"

It had been wonderful. Better than perfect. More than she could have imagined. When his lips had touched hers, she felt as if her body had finally been woken up, like some fairy tale princess. Colors seemed richer. Sounds sweeter. And Brian all the more handsome.

She knew he was kind and funny and all the things she liked in a man, but the fact that he was such a good kisser made her want him more. He was a great guy, well respected and genuinely liked. She would be silly to let someone like him go. She didn't want to.

She bit her lip and nodded. "I've never been kissed like that."

Cec whistled. "He's the whole package."

"He really is." Vivi sat up and grabbed Cec's arm. "He told me tonight that he's falling for me, and…maybe… I think I'm falling just as hard."

"Of course, you are. Because you're not going to let something like this so-called curse, or bad luck, or whatever it is ruin a good thing. You deserve someone like Brian, Vivi. You deserve to have a good life."

The smile faded from Vivi's lips. "But what if the curse does ruin it? What if…"

Cec scoffed and tsked.

"Stop talking like the end is inevitable." Cec scooted closer to her and pointed her finger at Vivi's heart. "You can be happy without worrying about what could go wrong. It's okay for you to have a happy time that doesn't have a shelf life of seven years."

"That's not what I'm doing."

"Isn't it? Because you seem to put too much stock in this idea that you can't be happy for longer than that."

"History has proven that it's true."

"No, your believing that it's true puts limits on your happiness. You let it define what you do and what you feel." Cec rose to her feet. "You're my best friend, and I love you to death. But it really angers me that you won't let this go."

"You think I want to get my heart broken?"

"I think it's easier for you to give yourself an out so that you can blame it on something else rather than just the bad luck that it is."

"So, you're saying I sabotage myself every seven years?" Cec was the one who was missing the point. Vivi gave a dry laugh. "Did I force Ray to call off our wedding? No, it was all him. And I didn't cause the skiing accident or break up my parents' marriage."

"But you allowed those things to have control over you and your future. Your plan for this year was to hide in your room and let life pass you by for twelve months rather than realizing that life is pain sometimes. It doesn't matter whether it's every seven years or every three months. To live is to experience pain."

Vivi shot to her feet and started to walk out of the room, but Cec grabbed her arm. "But life is also about happiness and joy and peace and all the good things that you're avoiding in order to protect your heart."

"You're wrong."

Cec gave a shrug. "Maybe I am, but what if I'm right? You haven't allowed yourself to have a serious relationship since Ray. And now here's this great guy who you could really fall in love with but you're going to keep him at a distance because what if he hurts you? What if he leaves just like Ray?"

"That's not fair."

"You're right. It's not fair. To Brian or to you." Cec dropped Vivi's arm and shook her head. "I'm going to bed. But you need to think about what I said."

Vivi watched her roomie leave. She thought about following her and arguing that Cecily was wrong, but something in her heart told her that her best friend might just be telling her the hard truth.

CHAPTER SEVEN

BRIAN STOPPED BY Jamie's house Saturday morning since she'd promised to cook breakfast for him. He sat on one of her stools at the kitchen island and replayed the moment he'd kissed Vivi the night before. Had she really responded so eagerly? Had she wanted him as much as he wanted her? And known that they were possibly on the precipice of something amazing?

Jamie waved her hand in front of Brian's face. "Earth to big brother." He blinked at her, and she gave him a knowing smile before turning her focus back to the pancakes on the griddle. "Have a good time at the charity dinner?"

"It was…" He felt his thoughts drift again toward kissing Vivi, and felt his cheeks warm. "I've never attended a charity dinner that was so wonderful before. But I think it was due more to the company than the actual fundraiser." He paused, then asked, "How do you know when you're in love?"

Jamie's eyebrows shot up into her hairline. "Did Paul have the caterer put something in the food or what?" She put a hand to his forehead. "Are you feeling well? Do you have a fever?"

Brian moved her hand away. "If I do, I never want to get rid of it. Vivi is… I mean, I knew she was special when I met her. She's beautiful. Smart. Funny. But she's so much more."

"Man, you've got it bad for this woman." She placed two pancakes on a plate and slid it across the counter to him.

He took a dollop of butter on his knife and smeared it over the cakes. "I do, James. She's everything I've ever wanted, plus things I never realized that I needed."

He put the knife on the side of his plate then took his phone out of his pocket and started to scroll for her name in the contacts. Jamie put her hand on his wrist and pushed it down. "Don't do it."

"I think I'm in love with her. I don't quite understand it, either. Just that I've never been so drawn to someone before." He stopped talking and realized what he'd said. A smile began to grow on his face. "I'm in love with her, so why wouldn't I tell her?"

"That's a conversation you might want to have with her in person."

He nodded and put his phone back in his pocket. "You're right. I'll tell her tonight when we go out again."

"You're going to have to slow it down or you'll scare her off. These are strong feelings you're talking about. It doesn't happen often, but clearly you've been struck by Cupid's arrow in a way that hits maybe only one in a million of us. You tell her this now, and you might as well plan on spending the rest of your evenings alone."

"Why wouldn't she want to know that I'd like to spend the rest of our lives together?"

"You're only proving my point. This woman is cautious, a slow mover, so step on the brakes and back off with this kind of talk."

"Doesn't everyone want commitment?"

"Some do, but I'm not sure about Vivian." Jamie peered at him. "I know you're feeling really good and in love and all, but think about it, Bri. You don't want to mess up something that you think is this good, right?"

A very small part of him knew that she spoke the truth. That Vivi was hesitant about relationships, especially with her insistence that anything that happened in the next eleven months would end up in heartbreak. And that small part knew he could be patient. He could wait.

He'd just have to prove to Vivi that he was in this for the long haul. It would take longer than he wanted, but when she was by his side in the end, all the waiting would be worth it.

Cec knocked on Vivi's open bedroom door. Vivi looked up from the half-made bed and took in her friend's red-rimmed eyes. She walked over to her and put a hand on her shoulder. "Bad news about your grandfather?"

Cec gave a short nod. "I just got off the phone with my mom. It's terminal cancer."

Vivi led her to the bed and sat next to her. "How long does he have?"

"With treatment, maybe a year, if we're lucky." Cec stared into her lap and wrung her hands. "But he's refused chemo. Says he's lived long enough and doesn't want to spend whatever time he has feeling horrible." Cec raised her eyes to Vivi's. "Without treatment, I don't know how long…"

She let her words trail off, and Vivi pulled her friend into a hug. She held her while she cried out her feelings. When the tears slowed, Vivi retrieved a few tissues from her bedside nightstand. She gave them to Cec who wiped her face, then blew her nose. "What can I do to help?"

Cec wiped her eyes again. "He can't live on his own anymore, and none of us want him to, anyway, so I've volunteered to move in with him until…" She gave a shrug, unable to say the words. "Being without a home has its advantages since I can pack up and be at his place this afternoon."

"I can help you pack."

"I also called Tom. There are a few things that I want from the house, so he agreed to be out of the house later today. You know someone with a truck we could borrow?"

Vivi nodded. "I know someone who knows a guy that does." She patted Cec on her shoulder, then took her cell phone into the other room to call Brian. His voice sounded winded, as if he'd been running when he answered the phone. "Are you okay?"

"Great. I was just thinking about you."

His words brought warmth to her cheeks, and she felt her lips twitch into a grin. "Well, I was just talking about you."

"Good things, I hope."

"Please tell me you know someone who has a truck that I can borrow for a couple hours this afternoon? And maybe some movers with muscles?"

They made arrangements to meet at one o'clock in the parking lot of city hall, then Vivi returned to Cec to help her collect what belongings she had brought with her. Most of it was clothes and shoes, but she had several boxes of books and knickknacks that held sentimental value. They loaded these into Cec's car. Once that was full, they put what was left in the back of Vivi's Jeep.

At one, Vivi drove to meet Brian at city hall while Cec drove to her old house. Brian got out of his car once Vivi had parked. He opened her car door, then engulfed her in a hug. "How's your friend doing?"

"She's the strongest woman I know, so she'll be okay eventually."

Brian turned and introduced her to Gary and Jill and their three teen sons. "Why don't I drive with you, and they can follow us in their truck to Cecily's house."

When he got into her car, she reached over and turned down the volume of the radio. He turned it back up. "I need to hear this. I survived my high school years by singing it loud and proud."

"Survived high school? Wasn't that your best time?"

"Hardly. Because my dad was air force, we moved a lot when I was growing up. I went to three different high schools, and I had that awkward ugly duckling phase of my life then." Brian gave a shrug. "Luckily, I was a charming kid, so I made friends quickly." She chuckled at that. He grinned and peered over at her. "What about you? You've probably been a swan your whole life."

"Hardly. My parents divorced my freshman year, so I went through a rebellious phase for most of high school. One of my teachers got me to realize that I wasn't hurting my parents with my behavior, only my-self. She challenged me to be better than I was."

"So, you became a teacher because of her. That is inspiring."

"No, I became a teacher because I wanted summers off." She grinned at his befuddled face. "Yes, she's the reason I am who I am today. In more ways than one, she was a big influence. We still keep in touch."

"What's her name?"

"Mademoiselle McClelland."

"Ah, a French teacher. I thought maybe she taught history like you do."

"She used to make learning French really fun. We would have potlucks where we brought French food and had to speak French while we ate. She would have us write poetry and short stories in French. And it became more than just conjugating verbs and learning vocabulary."

"So, you're beautiful, smart and you can speak French? Are you fluent?"

"Certainment, non. Seulment un peu." She put her fingers up and kept them an inch apart. "Only a little."

"Too bad. I thought maybe you had just

fulfilled all my requirements for a perfect match."

"You want a woman who is fluent in French?"

He gave an exaggerated shrug. "But alas, I guess I'll just have to somehow put up with your smattering of French."

"Or we could take a class together?" She turned to look at him. "Wait. Did you just mention us in a relationship?"

He winced. "Too soon?"

She considered the idea of them in a relationship. "I'm warming to the idea."

"Anything I can do to help you get warmer?"

The stoplight turned red, so she braked, then reached over and took his hand in hers. "Just be you and let me be me."

"That sounds too easy."

"Isn't there enough hard stuff in the world that we can make things easy with each other?"

He gave her hand a squeeze, then motioned to the road ahead. "I think we're on the right track for that, don't you?"

She smiled at him and startled when Gary beeped the truck's horn behind them. The light had turned green, so she hit the accelerator.

Once they got to Cec and Tom's house, she noted that one of the neighbors had found a reason to shovel an already cleared sidewalk. Cec opened the front door and walked outside, lifting a hand to the neighbor before waving everyone inside.

Once in the house, Cec pointed out the pieces of furniture she wanted to take to her grandfather's place. Brian's friends moved each item. Cec walked into her old bedroom she had shared with Tom and opened the doors of the armoire. Some of Tom's clothing was still stacked inside on the shelves. She grabbed the items with both arms and dumped them unceremoniously onto the bed. "You remember when I found this piece at the thrift store? It was in horrible shape, and I spent months sanding and re-staining it. Tom says he wants it, but there is no way the jerk gets to keep it. He can buy his own dresser. It's a fair trade for breaking my heart, after all."

Brian knocked on the bedroom door. "We're ready for the next item."

Cec pointed to the armoire. "The only

thing I want in this room is this. I've got blankets we can wrap around it to keep the finish from being scratched."

She left to retrieve them, and Brian glanced around the room. "It's got to be tough for her to be here again."

"It's tough for her to be anywhere, but she's just as tough."

Brian nodded, then took the blankets from Cec when she came back. "We'll take good care of it."

Gary entered the room, and the two men wrapped the armoire in blankets before lifting it and carrying it out. Cec's gaze moved around the room, and the corners of her mouth drooped with each look. "This is it, isn't it? All but the legal part, and my lawyer says I'll be a free woman by summer break."

Vivi walked to her friend and put her arm around her shoulders. "I was just telling Brian that you're one tough cookie."

Cec laughed at that, then had tears slipping down her cheeks, which she wiped away with a flick. "I'm something. Just not sure what exactly."

Vivi rested her head against Cec's. "You're stronger than before. And resilient.

And you're going to be better than ever once this is through."

"I wish I felt like that at the moment."

"You felt like it before, and you'll feel that way again. Soon."

Cec gave a nod and took a deep breath. "Let's get out of here. I don't want to waste any more time thinking about the might-have-beens."

BRIAN SHOOK GARY'S HAND and then Jill's and handed them several bills. "Please take the boys out for pizza. My treat. We appreciated your help today."

Gary handed the money back. "We didn't do this to get paid. We're trying to teach the boys that hard work is its own reward."

"But you still got to eat, right?"

Brian handed the money to Jill who put it in her coat pocket before slipping her hand in Gary's. "The boys deserve something after all that heavy lifting. Thank you, Brian." She reached over and kissed Brian's cheek before leading her protesting husband to the truck.

He waved goodbye and entered the house where Mr. Karsten sat in his recliner. He glanced up at Brian, then pointed to a matching recliner. "Why don't you join me while the girls set up Cec's new bedroom?"

Brian took off his coat and folded it over the back of the chair before taking a seat. "You have a nice home, Mr. Karsten."

The older man waved off the compliment. "It was all my wife's doing. And call me Pops." He lifted a stein of beer half-full. "Want a drink?"

Tempting, but Brian shook his head. "I'll be driving later, so I probably shouldn't."

Mr. Karsten gave a shrug, then took a healthy swallow. "My neighbor has gotten into craft beer lately, so he brings over some of his favorite finds. Some are good. Some…meh." He took another drink. "This one tries, but meh." He eyed Brian. "Now, he brought me this Belgian ale around Christmas that was fantastic. Wish I could remember the name of it so I could buy more."

"I'm not much of a beer drinker."

"I was never much of a drinker except on special occasions. But my neighbor seems to think that a beer now and then can be good for me. And especially given what's happened, what's a beer or two going to hurt, right?"

Vivi walked into the living room to ask Mr. Karsten where she could find a hammer, and Brian turned to her. She had pulled her hair back into a ponytail, which gave her a youthful appearance in her hooded sweatshirt and jeans. She shouldn't look as beautiful as she did in such casual wear, but a runway model couldn't hold a candle to her. While she had looked smashing in the fancy dress and heels the night before, here she looked more approachable. At ease. He longed to cross the room and pull her into his arms.

As if sensing his thoughts, she smiled at him. Earlier that day, he'd asked Jamie how he would know if he was in love. But seeing her now, knowing how she'd stepped up to help out her friend who needed her, and also knowing that she'd do the same for him if he asked... He was head over heels for this woman. The thought of it should have scared him since he'd never been in love like this. Instead, the thought only made him want to start their future as soon as possible.

On the other hand, Jamie was right. The

last thing he wanted to do was scare Vivi off. So, he'd have to slow down before he spoiled things and she leaned into her streak of more bad luck.

She left the room with Mr. Karsten, then returned with a hammer. "I need about another thirty minutes to get Cec settled, then we were talking about ordering dinner in. How does Chinese sound?"

"Take your time."

He only wished he could be as patient as she needed him to be.

Vivi drove them back to city hall where Brian's car stood alone in the lot under a bright light. "Thank you for postponing our plans for tonight. Cec needed me with her today."

He waved off her words. "I'm just glad that you included me in helping out."

"I'm glad you knew someone who had a truck that was available on such short notice."

Brian took off his seat belt, then motioned to Vivi. "Come here."

She leaned over the console to kiss him, letting her eyelids flutter closed. The heat of his mouth on hers seemed to keep the winter chill outside. He put a hand to the back of her head and tugged the tie out of her hair, so that the strands fell to her shoulders.

She backed away for a moment to catch her breath. "Wait."

He sat back and looked at her. "Everything okay?"

"It's perfect." She frowned and released another long breath. It was too perfect. Last night. Today. This kiss. Even Brian was more perfect than she could have imagined. "Do you mind if we call it a night?"

"If that's what you want."

She looked at him. "It's not what I want, but I'm exhausted after today."

"I understand. And agree. Especially after we had a late evening out last night." He reached over and put a hand to her cheek. "And, hey, it's just one night."

"I don't want to miss many more." She smiled.

He smiled back. "That's one of the nicest things anyone's ever said to me."

"And you're really not bothered about our plans getting hijacked?"

"Vivi, just spending time with you is

enough for me. However, whenever, wherever that happens. We could have been sitting on the side of the road watching cars pass by, for all I care. I was glad to help you with your friend. And grateful that you included me."

"Are you for real?"

He grabbed her hand and put it on his chest where she could feel his heart beating. "I assure you that I'm as real as it gets."

"Maybe that's what scares me."

He scooted closer to her. "You don't have anything to be afraid of. I know that this seems to be moving fast, but I'll wait for you as long as it takes, Vivi, if that's what you want. You're one of a kind."

"What if we do date, and it gets to be comfortable and then one Christmas you tell me that it's over and I end up having to move in with a friend to get back on my feet?"

"We're talking about you, not Cecily."

"But it could happen to us just the same. I saw Tom with her when they first got together, and I'll admit I was a little jealous of the love they had. But it ended, at least for Tom. It's inevitable, isn't it? Relationships end."

He dropped his hand. "Is this the curse talking or your fear?"

Vivi brought her hand back to her side. "I think I need to go home now."

"And I think that's my cue." He opened the car door and turned back to face her. "I know you won't believe me, but I have no intentions of leaving you. And I'll prove it to you one day."

"And what if I'm the one to leave you?"

The words were out of her mouth before she could stop them. Brian blinked at her several moments, then shut the door, walked to his car and got inside. Vivi started the Jeep and left the parking lot before she could do something foolish like tell him she wished she could take back the words. That they hadn't meant anything. And what if that was a lie? That she feared she might be the one to let a good thing like him go?

BRIAN PUSHED HIMSELF to crest the next hill, slogging through the knee-deep snow and using the hiking poles to keep him upright and moving forward. At the top of the hill, he looked across the pristine snow. He could see a few animal trails but there were huge expanses of untouched snow. He adjusted his goggles and snowshoed down the hill and toward the next one.

After last night, an early morning of physical exertion sounded like a wonderful plan. He still didn't understand why Vivi had gotten so upset. It was like a perfect day spelled trouble for her somehow. And it had been perfect. He thought they'd gotten closer and discovered they worked well together. That they could spend time together and be content in that simple fact. While the fancy evening spent together had been like a fantasy night out, he'd enjoyed yesterday more because it had been real.

Or maybe it was the reality of her friend's heartbreak that had made her feel like it could happen to them. That he would leave. He paused. She had said she would be the one to leave. And those words had felt like a crushing blow to the heart.

He'd gone home and pondered those words. Wondered why she seemed to be quick to end a relationship that had barely started. She'd been ready to run in the other direction because the day had been a good one, so what would happen if something went badly?

His heart pounding from exercise, he stopped moving and paused. He was in danger of losing his heart to someone who couldn't give him hers. And what was worse was that he still wanted her just as much as he had before.

His cell phone buzzed from his inside coat pocket. The display indicated it was Vivi. Taking a deep breath before answering, he braced himself for what she might have to say. "Hey, there. I was just thinking of you."

He swore he could hear her smile over the phone. "I was thinking about you, too. And how I really messed up last night."

Brian wanted to contradict her but couldn't disagree. "Okay."

"I don't know what was wrong with me." She paused. "No, that's a lie. I know exactly what I was doing. I was afraid it might actually work."

"Vivi, I think this is a conversation we should have face-to-face. I'm out hiking right now, but I can meet you later."

"I have plans with my mother. Besides, I

don't know if I could say what I need to if I was facing you. I'm pretty embarrassed."

He waited for her to continue. Despite the snow and the chilly temperature, he'd wait for her always.

She finally spoke. "Brian, I'm sorry that I'm disappointing you."

"What makes you think that?"

"Because I'm not brave like you. I can't jump into a relationship and figure it out as we go along. I need to know what is going to happen before I start something."

"We're discussing a relationship, not a project. You can't predict some things."

"But I want to." She chuckled softly. "Even I realize how ridiculous that sounds. As if we could sit down and make a time-line of when things will happen. But I still want to have some reassurances before we get more serious."

"If you're asking me to guarantee that I will never hurt you or leave you, I can't make that kind of promise. No one can. But I can promise that I will do my best to show you respect and to love you as best as I can. I'm only human, after all."

"I know that."

"So that means I will mess up, and you might get hurt in the process."

The volume of her voice dropped to a soft whisper. "I know that, too."

"Just like you will mess up and hurt me. What matters is what we do after we screw up. Do we ask for forgiveness and work to make things right or do we give up and walk away? I'm willing to do the work necessary to make things work. My question is, are you?"

"I want to be."

"But…?" Vivi didn't answer his question. "This is why I wanted to do this face-to-face. I can't tell what you're thinking when I can't see your face."

"I think we need to take a little break."

He closed his eyes and took a deep breath. "What do you need a break from?"

"I think we're moving too fast."

Jamie had warned him of this. "I can slow things down, Vivi. But I don't think we need a break for that."

"You say that, but then you tell me you're falling for me. And it scares me."

"I can give you all the time you need but don't push me away. Please, Vivi." If she was so ready to walk away this soon, how would they ever make this work in the long run? "I don't want to lose you."

"Brian…"

In his mind, they were good together. End of story. If he wasn't afraid that she would crush his heart by leaving him so soon, he'd be looking at rings and researching wedding venues. She was the one for him. He knew it down to the core of his soul. He didn't have any doubts about her, but he also realized that she needed to work through what was holding her back. "How about you make the next move when you're ready? But please don't wait too long."

"We will still need to meet later this week about the history project."

"We can meet at my office on Thursday after school?"

"Fine." A beat passed. "I'm sorry, Brian. I really wish I could just jump into this with both feet, but that feels so reckless. I need to take this slower."

He only wished that she wouldn't take it so slow that she'd lose interest in him.

CHAPTER EIGHT

VIVI CARRIED THE empty dinner plates to the kitchen sink and turned on the faucet to rinse them before placing them in the dishwasher. Her mother brought in the half-full casserole dish and started to fill plastic containers with the leftovers. "I'm glad you liked this recipe. I found it online last week and figured it would be a nice dinner for tonight."

"It was nice." Vivi rinsed the silverware and placed the knives and forks in the rack before glancing at her mother, who hummed as she filled the containers. "You're in a good mood tonight."

"Am I?" Connie chuckled as she placed the lids on each of the containers, "I guess you could say that."

Vivi peered closer at her mother to notice a telltale blush creeping up the sides of her neck and blooming in her cheeks. "Any particular reason why?"

Her mother turned her back on Vivi as she placed the containers in the refrigerator, then returned to the dining nook to wipe off the table. "I might have met someone."

Vivi paused in rinsing the now empty casserole dish, her mouth open, not believing what she was hearing. "Someone you're interested in? Like dating?"

Connie turned and flicked the dishcloth in her direction. "It's not what you think. I was at my friend MaryLynn's house for dinner last night, and there was this guy there. We got to talking, and he's an interesting man who wants to retire early and do some traveling."

"But you hate going anywhere."

Her mother frowned. "I didn't say I was booking a ticket to go with him, for heaven's sake. But the look on his face as he talked about all the different places he wanted to see..." Connie sighed, and a dreamy look came over her, one Vivi hadn't seen on her mother's face since she was married to her dad. "It almost made me want to pack a bag." She glanced at Vivi, then cleared her throat and straightened up. "But like you said, I don't like to travel. I must be mad to think that I might have anything in common with him. Or…" She hesitated. "Or that he might be interested in someone like me."

Vivi stepped closer to her mother. "Don't say that. How long did the two of you talk?"

Her mother shrugged. "Most of the night."

"I'd say that if he talked to you that long, he is interested. Did he give you his number?"

"No." Connie blushed even deeper. "But he did ask for mine."

"See? He's interested."

Her mother leaned on the back of a chair. "I haven't felt like this in a very, very long time."

"I'd say that it's about time, then." Vivi put a hand on her mother's shoulder. "And I think you deserve to have some fun with a new love."

"Love?" Her mother scoffed and shook her head. "It's way too early for that. Besides, I think I'm too old for that kind of thing."

"First off, I hope you're never too old to find love. But you'll be okay as long as you take it slow. Don't rush into things." Vivi's thoughts went to Brian. It was too soon for love with them, too. Sure, she liked him and liked him a lot, but he seemed to be moving way too fast. Which is why she would try to put some distance between them. But it only seemed to make him sad, and her, too. It's not like she wanted to stop seeing him, period. Just maybe taking it one small step at a time, so she wouldn't get all confused.

"Uh-oh. What does that face mean? What's wrong?" Connie asked.

Vivi put a hand to her cheek. "Nothing's wrong. I don't know what you mean." Her mother pursed her lips in a way that Vivi knew too well. She was about to get a lecture. Before her mother could get going, Vivi gave her a smile that she didn't feel. "Things are good with me. I'm dating someone, too."

"But it's not going well."

"No, it is. Was. Going too well, actually." Friday night had been elegant and magnificent, while Saturday had been comfortable. She had discovered that they worked well as a team, whether it was loading furniture or making small talk with a table full of strangers. "He's a really nice guy."

"Oh no. You used the *nice* word on him."

Her mom shook her head. "Poor guy never had a chance."

Vivi frowned at her words. "What is that supposed to mean?"

"Well, you don't usually fall for the nice guys. Complicated, yes. Completely bad for you, definitely. But the nice ones?" Her mother shrugged. "They don't last very long."

That couldn't be true. "Ray was a nice guy."

"Don't try to fudge things. He acted nice, but deep down he was all wrong for you."

"Then why didn't you say something before I wasted months planning a wedding with him?"

"If you remember, I did warn you. But you told me that you knew what you were doing. That you were in love with him and that he was the one for you." Connie approached her and gently put her hands on her upper arms. "Sweetie, he was never the right man for you. I knew the moment you introduced me to him. He never looked me in the eye but looked around the restaurant as if searching for someone more interesting to talk to."

"He didn't do that."

Her mom nodded. "And he did the same thing whenever he talked to you. As if he couldn't keep his eyes on you just in case he might miss out on something better."

Vivi tried to remember the last times she'd been with Ray but couldn't recall him doing something like that. What else had she missed? "Well, Ray is my past. And Brian is more than just nice, though. He's kind and smart and funny. And…"

"And?"

"I think he's in love with me."

Her mother smiled. "And, of course, that terrifies you."

"Yes, thank you. I've been trying to put this feeling into words." She frowned. "But what doesn't make sense is, why would that terrify me?"

"Because if this Brian loves you and you allow him to get close, then he could hurt you." Connie looked her in the eye. "I understand it's a risk, a scary one, but you shouldn't run away."

"I don't do that."

Her mother's expression was skeptical. "What was your plan for this year?"

"Keep my head down. Don't make any big changes."

"And why were you doing that?"

"To avoid the curse. You know that."

Connie put a hand on her shoulder. "To avoid pain. It makes sense, of course we all do it. But it means you don't talk about your feelings."

"It seems like that's all I do is talk about them."

"Did you and Ray talk about how you felt about things? Did you share how our divorce changed you? Or how the accident altered your life plans?"

"Well, no. He said the past was the past, and it was best to leave it there."

"Do you talk about how you feel with this Brian?"

He tried to talk to her, but she found herself unable to share what she was feeling. Well, she tried but she seemed to make a mess of it rather than resolving anything. That's why she needed this space from him, so that she could figure out what it was that she wanted. What she needed. But talking to him only seemed to make things murkier. She glanced at the clock. "I've still got papers I need to grade tonight." She leaned over and kissed her mother on the cheek, then accepted one of the plastic containers of leftovers.

"You don't need to run away. We can talk about this."

Vivi shook her head. "I'll see you next Sunday."

BY THURSDAY MORNING, Brian missed Vivi. They had gone on only two dates and spent another afternoon with each other, but he missed hearing the sound of her voice. He'd debated texting her, but she needed some space, so he had kept his words to himself.

Josh entered the office and shut the door behind him. When the mayor turned to face him, his expression was worried. "Oh no, what's happened?"

"I don't want you to panic."

Those were not the right words to say to keep him calm. "Josh, seriously. What's going on?"

"Marjorie contacted me this morning about the booklet's production. It's not good. You need to call her."

The publisher of the senior citizens' stories had bad news? He took a deep breath, then picked up his cell phone. Marjorie explained the supply chain issues that were plaguing the company, leaving them to cancel contracts. Including theirs. "Marjorie, there's got to be something we can do. We can change the type of paper or ink we were planning on using."

"It's more than just that, Brian. Because of shortages, I've had to lay off staff and we're on the verge of closing our doors for good. I'm sorry, but we have to cancel the contract. You'll need to find a different publisher."

Brian made some notes. "It's not your fault. Can you recommend another company who could work with us?"

He ended his call with her and looked at Josh, who looked back at him expectantly. "Did she have any ideas?"

He held up the notepad where he'd jotted down a few names she'd recommended. "These other publishers may or may not have space to do this for us. And possibly at a higher cost than what we negotiated with Marjorie." He collapsed into his chair and spun around to glance out the window behind his desk. "How am I going to break this to Vivian?"

"I'd recommend doing it very gently."

Brian spent the rest of the morning calling around to find an alternative but came up with nothing by the time he was to meet with Vivi. When she walked in looking as beautiful as ever, he wished that her presence alone could get rid of this hiccup in their project.

She took off her coat and placed it over the arm of the second chair in front of his desk before sitting in the first. "You don't look so good."

He put his arms on the desk and faced facts. "I got a call from our publisher this morning." While he told her the bad news, she gnawed on her lip and dropped her gaze to her lap. "I'm sorry, Vivi. I've spent my day calling around and already contacted five publishers who are either not taking any more clients or will push the publication date to next year."

"But my seniors will be graduated and moved on by then. We wanted them to have copies of the book by this summer. And what about the library fundraiser in July?

This was all supposed to help them raise more money."

Brian knew this project was important not just to Vivi, but also to the kids and the senior citizens. He'd been reading the stories that Vivi had emailed him, and they were good. He'd even stopped by the center, where the director had mentioned that interest in the book had been growing. They already had a waiting list for those who wanted to buy copies and contribute to the next book. "I'll keep trying to find another publisher who can keep to our original timetable or as close to it as possible."

She ran a hand through her hair and kept her fingers intertwined in the strands. "What will I tell my class?"

"That sometimes reality stinks and things don't go as originally planned? My mom always said life's not fair, so it's best to learn that early on."

"Well, my mom always said that nothing's over if you keep trying." Vivi sat up straighter in her chair and kept her gaze on his. "You keep calling. I'll get my students to keep writing their stories with the original deadline. And I'll edit them with Arlene's help. We will keep going as if we can get the book published as initially planned. Understood?"

Brian's lips twitched. "Are you always this determined? I knew you were competitive, of course, but do you work just as hard to win in life?"

"When it's something I want badly, yes."

"Then why aren't you fighting for us? Is it because you don't want it as much as I do?"

The words were out of his mouth before he could stop them. He wished he could bring them back rather than blurting them out like he had. He looked across the desk to gauge her reaction.

Vivi blinked several times, her gaze on his, then her shoulders lifted as she took a deep breath. "It's not that I don't want something to happen between us."

"Then what is it?"

"I thought we agreed we were going to take things slower."

He agreed, and said, "But it's out there now. Can you answer the question?"

Vivi stood to retrieve her coat and purse from the other chair. "You know, I could call some of my friends and see if they know of any publishers who might be interested. I'll check with Marta who always does the yearbook at the high school. Maybe she will know something."

Brian followed her to the door. "Please, Vivi. Help me try to understand what you're running from."

"I'm not running away."

"All evidence to the contrary, I'm sorry to say." His gaze landed on hers. "I wish you trusted me, could confide what's going on. I'm not going to judge you or get upset."

Vivi shook her head. "Please, Brian. I need to go."

She stepped away from the office, then turned to look back at him once before rushing off. Brian watched her in the hallway until she rounded a corner and moved out of sight.

SINCE HER RELATIONSHIP with Brian seemed to be on hold for now, Vivi sat in Pops's living room while Cecily worked in the kitchen on Friday night after school. Pops glanced into the kitchen then turned back to Vivi. "We're glad you could join us tonight for dinner. Cecily has been talking about how she's wanted to pay you back for letting her stay with you."

"There's nothing to pay back. It's what any friend would do."

Pops shrugged. "Still, she had nowhere to go, and you opened your home to her. That's more than many people would do."

"Well, I'm not just people. I'm her best friend." She sipped the glass of wine that Cec had thrust into her hand when she'd arrived. "How are you feeling, Mr. Karsten?"

Pops waved off the name. "I told you to call me Pops. And…" He gave a shrug. "Not doing too bad for a cranky old man."

"*Cranky* isn't how Cec has described you."

"Ornery, then. Or maybe crotchety. I like that word. *Crotchety.* Makes me sound like I'm crusty and finicky, which of course I am."

Cec handed him a glass of water and a small cup of pills. "Don't listen to him. I never hear him complain or fuss." She leaned over and kissed the top of his head. "Dinner will be ready in about five more minutes, so take your pills."

"You see how she treats me?" he asked, then winked at Vivi before taking the pills out a few at a time and washing them down with water. "You'd think she cared about me."

"Take your pills, old man. And maybe I'll let you have dessert. But only if you clean your plate."

"It's like I've become a child again." He finished taking his medicine and handed Cec the empty cup. He opened his mouth and stuck out his tongue. "I took them all, Nurse Ratched."

Cec rolled her eyes and returned to the kitchen. She called out, "You should come to the table. Dinner's ready."

Pops moved his walker from the side of his recliner and anchored his arms on it before starting to rise but then fell back. Vivi shot to her feet and went to hold the walker steady. He shook off her help. "I've got it."

"Why don't I give you a hand?"

"I told you, I've got it."

Vivi stepped away, and Pops grunted for a moment before starting to clop his way into the kitchen. She followed him just in case he lost his footing. Cec pulled out his chair for him, then took her spot in the chair beside him. Vivi sat across the table from Cec so that Pops sat between them. Cec started to make a plate for Pops. "Not too much of those green vegetables, now," he told her.

She gave him a look and put a second scoop of green beans next to the mashed potatoes, then placed his plate before him. "Vegetables are good for you. They keep you strong."

"There's nothing that can fight what I got, but I appreciate the effort." He put his napkin on his lap and began to eat.

Conversation over dinner centered on Pops's best friend and neighbor, Gus, who usually stopped over after dinner to talk with Pops and have a drink.

"Every night?" Vivi asked.

Pops paused to consider her question. "Most nights. He's got plans tonight, though. Maybe next time you can meet him."

Cec had an expression that Vivi couldn't decipher. Her friend asked, "Pops, did Vivi tell you about the project she's working on with her seniors?"

Vivi gave him the details then sighed, scraping her fork through the mashed potatoes. "We've run into a hiccup with that, actually. The publisher canceled our contract, so now I don't know if we'll be able to do the book after all."

Cec stopped eating. "But the students are looking forward to it. Not to mention all the residents at the complex."

"I know, but if we can't find a replacement, what are we to do?" Vivi played with her fork for a moment, then set it back on her plate, discovering that she didn't have much of an appetite. "Brian seems to think we can find someone else, but it could delay the release of the book until after the library fundraiser and after the seniors have already left for college." She shook her head. "Maybe I was trying to do too much. Maybe it's best that the project dies now rather than later when their hopes are up."

"Their hopes are already up." Cec glanced at Pops. "You wouldn't happen to know of a publisher, would you? Or a printer that would be interested in an important local project like this?"

Pops pushed more green beans onto his fork. "I wish I did. Something like this could really generate interest in the community. Maybe I should ask Gus. He might know of someone."

Cec rolled her eyes at this.

After apple pie for dessert, Cec settled Pops back into his recliner, then joined Vivi in the kitchen, where she was washing dishes. Cec took a towel out of a drawer and dried the dishes after Vivi rinsed and placed them in the dish rack. Pops didn't own a dishwasher. They worked in silence for a while, then Vivi said, "This Gus seems to be a good friend to your grandfather."

Cec made a noise as she placed a glass in the cupboard before picking up the next one to dry. "It's all Gus this and Gus that. You'd think the guy was a saint or something."

"Have they been friends long?"

"Ever since Gus moved in next door a couple years ago. But I didn't meet the man until this week." Cec shook her head. "With a name like Gus and the way Pops talked, I expected an old man like my grandfather."

"I take it he's not."

"No. And you'd think I'd know better than to judge someone by their first name since you're my best friend and you have a grandma's name." Cec slammed the silverware drawer shut on her last word, which made Vivi jump and stare at her. "But Gus is our age. And he's opinionated and ingratiating and gets under my skin." A smile flirted around Cec's mouth. "And he's also completely hot."

"Completely?"

Cec nodded, the smile fading into a grim line. "Not that I should be looking."

"And why not?"

"It's only been a little over a month since Tom…" She wiped off a plate and placed it on the counter before taking another. "It's too soon. And besides, I'm still married."

"I don't believe there's a timetable for when you are allowed to be interested in another man. I mean, my mom hasn't dated since the divorce but that's her." Vivi rinsed a plate and placed it on the rack. "Did I tell you she met a guy at her friend's house?"

"Connie's found a man?"

"Well, she said she liked talking to him, but dating's a big step for her."

"Wow, good for Connie. And I'm not saying I'm going to wait twenty years like your mom before I'm interested in another man. Besides, Gus is so obnoxious. He actually told me last night that he will shovel the sidewalks and driveway after the next snowfall. As if I'm not perfectly capable of doing it myself."

"He just wants to help…"

"No, he's saying that I'm incapable of doing it. Like the way he takes the trash cans out to the curb and puts them back the next day before I even get a chance."

"He sounds like a sweet guy."

"He's interfering and annoying."

"And completely hot."

Cec sighed again. "Completely."

The dishes had been washed and put away, so Cec poured more wine into their glasses, and they joined Pops in the living room, where he had fallen asleep in the recliner while watching his game shows. Cec placed a crocheted afghan over him before sitting on the sofa with Vivi. She took the remote control from the side table by Pops's recliner and turned the volume down on the television.

"So have you heard from Brian?" Cec looked at her over the top of her wineglass. "Besides him telling you that the publisher dropped out?"

Vivi stared down into the depths of her glass. "I don't know what to say to him."

"How about 'I'm as wild about you as you are about me'? That sounds like a good start."

"But it's not true."

Cec reared back. "Girl, please. You are so crazy about him that you're creating excuses to keep him at arm's length. Because if you were to admit how you feel about him, then you might have to be truly vulnerable to him and give him your heart. And you can't have that, can you?"

"Are you going to tell me I go out of my way to avoid my feelings? Because my mother seems to think that I won't be able to have a real relationship with Brian until I open myself enough to let him hurt me."

"Connie has a point. Wait. What? Not about letting Brian hurt you—that can't be right—but about being open to him."

"Not you, too."

"I'm just saying that you really like Brian but you're working overtime to convince yourself that it's not going to work. Because you've finally met a guy who might stay for the long run. And that scares you to death."

"Can we change the subject, please?"

"Fine. We will for now." Cec glanced over

at Pops who snored softly, his head leaning to one side. "How does he look tonight to you?"

"He seems to be in better spirits since you moved in last weekend."

"I think he is. Sure, he fusses about what I feed him, but he's not serious about it. And he doesn't complain about how he feels. Not really. Sometimes, I think the doctors are wrong about his diagnosis because he doesn't seem sick. Other days, I'm afraid that I'll leave the room and come back to find that he's gone."

"Are you going to be able to take care of him on top of working?"

She nodded. "A nurse stops in twice a week to check on him, plus Mom comes over several days when I'm at work. It's a group effort."

"Plus, you have Gus trying to help you out."

Cec rolled her eyes again, but there was that small smile that appeared then disappeared just as quickly. "I think help is a relative term. He might think that's what he's doing, but all he's really doing is making me feel like I don't know what I'm doing."

"You do know what you're doing. Pops looks happy that you're here."

"That's because I am happy about that." They turned to find Pops looking at them with one eye open. "And you're doing a great job of taking care of me."

"That's not what Gus says."

"Listen. The man is my best friend. But you're my granddaughter, and I love you. I couldn't ask for better."

Cec shared a smile with her grandfather, and Vivi realized that her best friend was right where she needed to be to not only help Pops but heal herself as well.

VIVI STOPPED AT the grocery store on her way home Tuesday night. Since Cec no longer lived with her, cooking for one had turned into a pointless chore rather than the pleasure it had once been. She'd lived on her own for so long after Cec had gotten married, but now that she'd experienced having a roomie again, her life had become emptier. Lonelier.

She stopped at the deli department to see what they had available to take home for dinner instead of cooking. The scent of freshly fried chicken lingered in the air, making the decision for her. She clutched the paper tag with the number seventy-two printed in bold black. She glanced up at the digital display to discover they were only on fifty-eight. She leaned against the handles of her grocery cart.

"Imagine bumping into you here."

She turned and spotted Brian's sister standing a few feet away from her. She racked her brain. "Jamie, right?" She glanced behind Jamie but there was no sign of her brother. "Brian's not with you?"

"City council meeting."

The knot in Vivi's stomach loosened, and her shoulders dropped back to their relaxed position. "That's good. I mean, it's good the council is meeting. Not that I meant it's good that he's not here." She shut her mouth before she dug the hole she was in any deeper.

Jamie laughed. "I usually think it's a good thing when he's not always around. Bad enough that we hang out together and eat together at least twice a week, but I don't want to spend all my time with him." Jamie glanced into Vivi's cart. "Doesn't look like you're buying much."

"I didn't feel like cooking dinner tonight, so I figured I'd pick something up." She looked into Jamie's empty cart. "You, too?"

"Cooking for one is one of the worst things in the world."

"Right? Sometimes I don't know why I even bother. Besides the fact that I need to eat."

"Exactly. And then when I eat, I sit in front of the television because at least there's some noise. Doesn't matter what program is on."

It was like Jamie was speaking Vivi's language.

"Number fifty-nine?" the deli clerk called.

An older gentleman stepped forward, the coveted ticket held high in the air. Vivi glanced down at her seventy-two and sighed. Then she looked over at Jamie. "Want to skip this line and grab dinner together?"

"You're reading my mind."

They met at a nearby Greek restaurant that Jamie loved and Vivi had never tried before. Once they had ordered their meals, Jamie looked across the table at Vivi. "So, you and my brother. What's going on there?"

"You don't beat around the bush, do you?"

"What's the point in that?" Jamie narrowed her eyes, and Vivi could feel an uncomfortable heat creep up her neck. "Are you dating him or not?"

"Right at this moment? Not." Although she'd regretted it terribly over the weekend. She'd had dinner with Cec at Pops's on Friday night, spent Saturday cleaning and lesson planning, then gone to her mother's on Sunday. And she'd missed him every single second. "It's complicated."

"That's what people say when they don't know what they want."

Vivi opened her mouth to protest, but Jamie was right again. She thought she knew what she wanted with Brian, but it wasn't so cut and dried.

"I mean, I know the man is hideous. But underneath all that, he's a really nice guy."

Vivi burst into laughter. "The man is gorgeous. How in the world can you call him *hideous* of all things?"

"So, you do think he's hot."

Ouch. She'd stepped into that one. "Of course, he is. That's not the problem."

"There is a problem, then?" Jamie leaned over the table and dropped the volume of her voice. "Is it because he's mean, especially to kids and old people?"

"You know that's not true. He's one of the kindest people I've ever met."

"Then what is the problem?"

"Are you an interrogator for the police? Because you're gifted at it. I feel like I should be sitting under a hot light in a metal chair."

"Actually, I am a cop. I hope to be a detective someday." Jamie laughed and reached for her water glass. "Brian accuses me of the same interrogation thing. He also says that I'm a stalker until I find out the information I'm looking for." Jamie put two fingers in front of her eyes then pointed at Vivi with them. "I've got my eye on you now, so you might as well tell me what I want to know."

"I don't know what the problem is, okay?"

"That's a lie. You glanced to the left when you said that." Jamie held up her hands. "This is a safe space. If there's something you want to share with me that you don't want Brian to know, say the word. It will stay in the vault. So, you can be honest with me, okay?"

The words sounded nice, but Vivi debated

the wisdom of sharing intimate knowledge with Brian's sister. She tried to stall by taking her glass of ice water and sipping it slowly. But Jamie didn't seem like she was going to let this line of conversation go. She let the silence stretch between them to the point where Vivi wanted to say something, anything, to break the quiet.

The server set down fresh pitas and bowls of tzatziki on the table before walking away. Jamie grabbed a pita but kept her eyes on Vivi as she broke a piece off and dipped it into the creamy mixture. Vivi also took a pita from the basket and discovered that it was still warm from the oven. She broke off a piece and popped it into her mouth. "This is amazing."

Jamie grinned from ear to ear, as if she'd won, but still she didn't say anything. Vivi sighed and placed the remainder of the pita on the small plate in front of her. "I'll admit that I like your brother a lot. And I'm not saying that I don't want to see him ever again, but I need some space from him right now."

"That's what I figured. He came on too strong, right? I tried to tell him it would scare you off, but he insisted that he knew what he was doing." Jamie shook her head as she dipped more pita into the tzatziki. "I love him dearly, but sometimes the man is maddeningly clueless."

Vivi thought Brian's confidence in himself was charming rather than misplaced. He knew what he wanted, and he went after it. It would be admirable if what he wanted wasn't her. "I tried to tell him, to explain but I don't think he understood."

"He understood. He was just hoping for the opposite."

"This isn't a good time for me. I don't want to fall in love with him when the moment really sucks."

"Wait." Jamie stopped chewing and held up a finger. "You're falling in love with him?"

"I didn't say that."

"Yes, you did."

"No, what I meant was that I'm not in love with him. And I absolutely can't fall in love with him right now."

"You're in love with him. You are. Now I can see it."

Vivi cocked her head to the side and stared at Brian's sister. "There's nothing to see because I haven't fallen in love with him yet."

"Yes, you have, which is why you're reluctant and asking for space." Jamie held up a hand when Vivi started to protest. "It's okay. I totally understand. It's not easy to admit, especially to the sister of the man you love. But now that you've admitted how you feel, you can work out the issues you have with Brian."

"I haven't admitted a thing."

Jamie's nose wrinkled, and her lips curled into a smile. "Haven't you, though?"

Thankfully, the server arrived with their meals, and the dinner conversation turned to topics less intrusive and uncomfortable.

By the time Vivi left the restaurant that night, she felt as if she had been turned inside out and had all of her secrets exposed. But she didn't feel as if Jamie would use them against her or share them with Brian or anyone else. She knew she could trust Jamie despite her insisting that Vivi was in love with Brian. Which was completely wrong. She wasn't.

She couldn't be.

Could she?

CHAPTER NINE

BRIAN LET HIS sister into the house and watched as she hung her coat on the rack by the front door. She turned and faced him. "I didn't expect to find you home this early. Quick meeting?"

"Short agenda. What's up?"

"First of all, let me say that I don't want you to be angry. It wasn't something I planned, but we just ran into each other at the store, and we started talking."

"Who did you run into?"

"And dinner was technically her idea. Not mine."

His senses started to tingle, and he frowned. "Whose idea? Who did you have dinner with?"

Jamie gave a shrug that he assumed she meant to be nonchalant but came across as more calculated. "Oh, you know, just Vivian."

Brian stared at her as if Jamie had said Santa Claus or the Tooth Fairy instead. This was bad, right? He loved his sister, but she had a tendency to go too far while questioning his dates. He'd lost more than one girlfriend to her habit of pushing and prodding into their lives. Jamie and Vivi alone at dinner could spell disaster when his relationship with the unlucky schoolteacher was already on shaky ground.

But Jamie also had the gift of getting people to open up to her. And offering insight they might otherwise have missed. It's why she would one day make a great detective.

He took a deep breath. "So, what did she tell you?"

"Without violating any kind of promises to her, I can only tell you this. She's not ready."

"I know that. You didn't find out anything else?"

"She wants some breathing room, and you need to give it to her."

"She told you about the curse, too?" He groaned and held his head. "I thought we had gotten past that at least a little."

Jamie's face scrunched up. "Wait. What curse?"

He dropped his hands to his sides and looked away. "She didn't mention it?"

Jamie took a step toward him. "Just said it wasn't great timing for her. But I assumed that something else was going on in her career or family that would keep her from dating you right now."

"Oh. Well, that's good, right? Maybe she's realized there is no such thing as this curse."

Jamie stepped closer and looked directly at him. "I'm going to need you to go back a little and take me through this. What curse are you talking about?"

He shrugged. "She has this idea that every seven years she has a year full of bad luck. Calls it a curse. And this year is…"

"Number seven. So, she thinks that meeting you right now will only bring her bad luck. Now things are starting to make sense."

"Things make no sense. Not at all, James. I love this woman and want to be with her, but she's running in the other direction because she thinks something bad is going to happen. In what world does that make sense?"

"Let me ask you this. You just said you love her."

He nodded. "I do. Since the moment I met her she's had my heart."

"You think you have a future with her?"

"I know I do."

"And because you love her and want a future together, you'd be willing to give her whatever she needs to accept that and love you, too, right?"

"I can see where you're going with this."

"So, if she needs the rest of the year, you'd be willing to wait."

He took a seat on the edge of the sofa. They were only a month and a half into the new year, so would he be able to wait for her the next ten-plus months? He didn't doubt his answer. "If she asked me to wait, I would. Would it be easy? No. But if that's what she wanted, I'd do it."

"So then let her get her feelings for you where they need to be. Even if it takes the rest of the year."

"And what if her feelings never get there?"

Jamie bit her lip and opened her mouth, then closed it. She looked as if she was about to say something more. "Just give her time."

Brian smiled at what she didn't say. "I

told you before. I have a good feeling about me and Vivi."

"Then don't scare her off by coming on too strong, okay? Listen to me for once."

"I listen to you all the time. I just don't take every piece of advice you pass along."

"No kidding. That's the reason why you're still single."

He narrowed his eyes at her. "If you know it all, then why are you still single?"

"Because I have high standards and have yet to come across a man who meets them." She looked at him for a long moment. "Are you sure you're okay with this?"

He nodded slowly. "Actually, I'm better now than I have been in the last week and a half. You've given me hope."

"Are you going to call Vivi?"

He shook his head. "You're right. I need to give her the room she asked for."

Jamie dug out the cell phone from her pocket and held it up to him. "I'm sorry. You're going to have to repeat that again so I can record it for posterity."

Brian laughed, then grabbed Jamie into a hug. "Thank you for being the best sister and best friend ever."

"Considering I'm your only sister and probably your only friend, that's not much of a compliment." But she hugged him back. "This one is special. Don't mess it up."

VIVI FOCUSED ON the target about ten feet away from her. She lined up her aim, drew her arm back, then brought the axe forward and embedded it near the outer rim of the inner circle. *Yes!*

Vivi turned to Cec who held up her hand for a high five. "Good job. You've done this before?"

"It's not that different from bowling, apart from throwing overhand." She went to the bull's-eye and removed the axe to bring it to Cec. "Your turn."

"I'm not much of a bowler."

"I know. So, focus on the inner circle, and bring your arm around so that it goes through the target."

Cec stared at the bull's-eye, her face scrunched, her intent clearly visible. "Here goes nothing."

She brought the axe back but released it before her arm had made it over her head. Unfortunately, the axe stopped several feet in front of the target. Cec groaned as she picked it back up. "I'm no good at this."

"Hey, don't give up already. Release the axe when your arm is at about a thirty-degree angle from your shoulder."

"You put it in math terms. I can get behind that." Cec stood at the line. She took a deep breath as she brought the axe back and released it when her arm was at a thirty-degree angle from her shoulder. The axe flew through the air and hit the target's middle ring. Cec gave a fist pump. "Yes!"

They continued to play, but Vivi had the better skills and won. They took the axe back to the front desk, then entered the bar. "Loser buys the drinks," Vivi said as they took a seat at a high table with stools.

A server approached them, and they ordered their drinks, plus a platter of nachos. Cec settled back into her chair once the server left to put in their order. "Thanks for bringing me out tonight. I needed it."

"Everything going okay with Pops?"

Cec shrugged. "He's hanging in there. That's the best I can say right now. It's adjusting to living under his roof that is the bigger issue." She held up a hand. "Not that

I don't love him, but Pops can be stubborn. And he doesn't like change."

"Most of us don't."

"And Pops more than most. I'm only trying to help him."

"And you're doing a good job."

"I hope so."

The server set their drinks in front of them. Vivi took hold of her wineglass and took a long sip. It was sweet and crisp, just as she liked it.

"So have you heard from Brian?"

Vivi looked over at Cec. "No."

"Do you want to hear from him?"

"Yes. And no." She put her head in her hands. "I don't know." She looked up at Cec. "I really care about him, but I'm so…"

"Scared?"

"Of course."

"Because of this curse."

"Partly. But more because I could really fall for him, and that means I'd be vulnerable. And I don't like that."

Cec took a mouthful of her drink, then started to cough as if it went down the wrong way. She shook a finger in the direction behind Vivi. Vivi shifted in her seat and spotted Brian sitting at another table on the other side of the bar.

Vivi turned back to Cec. "Do you think he saw us?"

"Yes. And now he's coming over here."

Vivi took a deep breath before turning. Brian approached their table, smiling. "Imagine running into you two here. Did you try throwing the axe?"

Cec nodded. "And Vivi soundly beat me."

"You're really competitive, aren't you?"

"That should be obvious by now." Vivi took in how he looked. He wore a shirt and tie, which meant he had stopped here on his way home from work. "What brings you here?"

A woman called his name, and he waved to her. Vivi tried to ignore the flare of jealousy that erupted as Brian faced her again. "I'm meeting with Kayla about a new pop-up shop she's interested in opening. She asked to meet here."

Vivi looked over Brian's shoulder to take in the woman's carefully applied makeup and hair that appeared perfectly in place. She also wore a smart dress and heels despite the cold weather and casual spot. Vivi narrowed her eyes. "So this is a business meeting?"

"Yes. She wants to bring her business to Thora."

"And she's not interested in anything else?"

Brian grinned at her. "You're not jealous, are you? Because as I recall, you were the one who wanted us to take a break."

"I did. Do."

"Then there's no problem if she is interested in me."

Vivi glanced again at the woman, then back at Brian. She didn't have any room to be jealous of her. And Brian was free to date whomever he wanted.

Even if she was jealous.

"I hope your meeting goes well."

Brian blinked a couple of times, then gave a nod. "I should probably go meet with her. Good to see you, Cec, Vivi."

Vivi watched him leave, then turned back to Cec. "He looked good, didn't he?"

"Why don't you admit that you want to be with him? He's still interested in you."

"You don't know that."

"I have eyes, don't I? And it's obvious to

me, along with everyone else, that you two belong together."

"Belong?" Vivi scoffed at that. "I don't know if that's true."

The server brought their nachos platter to the table. "Can I get you anything else?"

Cec shook her head. "I think we're good." She looked across the table at Vivi. "Right? You're good?"

Vivi nodded at the server, but she felt anything but good. If anything, she questioned what she felt. And whether she should change things to make her life better.

Vivi dismissed her midmorning tenth-grade US history class with a reminder to them to go over the notes before the exam the following day. "And pay special attention to the timeline of western expansion."

She put her books in her messenger bag, then tried to determine if she'd have enough time to run down to the library for the book she'd ordered. Mrs. Beasley had called her to say it had finally arrived, and she really wanted to start reading it this weekend.

"Ms. Carmack?" She glanced up to find Devonte standing at her desk. "I don't think

I thanked you enough for what you did for me and my family."

"I didn't do anything, Devonte. It was all Mr. Redmond."

"If you hadn't told me to get ahold of him, I don't know what would have happened. We moved into our new place this weekend, and my mom is going to get all her back pay since she's been in the hospital." He swallowed, and his voice broke. "So, thank you. And please thank Mr. Redmond for me. He's a good man."

Vivi nodded. "I know he is."

Devonte slung his knapsack over his shoulder and ran out of the room, presumably to get to his next class. Students had started to enter the classroom for her American Civil War history class. So much for the library, but Devonte's message echoed in her head as she talked about the South's eventual downfall.

He's a good man. Brian had helped her student and his family. He'd helped Cecily. She found her thoughts drifting to the image of him, the one she thought of when she fell asleep at night. He had been talking to Pops in the living room, laughing at something the older man had said. Brian didn't know that she watched him as his face grew animated and split into a smile that she recognized was mirrored on her own. He hadn't talked to Pops to get something from him or because he felt obligated to be polite. He'd reached out to the older man because it was the nice thing to do. To help him feel included in the move, even though he couldn't lift boxes or carry furniture. He had talked to Pops and made him feel special.

Just like he had made her feel special when they were together.

She blinked and discovered her students staring at her. She'd gotten lost in her thoughts of Brian. To get back on track, she cleared her throat and focused on the textbook. "Can someone explain the importance of manufacturing to what eventually led to the South's defeat?"

A hand shot in the air, and she called on Jordan. While her student spoke, she reminded herself to leave images and thoughts of Brian for after school. Or at least until her lunch hour.

But he intruded on her lessons for the rest of the day and on her drive home. She was a block from her house when she suddenly turned down a side street, leading away from her place and heading toward city hall. Practicing what she would say when she saw him as she drove and then as she got out of her car and strode to his office, Vivi told herself that she'd finally tell him what she wanted.

The door to his office was closed, so she knocked and waited for his call to enter. Nothing. She knocked once more. Maybe he had gone home early for the day. Or maybe he was sick and hadn't come in at all.

"Looking for me?" She whirled around to find that Brian had walked up behind her.

Vivi jumped. "What are you doing, scaring me like that?"

"I was in the middle of a meeting when I saw you walk by and head to my office. So of course, I had to follow." He grinned at her. "What did you want, Vivian?"

"Oh. You're in the middle of a meeting. I can come back another time."

Someone called his name, and Brian unlocked his office door and ushered her inside, shutting the door quickly behind them. He held a finger up to his mouth. The person calling his name got closer, the voice louder, then faded. He sighed and rested his head on the door. "Mrs. Vincenza is a lovely lady, and a dedicated advocate for her neighborhood, but I can only take so many of her complaints that don't really have to do with the town before my eyes start glazing over." He looked Vivi up and down. "I'm glad you interrupted me. I owe you one."

She studied his hazel eyes and found humor and affection there. Affection for her? "Well, since you owe me, do you think that would extend to forgiving me?"

Brian frowned at her words. "What have you done that needs forgiving?"

"I pushed you away."

He reached up and brushed back a strand of hair that had fallen over her eye. "No, I scared you off. I'm the one who should be asking you to forgive me."

Vivi stood there, trying hard to figure him out. "Are you for real? I mean, not even Ray, who called off our wedding and broke my heart, asked me for forgiveness. Not once did he say he was sorry."

Brian put his hands on both sides of her

face. "I assure you that I am one hundred percent real."

He started to lean in to kiss her, and she closed her eyes, anticipating his lips on hers, when a sharp knock on the office door broke them apart. "Mr. Redmond? Are you in there?" Mrs. Vincenza asked from the other side of the closed door. She continued to knock a couple of times.

They both held their breath, waiting to see if the woman would leave.

More knocking on the door came, and Vivian groaned. "I don't think she's going to go away."

Brian groaned and tucked Vivi behind him as he opened the door a crack. "Mrs. Vincenza, was there something else you needed to tell me?"

"Is there someone in your office with you?"

Vivi held her breath as if that would make her disappear, but Brian opened the door to reveal Vivi's presence. "As you can see, my next appointment has arrived. Is this something we can wait to discuss next week at our usual time?"

Mrs. Vincenza looked Vivian up and

down, and Vivi reached up to pull the collar of her coat closed. The older woman huffed. "It can wait."

"Great. I look forward to seeing you at our usual time next week. Goodbye." He gave her a wide smile before shutting the office door and sagging against it. "I really owe you one now. I love the spirited lady, but we have a standing meeting every week for her to complain about things she sees around town."

"I didn't know that fielding complaints was your department."

He gave a shrug. "It's not, but she's old and lonely and needs someone to talk to. I don't think she's eating very well either, so I order lunch in on those days. That way I know she's at least getting one good meal a week."

Vivi looked at him, then pulled him to her and kissed him hard on the mouth. Brian backed away for a moment and held her at arm's length. "Not that I'm complaining, but what is that kiss for?"

"Because you care about old ladies and kids with moms who have gotten hurt." She felt a tear at the corner of her eye. "And you're extremely patient with women who are afraid and need time to work through those fears."

"So, you're not afraid anymore?"

She whispered back, "No, I'm terrified. But I think I won't be nearly as scared if we can figure this out together."

Brian smiled at her. "Does that mean what I think it means?"

"I'm willing to try again. I mean, if you are."

He placed a hand on her waist and pulled her to him, his hands joined behind her, resting at her lower back. "I'm always willing, Vivi. And we'll take it as slow as you need to."

She reached up and gently touched his face. "I might need some encouragement to move a little faster at times."

He smiled again. "I think I can do that."

"And if you're in the mood to feed cranky women on a regular basis, I'd be agreeable to that, too."

"What are your dinner plans tonight?"

"DID I TELL YOU about my student who was invited to join the senior center's euchre game? I guess he really hit it off with the gentleman he was interviewing, so Jeremy now joins Rod's weekly game." Vivi chuckled. "Who knew this project was going to spark a friendship like that."

"And Christopher told me that a few of your students are now stopping by on a regular basis to visit the residents and their friends."

"I'm glad to hear that."

"I've got an update on the publishing company. I've been in talks with someone who could get it completed by the end of summer."

Vivi put a hand on Brian's arm. He enjoyed the feeling of her touching him, and he put a hand over hers. "That's great news, Brian. But I'd hoped we could have it ready by the end of June."

"I'm still negotiating with him, so there's room to get that date moved up before we can finalize the contract. If we want to make this an annual project with your graduating students, I need to make sure this is something that the publisher can commit to long-term." He rubbed the top of her hand, his fingers lingering over the knuckles. "I didn't ask you to dinner tonight to just talk business, though."

"I know." Vivi put her other hand over his and threaded her fingers through his. "I've missed you."

"I was always here, waiting for you." And if he'd had to, he would have waited even longer. Still, he was glad that she was next to him now. That they could finally give this love a chance. Because given time, he felt sure she'd realize that's what it was.

"That's so sweet." She leaned in and gave him a quick peck.

He did the same. "I'm all yours, finally. Good and bad. Thick and thin."

She jerked her head back at his words. "Things were going so well. Why did you say that?"

"What did I say?" What had spooked her? It's not like he'd said for better or worse, richer or poorer. And implied that he wanted to marry her. He'd only wanted to let her know that he could be counted on to stay with her no matter what.

"Why did you have to bring anything bad into it? Why can't we just keep our focus on the good? Not even bring up the bad that will… I mean, could happen?"

He rubbed her arm, wanting to reassure her. "Vivi, I'm not inviting the bad things to happen by saying that."

"But it's a sign."

"The sign is that I'm a good man who is crazy about you." He could feel her stiffen. Had he gone too far? Was he going to lose her so soon after getting her back? He took a deep breath, and looked her in the eyes. "I'm completely yours. You don't have to worry about anything with me by your side."

"I want to believe you."

"Then give it a try. Trust your instincts, Vivi, and we'll see where this goes."

VIVI STOOD SIDE BY SIDE with her mother as they chopped vegetables for the teriyaki chicken stir-fry recipe that Connie had found and wanted to try for Sunday dinner. The chicken pieces had already marinated in the teriyaki sauce and would soon be frying in the wok. The inviting smell of the ginger and soy made Vivi's stomach grumble, and she held back a giggle.

"You're in a good mood today." Her mom

stopped slicing the red pepper into thin strips and peered at her. "You met someone."

"Yes. I mean, no, I already met him. I told you about Brian."

"So, things are back on with you two, then?"

Vivi kept her gaze on the sharp knife and the onion she was cutting. "Yes." She felt her cheeks warm as she thought about the kisses they'd shared the night before while they'd watched television on her sofa. "It seems to be going pretty well so far."

"Good."

"What about you and that guy from the dinner party at MaryLynn's?"

"Stan? We're talking, but we haven't gone out. Yet." Her mom looked up at her. "Would you be okay with me dating someone that's not your father?"

"I'd say it's about time." She pushed the onion slices to the edge of the cutting board with her knife. "Daddy's moved on. It's time you did, too." She picked up a slice of the red pepper and popped it into her mouth. "You should ask Stan over for dinner some night."

"I'm not quite ready for a man to be in my house. But I wouldn't object to a dinner out."

"So, ask him."

"I'm not going to ask him out first."

"Why not?"

"Because I can't do that. He should be asking me. That is, if he's interested."

"Has he said anything that would make you think he's not? I mean, he's called you how many times since I was here last week?"

She could see Connie mentally counting the calls. "He called three times, but I called him twice." Her mother shook her head. "He's said that we should get dinner together sometime, but he hasn't come right out and asked me for a specific day and time."

"Then you do it. Tell him to pick you up Saturday night at seven."

Her mother shook her head again. "Oh, I couldn't do that."

"You could, but you're choosing not to. Mom, why not take a chance?"

"This from the woman who last week was telling me that she couldn't risk taking a chance at all on a man?"

"I'm taking that chance now."

"What changed?"

Vivi thought about the long ten days she'd lived without contact from Brian. The longest week and a half she'd ever had. Seeing him again had brightened up the February skies of her world. "I figured it was worth it to face the risk than avoid it altogether. Maybe you'll think that one day about Stan and ask him out."

Her mother looked at her, opened her mouth as if to say something but turned away to increase the heat under the wok. Vivi watched her, then put a hand on her mother's arm. "Is something wrong?"

"No." But the word came out soft, unconvincing to Vivi's ears.

A sense of dread gripped her belly. "Mom, what's going on?"

"I was going to tell you later. Over dinner." She faced Vivi. "I got a call from my doctor's office. They need to run some tests."

"What kind of tests?"

"I don't know. I was too afraid to ask. But it's like you said, maybe it's worth more to face the scary truth than avoid it or pretend everything's fine."

"Are you feeling okay?"

Her mother shrugged. "I feel fine. Maybe

a little more tired and worn down than usual, but nothing that should concern you."

"But if the doctor wants more tests…"

"I'm still young and vibrant."

They both fell silent, Vivi thinking of her grandmother who had died too soon at fifty-six. Her mother turned when the oil popped in the wok. She poured the chicken with the marinade into the hot dish and started to stir it. "I'm not saying that I'm going to ignore this. I will go for the tests." She stopped stirring but stared at the meat. "Baby, I'm scared of what they're going to find. What if it's cancer? Or my heart?"

It couldn't be. Wouldn't be. This stupid year couldn't take her mother away from her.

Vivi called Cecily when she got home from her mother's. She'd barely gotten two words out before she blubbered and cried through the rest of the sentence. "What if it's cancer? I can't lose her. I just can't."

"Vivi, the doctor said he wanted more tests, which could turn out to mean that it's nothing."

"Or it's something."

"But it could be nothing."

"I hate this year. I'm going to lose my

mom and probably lose my heart to Brian if I'm not careful."

"I thought you two were back together."

Vivi wiped her face with the back of one hand. "We are, but I'm still cautious. I don't want to be blindsided by anything."

"Which means you're already preparing for the worst. Just like you are with your mom's news."

"You're dealing with this with your grandpa. Why aren't you more upset?"

For several seconds Cecily was silent on the other end of the phone. Had Vivi said the wrong thing? Finally, Cecily said, "Just because I'm not crying all the time doesn't mean I'm not upset. I don't want to lose him, but I also don't want him to spend his last days consoling me when I'm the one who should be supporting him. I'm strong enough to face it."

"So, you're saying I'm not?"

"No. What I'm saying is that you are focusing on the negative of what might happen rather than enjoying the positive of what is."

"You're always so wise."

"I got that from my grandma. Now buck up and stop crying over the what-ifs."

"If I didn't love you so much, I'd never talk to you again."

She could hear Cec's smile in her voice. "Back at you, babe."

"How is your bowling game?" Brian asked Vivi.

"First off, it's not a bowling game. It's just bowling. Second, I used to be on a league with my ex-fiancé and had the best average on my team. Why are you asking?"

That was how they ended up attending the fundraiser for a charity that held after-school activities for children that might otherwise go home to an empty house. Brian had signed up months ago and figured he'd bring Jamie along with him tonight. The fact that Vivi had accompanied him instead and brought her own engraved bowling ball was just a bonus.

Part of their entry fee included a free T-shirt advertising the charity, so they had worn them as asked. Brian had to admit that Vivi looked a lot better in hers than he ever could. She'd worn a navy turtleneck underneath, then tied the T-shirt hem in a knot to one side. He had simply put the T-shirt on with his favorite pair of jeans and called it a night.

Vivi turned from where she'd been talking with someone on the lane next to theirs and gave him a bright smile and a small wave. He didn't think he'd ever get over looking at her. She shone like a star, but she wasn't aware of the effect she had on him. He tried several bowling balls that had been left on a stand to find one that had the right weight. Vivi joined him. "That was Evangelina. We used to bowl in the same league, and we were catching up on the last seven years." She looked at him as he weighed the ball in one hand. "Don't be concerned with the weight of the ball right now. What you're looking for is the finger positions. You want that to be comfortable first in order to have better control. Weight is secondary."

"And all these years I've been doing it wrong."

"And how is your bowling game?" she asked him, smiling warmly.

"First of all, it's just bowling. Or at least that's what I've heard. Second, I haven't bowled since high school at Matt McClary's birthday party, so I might be rusty."

"Score doesn't matter, though. We're just here to have fun, right?"

"That and raise money for a really good cause."

"I have to admit that I like this kind of fundraiser a lot better than the fancy frou-frou dinner we attended before."

"I'll have to tell Paul he needs to change up his fundraising plans for next year." He found a ball that fit the span of his two fingers and thumb. "This feels pretty good."

"And how does the weight feel?"

He held the ball in his hands and nodded. "Seems okay."

"Why don't you try it out before the game gets started?"

They bowled a few frames to warm up then settled in the plastic chairs while they waited for their lane mates to arrive. Brian put his elbow on the back of Vivi's chair and ran his fingers through her hair. "I'm so glad you're good at this. Jamie is as out of practice as I am, and I don't want to embarrass myself tonight."

"We're doing it for the charity. Not to win." She smiled at him, then her eyes glanced over his shoulder and lost their warmth, replaced by anger and something that looked like disdain.

"Vivi, what is it?"

"The couple we're bowling with has arrived." She said this through gritted teeth. "It's Ray."

"Who's Ray?" Brian turned to look at the young couple that joined them.

The guy helped the woman take her winter coat off to reveal a very rounded belly, then turned to look at Vivi. "Oh, hey, Vivi. Imagine running into you here."

She gave a quick nod. "Yeah. Imagine that."

Ray spoke to the other woman and pointed to Vivi. "Babe, this is the woman I almost married before you."

Ray's wife waved and smirked. "That's right. You told me about her."

Ray smirked, too, then returned to Vivi. "Guess we're sharing a lane, huh? Isn't that ironic?" He looked Brian up and down as if assessing him. "Finally get someone to commit to you?" He glanced at their hands. "But no wedding rings. That's too bad. Maybe someday, huh?"

Vivi bristled at his words but didn't say a

thing. Instead, she got out her bowling ball from the bright blue leather bag that had her name stitched on it and placed it on the ball retrieval. Brian walked over to her and leaned in close. "Are you okay with playing against them? I can talk to the organizer and get her to switch our lane. I know her pretty well."

Vivi scrunched up her face at him, her eyebrows gathered. "Why would you do that? You think I can't beat him?"

"That's not what I'm worried about. I'm more concerned about how you're feeling."

"I feel fine." She gave a smile, but it appeared forced. "It doesn't matter to me what Ray does or says. He's from a part of my life that has been over for a long time."

"Are you sure? Because it wouldn't be a problem to switch lanes."

"And make him think he scared me off?" She shook her head. "I'm fine, Brian. And I definitely want to beat the pants off of them."

"I'll do my best."

Cheri, Brian's friend and the event organizer, walked down a lane and stood in the middle, tapping a microphone that gave a short squeal. She welcomed everyone and reminded them about the fifty-fifty raffle tickets available for sale, and that the person with the highest overall score would win a large screen television and a trophy. Brian whispered to Vivi, "No offense, but I am starting to rethink the whole not winning thing. I'd like to take that TV home."

Vivi looked aghast. "What happened to we're just playing for fun?"

Brian laughed at Vivi's teasing look. She huffed. "But I admit, that thought went out the window for me when Ray joined our lane. I need to beat him." Vivi frowned. "Wow, I sound horrible."

Ray approached them. "Are we going to spend the night chitchatting or are we going to bowl?"

"Why don't you go ahead?" Vivi said, then linked her arm through Brian's. "Guys go first."

Ray gave her a smile that made Brian want to punch the guy. He shouldn't be looking at Vivi like that with his wife sitting next to them, her hand on her rounded belly. Ray stepped up to the line and threw a perfect ball. It rolled to the end of the alley for a strike. He pumped his fist into the air and hooted loudly. "You're up next, Big Bri."

Brian turned to Vivi. "Big Bri?"

"Ignore him. He likes to make nicknames for everyone he meets."

"But, Big Bri? What is that supposed to mean?"

"It doesn't matter. Keep your focus on the pins and try to throw the ball straight down the lane. Okay?" She pecked him on the cheek. "For luck."

Brian nodded, picked up his ball and walked a few steps to stop before he reached the foul line. He brought the ball up and rested it on the palm of the opposite throwing hand. *Deep breath. Keep it straight.* He swung his arm back, swung forward and let the ball go. It landed with a solid thunk and rolled straight to the gutter.

"Ouch, that's tough luck."

Brian could almost hear the snicker in Ray's voice. He went back to the ball return without a glance at the others. Vivi approached him. "Let the ball go when your arm is at about a forty-five-degree angle from your leg. And you'll want to give it a little more force than this last one, okay?"

He nodded and picked up the ball when it returned. He walked to just before the line. *Deep breath. Focus on the pins.* Swing the arm back and let go when the ball was at a forty-five-degree angle from his leg. This time the ball sailed to the end of the lane, but it had a slight spin and knocked down six pins.

When he sat back down next to Vivi, she put her arm around his shoulders. "It's okay. It's just the first frame. Plenty of time to make up ground."

He smiled, then leaned his forehead against hers. "Thanks."

Ray's wife slowly rose to her feet and put a hand at the small of her back before waddling to the ball return. She grabbed a bright pink ball and slowly went to the line before tossing the ball with both hands and waddling back to Ray. The ball hit several pins on the first throw, and on the second she got the spare. Ray gave her a high five when she claimed her spot next to him again. "That was great, babe. You definitely earned some nachos with that one."

"Extra guacamole?"

"You betcha."

Vivi watched them, her mouth in a grim line, then stood. She only took a second to glance at the end of the lane before throwing the ball. It sailed down for a strike. She returned with a small smile on her face. Brian gave her a high five as she took the seat next to him.

"Good job, Vivi. I thought you might be rusty after all this time," Ray said.

Vivi turned to Ray. "Just because I quit the league after we broke up doesn't mean I haven't been bowling since."

Ray held up his hands. "I didn't mean to get you all huffy."

"I'm not," she said with gritted teeth. "It's your turn."

As the game progressed, it was clear that Ray and his wife had an advantage over Vivi and Brian. It wasn't only that Brian clearly lacked any bowling skills, but the way Ray talked to Vivi started to affect her game. She had bowled three strikes in a row, but the fourth and fifth frames gave her only spares. They decided to take a break after the fifth frame, and Ray's wife finally got her nachos with extra guacamole. Brian leaned toward Vivi. "Are you hungry? I could go get us something from the grill. Those nachos look pretty good."

"I don't want nachos, thanks."

"Burgers. Hot dogs. Pizza. Whatever you want."

"I want to win this game." She slipped her hand into his and tugged him away from the lane. She brought them outside the bowling alley and took a deep breath of cold air. "You're twisting your body when you throw, which is why your ball has that weird spin." She moved behind him, drew his arm back, then pushed it forward so that it came across his chest. "See? It's going to the left because you're moving your body in that direction." She brought his arm back and hooked her leg through his so that it anchored him in place. This time when she brought his arm forward it stayed straight. "Plant your legs firm. Keep your focus on the pins. And you'll start knocking them down."

He twisted and smiled at her. "Thanks. You're really good at this."

"Not that you can tell from those last two frames."

"Because you're letting Ray get to you. He's in your head." Brian put his hands on either side of her face. "Take a deep breath. Focus on me. You are so much better than that guy. He's all smarminess and innuendo. He's not nice."

She nodded. "He's horrible. I don't know what I ever saw in him."

"He is good-looking."

"That's no excuse for his behavior."

Brian leaned forward and gave her a quick peck. "Okay. Let's go back in there and show them who's the boss of this last half."

"To be honest, I can't wait for the next round when we'll get paired with another team."

"That would solve everything."

They returned to their lane, where Ray sat with his wife's feet on his lap as he massaged them while she ate her nachos. He gave Vivi a smile as they took their seats across from them. "Her ankles get swollen at this point of her pregnancy. It's our third kid, you know."

"Congratulations, Ray. That's wonderful news."

"Yep. Three kids. Great marriage. And I just got promoted at work. I'm living the dream better than I ever imagined."

Brian felt his blood start to boil and he glanced at Vivi, but she only smiled and offered the couple more good wishes. *Right. Focus on the game, Brian.* He only hoped that his technique would improve in the second half.

Plant your legs...plant your legs...

BY THE END of the ninth frame, Ray and Jenna led by only twenty-seven pins. Vivi's string of strikes had returned once she stopped thinking about Ray, which had boosted their score, along with Brian's improvement in his stance. He had even gotten a strike in the last frame. He jumped up and down, lifted his arms in victory before running to her and giving her a huge kiss. "I did it."

"You really did."

"It was all you. That advice you gave, it was spot on." He smiled as the scoreboard lit up with a huge X. "Look at that. Isn't that amazing?"

She smiled at him, enjoying how such a small thing as a strike had turned him into a little kid for a moment. "You're the one who's amazing."

He looked at her, smiling, then kissed her

again. "Maybe we both take that title. I'm proud of you for putting thoughts of him aside."

Brian ended the game in last place, but with a respectable finish as he bowled his last two balls, knocking down eight more pins. That meant Vivi and Brian were down by nine pins before the women bowled their last frame. Vivi calculated that she might be able to still eke out a win if she bowled a perfect frame, depending on how Jenna bowled her last balls. It would be close, but not impossible.

Jenna rose to her feet, a little unsteadily, then walked with her ball to the foul line. She started to swing the ball back with both arms, then let it drop to the floor and bent over. Ray rushed to her side as Vivi quickly followed. "Is she okay?" Brian asked but Ray waved them back.

Ray helped Jenna walk back to her seat. "Babe, what's going on?"

"Nothing," she said, but it came out strained and weak. "Let's just finish the game."

"We can have a break." Ray glanced at Vivi and Brian. "Maybe take five?"

They both quickly nodded and gave the

couple room as Ray bent over his wife, talking softly. Vivi glanced at Brian. "Do you think she's okay?"

"I hope so. I have to admit they're hardly my favorite people ever, but I wouldn't want anything bad to happen to them."

Vivi grunted. "I wouldn't mind if Ray suffered a tiny bit. You know, just..." She held up her fingers less than half an inch apart. "Part of me thinks it would serve him right for hurting me seven years ago."

Brian glanced at her. "Let it go, Vivi."

"I'm trying."

Brian reached over and squeezed her hand, then stood as Ray and Jenna got to their feet. Ray called over to them. "I'm going to help Jenna to the restroom."

Vivi stepped forward. "I'll take her."

Ray glanced at his wife who gave him a short nod. Vivi went to Jenna, who was slightly hunched over and had a hand on her belly. "You can lean on me if it'll help?"

The other woman nodded, and Vivi put her arm around her waist and kept her steady as they walked to the ladies' room.

Once inside the bathroom, Vivi led Jenna to the tufted bench beside the door. She then moistened a few paper towels at the closest sink and pressed them to Jenna's forehead. "Are you sure you're okay?"

Jenna took the towels from Vivi and wiped her face. "It's the jalapenos. I knew I shouldn't have eaten them, but I've been craving spicy things lately. And then I pay the price after. It's probably indigestion."

Vivi took a seat next to her. "Do you think we should have you get checked out by a doctor or something?"

Jenna looked up at her with wide eyes. "No, it's fine. Ray would hate that. He really wants to beat you tonight."

"Isn't your health and the baby's health more important to him than a silly game?"

"I'm okay. Really. I don't need a doctor."

Vivi looked her over and wasn't convinced. "If you're sure…"

Jenna agreed and put the paper towels against the back of her neck, leaning forward. "You know, you're not at all what I expected."

"What do you mean by that?"

"Ray can be so critical sometimes. So I guess I expected this…shrew. But you're really nice."

Vivi tried to ignore the twinge of guilt. She'd been having less than charitable thoughts about Jenna all evening. She'd even been comparing the two of them to figure out why Ray had married her instead. She smiled at how silly she felt in that moment. "You're not what I figured, either."

"In a good way?" Jenna asked as she gently rubbed her belly.

Vivi nodded and put her arm around the other woman's shoulders. "Do you have pictures of your other kids? I'd love to see them."

Jenna beamed and pulled her cell phone from her pocket.

Brian had his eye on Ray but then glanced away. What had Vivi seen in this guy to want to marry him? He didn't get it.

Ray let out a sigh. "So, you and Vivi, huh?"

"Yep."

"She tell you about the curse?"

"Yep."

"You believe in it?"

Brian thought about his answer before he said it. "I believe that she believes in it."

Ray let out another sigh. "It's like she expected me to leave her. Even after I proposed, she watched me as if waiting for me to go."

"Then why did you?"

He shifted in the plastic seat, facing their lane. "I realized we couldn't give each other what we needed. And I couldn't see myself marrying someone that wouldn't make me happy. Nor would I be able to make her happy. Why spend the rest of our lives miserable?"

Brian was impressed by the self-awareness the other man possessed. "That's pretty wise."

"And you've seen Jenna. She's smoking hot."

Brian's good opinion of Ray evaporated. "Vivi is attractive both inside and out."

"If you say so."

"I do."

Ray looked past Brian and stood as the two women approached them. Ray walked to his wife and put his arm around her. "You doing okay, babe?"

She nodded and took a seat in one of the plastic chairs. "Vivi and I were talking in the bathroom, and we agreed you should bowl my last frame to finish the game."

Ray stared at Vivi. "You're sure?"

Vivi sat, too. "Jenna's in no condition to play right now. Go ahead."

Ray rubbed his hands. "This round is ours. I knew we would win."

Jenna and Vivi shared a look as Ray grabbed his ball and bowled a strike. He punched the air. "Booyah. That's how it's done."

He waited for the return to bring his ball back, then bowled two more strikes. Brian felt Vivi stiffen next to him. He put his arm around her shoulders. "It's okay."

"I really wanted to win."

"I know." Brian noted how content Jenna seemed with her feet propped up on a chair, her hands on her belly. "She's going to be okay?"

"She thinks it's indigestion."

"Good." He pulled Vivi closer to his side. "I know we didn't beat Ray and his wife this round, but I can't help thinking that I still won."

A minute, maybe two, passed and Vivi let out a deep breath and stood. She went to

Ray, who smirked at her. "Who's the best man now?" he asked.

She held out her hand to shake his. "Congratulations on a good game."

"Aren't you going to finish?"

Vivi seemed serene. "No need to. Best of luck on the new baby. I'm happy for you."

She returned to Brian and reached for his hand. "I'm in the mood for something from the snack bar. What do you say?"

He'd say that he might not be the best bowler, but he was the luckiest man in the room. He put his hand in hers, and rose to his feet so that their eyes met. "I say that it would be my honor to share a hot pretzel with you."

"With nacho cheese dip?"

"Is there any other way to eat one?"

CHAPTER TEN

BRIAN DROVE THEM to Vivi's house in silence. Their score in the first round had been enough to get them paired up with another couple for the second round, but they hadn't made the top six teams for the third and final round. Fortunately, the program had raised a new record for funds donated.

He stopped the car for a red light, and looked at Vivi, only to find that she had been watching him. "I'm sorry about earlier tonight and letting Ray get to me. I don't really have an excuse," she said, her voice soft and full of something that he assumed was regret.

He gave a nod, not knowing what to say.

Vivi focused on what was outside her window. In a soft voice, she said, "I loved Ray so much that I was blinded to the kind of guy that he is. There were warning signs all along, but I chose to ignore them." She kept her gaze out the side window. "I hate to think of what my life would be like if he hadn't called off the wedding. Because I know I would have gone through with it. That's scary. I think I would have been so miserable."

"You don't have to explain it to me."

"But I do." She turned back to him and put her hand over his on the steering wheel. "My mom says that I fall for guys who I know will let me down. The ones who will leave. I'm not sure she's right, but there's Ray..." She shook her head. "But you're different. You're...you."

He sent her a small smile. "You couldn't have picked sexy? Or successful? Or even smart? I'm just...me?"

"You're all of those and more."

He pulled into her driveway and shut off the ignition before moving to face her. "Vivi, I love you, but I have to tell you that tonight was something else."

She swallowed and gave a soft nod. "I know. And I'm really sorry. I behaved badly, didn't recognize myself for a moment."

"Why did you let him get to you like that? Have you really moved on from that relationship? I feel like I have to ask."

"I have. But seeing him tonight took me right back to the day he told me that he didn't want to get married. That he didn't love me anymore."

Brian reached over and took her hand in his. "He never deserved you, Vivi, because he never realized the treasure that he had in you."

She removed her hand from his grasp. "How can you say that after how I acted? I was horrible. I cared more about winning a stupid game than what was going on with Jenna. You should be running in the opposite direction of me right now."

"I meant what I said earlier. I love you. All of you. Even the parts of you that you don't recognize sometimes because they belong to you."

She turned away from him. He continued. "I'm not saying you have to say that you love me, too. I fell in love with you the moment I bumped into you on the dance floor. And I know you're not ready to hear it, which is why I didn't mean to say it so soon, but it's the truth. I'm in love with you."

She shook her head, then got out of the car, and sped up the sidewalk to her house. He got out of the car and ran after her. "What's wrong?"

She put a hand to her heart, her eyes teary. "I've told you that it's the worst time for this to be happening. But I want to be with you because I care about you a lot."

"I care about you, too."

"But you can't love me. You just can't."

"Why not?"

"Because that makes what happens later hurt the most."

He swallowed and took a step toward her. "I don't know what you think is going to happen, but I don't intend on hurting you or leaving."

"Of course, it won't be intentional, but it will still happen."

"Vivi, this is not about a curse or bad luck or whatever you call it. This is about two people who want to be together and are willing to work at a relationship." He paused and said the words that he feared, "Unless that's not what you want."

"I've got to stop running sometime. Have to face this or there won't be a future for us." She looked down, her head bowed. "And I find myself wanting a future with you."

"So, if you want us to be together, why do you keep pushing me away?"

This time, she lifted her head to look at him, her voice soft and a little strangled as if the effort to say the words cost her something. "Because I'm terrified of you."

SHE PUT HER HANDS over her mouth as soon as she said the words. She hadn't meant to say them. Hadn't meant to even think them. She glanced at his face, dreading what he must think of her. But rather than looking hurt, he was grinning? Maybe even snickering a bit? She smacked his arm. "It's not funny."

"Oh, believe me, this is hilarious. I never thought there would be a day when anyone would be afraid of me." He put his arms out and looked himself over. "I mean, what in the world do you have to be so scared about? I'm a pushover. Just ask my sister."

"What if I fall in love with you and you leave me one day?"

Brian took a step toward her. "What if you're already in love with me? And that's why you're so scared?"

She took a step closer to him. "And what if I pine for you for twenty years after you've replaced me with someone younger and prettier?"

He reached over and brushed a strand of hair from her eyes. "Not possible. Because you're the only one for me."

She reached up and squeezed his hand before he could take it away. "What if…"

He silenced her question by kissing her for several seconds. "No more what-ifs. Not tonight."

"But…"

He kissed her again until her doubts and protests revealed themselves to be full of empty air.

She reached up and brushed the bangs off his forehead. "Valentine's Day is in a few days."

He nodded and put his arms around her waist. "I know. Should we risk getting together that night? Or play it safe and wait a day or two?"

"Since it's the middle of the week, I vote we wait and have our special night later in the week when we don't have to worry about having to get up early to go to work the next day."

His grip tightened around her. "Deal. And

why don't we make it even safer and go out to dinner and a movie?"

"No fundraiser that you promised to help at?"

He grinned at her. "Not next weekend. But I have a few in the upcoming months if you're so inclined to go."

"Let's stick to a traditional date. You buy dinner first, and I'll buy the movie tickets after. I'm not even sure what movies are out in the theaters. What do you like watching?"

He rested his forehead against hers. "Anything as long as I'm with you."

VALENTINE'S DAY PASSED without a word from Brian. Vivi kept checking her phone between classes, but there was nothing, even though she had sent him a message earlier that morning. She checked again and placed the phone in the front pocket of her messenger bag. *Stop thinking about it. You said you'd get together on the weekend. It's no big deal.*

By the time school got out and she headed for home, she felt a little down. And it was all her fault, since it had been her idea to skip

Valentine's Day. And all because she wanted to play it safe.

Safe was boring, she decided.

She had graded most of her student papers before her stomach loudly reminded her that it needed some attention. In her kitchen, she opened the refrigerator. It looked like she'd need to go grocery shopping soon since there were bare spots. Deciding to reheat leftover spaghetti, she took out the large plastic container and retrieved a bowl from the cabinet. She placed about half of what was left in the ceramic bowl and set it in the microwave. A knock on her front door stopped her from pressing the start button.

When she opened the door, her heart leaped at the sight of Brian. "Hi!"

"Want to build a snowman?"

"Aren't you going to ask me in song?"

"Cute." He pointed behind him. "Come outside. It's been snowing this afternoon, and it's perfect for packing."

"I was about to eat dinner."

"I've got that covered. It will be delivered in about an hour. But let's work up an appetite first." He slipped his hand in hers and tugged her forward. "Come on. It will be fun."

"I haven't built a snowman in years."

"Then you're overdue."

She looked into his eyes, then grinned. "Fine. Give me a minute to get my coat."

She ran back to the kitchen, put the pasta in the fridge after eating a few noodles and grabbed her coat and gloves.

Outside on her front lawn, Brian looked her over. "You don't have a hat or scarf?"

"It's not that cold."

He reached down, made a snowball in his hands and tossed it at her. "It will protect you in case the snowball in my hands gets slippery. I can't guarantee you won't get wet in the process of making our snowman."

"You threw that on purpose."

"Did I?" He reached down and made another snowball and tossed it again at her. "Oops. Slippery hands."

She grinned at him, holding up her hands in surrender. "Okay. I'll get a hat and scarf."

She returned a minute later with the scarf wrapped widely around her neck and a stocking cap pulled low on her head. "Better?"

"Much." He pointed at the small stack of

snowballs he'd already formed. "But you're behind."

"Are we on a time schedule?"

"Knowing how competitive you are, I figured we'd have a contest to see who can build their snowman the fastest."

"Who builds a snowman fast? You're supposed to worry about structural integrity, not speed."

He froze and blinked. "I thought you said you haven't built one in years?"

"I haven't, but I still remember how to do it."

"Well, I say we see whose can be built the fastest."

"And not fall apart."

"Okay, fine. Fast and sturdy. Right?"

She agreed, then took a deep breath. "When does the timer begin?"

Brian looked at her and shouted, "Now!"

For the next few minutes, Vivi concentrated on building solid snowballs of graduated sizes. She placed the largest on the bottom and packed snow around the base to keep it from rolling. Then she stacked the other two snowballs. She broke branches off the barren tree in her front yard to make arms.

She snuck a peek at Brian's snowman. He'd chosen to make a mound of snow for his base. Smart considering they would have to judge them on their sturdiness. But it looked like he'd fallen behind on his structure.

Liking her chances, she searched for items she could use for eyes, nose and mouth. She found some pebbles in the snow-covered flower beds, along with a vine that she could use for a mouth. The nose proved to be harder to find. She finally decided to run into her house for the traditional carrot and retrieved two from her refrigerator. She handed one to Brian when she returned.

He didn't look at her as she handed it to him. "I'm in the zone. Don't distract me."

She watched him for a moment, then packed a snowball and tossed it at him. He waved her off. "I'm serious. I'm going to beat you this time."

She packed another snowball and threw this one with more force. It hit him in the shoulder, and he looked up at her, his mouth open. "Are you really declaring a snowball fight now? Because I've got as good as you've got."

This launched the two of them into throwing snow at each other, laughing and shouting when the other got hit. Good thing Brian had suggested the hat since one of his snowballs caught her on the side of the head. "Gotcha!"

"I'll get you back." She pulled some snow together to form a ball but lost her footing and pitched forward into the base of Brian's snowman.

Brian bent down over her. "Are you okay?"

"Just lost my step." She sat back to look at the chunk missing from the side of the snowman. "Sorry about your guy."

He took a seat next to her in the snow. "It's okay. But I think it proves that mine is built very sturdy since it didn't topple over."

"I'll give you points for that."

"And I'll give you points for being further ahead than me."

She looked over at him. "It's a draw?"

"I think so."

She sighed. "Then I tell you what. Why don't we help each other finish the snowmen, then wait for dinner to get here?"

Brian reached over and gave her a soft kiss. "This is the best Valentine's Day I've ever had."

Vivi nodded. "Mine, too."

ON SATURDAY NIGHT, the movie over, Brian stood and helped Vivi to get her coat on before picking up the tub of popcorn and empty drink cups. He thanked the usher as he placed the containers in the trash receptacle, then grabbed Vivi's hand and threaded his fingers through hers. She cuddled close to him, resting her head on his shoulder. "That was a good film. Didn't see that ending coming."

He nodded. "Lots of action."

"With a few kisses thrown in."

"I liked the kisses."

Vivi gave him a quick peck. "I know you do." They strolled toward the exit, and he let go of her hand in order to open the door for her. She gave him another peck before walking past him and stepping outside.

The crisp winter air hit them full force, and he put his arm around her shoulders and pulled her close to his side as they walked to his car. "Do you have plans tomorrow night?"

"It's Sunday. I visit my mom and have dinner at her place on Sunday nights. It's kind of a tradition we've kept since college."

"It's a nice one." He liked the idea of her

seeing her mom once a week. "Maybe you could bring me with you some Sunday, and I could meet her."

Vivi glanced at him. "She'd like to meet you, too, but do you think it's too soon for that?"

"It's like I told you. We'll go at your pace."

She laughed. "Going at my pace, the two of you might never meet." She gave a shrug. "I tell you what. I'll bring it up with her when I'm over there tomorrow, and maybe you can come with me the following Sunday."

"I like that idea."

They were still walking to his car, which seemed to be parked the farthest away from the theater. A car pulled into their aisle up ahead, and Brian brought Vivi closer to get her out of the path.

"She loves to try new recipes, so be warned that the cooking might be different from what you're used to."

"I'm sure it will be fine."

The car seemed to be edging closer to them. What was wrong with the driver? Couldn't she see them? Brian tensed as he noticed the driver's head down, probably texting.

Then, as if in slow motion, the car accelerated and headed straight toward Vivi. Brian pulled her out of the way of the oncoming vehicle, shielding her with his body. He heard Vivi scream, then felt himself falling. His head hit the pavement, and he glanced up to make sure she was okay before closing his eyes.

VIVI BENT OVER Brian's prone body, afraid to move him. The driver jumped out of her car. "Is he okay? I didn't see you guys there."

"Call 911." She felt along his body to see if anything was broken or bleeding. She wasn't a doctor and had only taken a single semester of biology in college, so she was no expert. She didn't even know if she was doing it right. "Please be okay, Brian. Please."

She pushed the hair away from his eyes and brought her hand back to see that it was stained with his blood. That couldn't be good.

It seemed to take twenty years, but the ambulance finally arrived. A paramedic jumped out of the passenger side with a bright yellow medical bag. "What happened?"

Vivi pointed to the driver. "She struck him with her car, and he fell and hit his head. He's bleeding." She showed her hand.

The paramedic nodded and started taking items out of the bag. "What's his name?"

"Brian Redmond."

The paramedic paused and took a better look at him. "That's him all right." She glanced behind at her partner. "Call ahead and tell them we've got a possible head trauma. It's Brian."

The guy winced and hustled back to the ambulance. The paramedic treating Brian looked up at Vivi. "He helped the department get a second ambulance last year. Found the money in the budget to cover it and all. He's a good guy."

Vivi nodded, her eyes streaming with tears. "He's the best."

"We're going to do everything we can to help him, okay?"

"Ma'am?" A police officer approached them, and Vivi stood to face him. "Can I get your statement about what happened?"

Vivi didn't want to leave Brian, so she looked to the paramedic. "Go ahead. We're going to load him in the ambulance. We'll be taking him to Sterling Center Hospital."

Vivi gave her statement to the officer about the car and the possibly distracted driver. How Brian had pulled her around then shielded her with his body so that she wouldn't get hurt. How he had gotten the brunt of the impact. The officer took notes, then nodded at his partner, who interviewed the young female driver. "The driver claims she didn't see you two."

Vivi held out her arms. She was wearing a bright lime-green coat. "There are parking lot lights shining and you can't miss this glow-in-the-dark shade of green, even at night."

He nodded again and stepped aside as the ambulance drove out of the parking lot. Vivi felt her heart convulse in her chest. Then the lights flashed and the sirens blared, and the ambulance zoomed off.

She wanted to run after it, demand to go with them. She hoped that Brian would be okay. Or that this was just a nightmare, and she would wake up in her bed and none of this had ever happened. She put a gloved hand to her forehead and closed her eyes.

"Ma'am?" She opened her eyes to look at the officer. "I know you're worried about him, so why don't we finish these questions, and I can get you up to the hospital."

"Yes, please."

"Is there any family we should contact?"

She gasped. "Yes. His sister, Jamie. I'm sure she would want to be at the hospital as soon as possible. But I don't have her number. Brian has it saved in his phone, which I'm sure is on him."

The officer's eyes widened. "Wait. Jamie Redmond is his sister?"

"Yes. You know her?"

His cheeks turned a deep red. "She's a cop in the next town over, and we might have dated a time or two." He pulled out his cell phone and scrolled before hitting a number. He stepped away from Vivi to relay the information to Brian's sister about the accident, then quickly returned to Vivi. "She's on her way to the hospital."

"I guess the advantage of living in a small town is that everybody knows each other."

"Sometimes it can be an advantage. Other times it's more of a curse."

Vivi paled at the word. She'd been so

happy the last couple of weeks that she hadn't thought about the curse. But of course, this accident would happen now. Brian had confessed he loved her, and just when she thought they might have a chance at a relationship, something bad had to happen. She groaned.

"Are you sure you're all right, ma'am? Maybe we should have you checked out when we get to the hospital."

She waved off the suggestion. "I'm physically fine." It was her mental and emotional health that was a mess.

Sometime later, the officers finished taking her statement as well as those of the driver and witnesses. Vivi's fingertips and toes had frozen while she waited. She stamped her feet and rubbed her hands to warm them, but it didn't seem to help too much. The first officer approached her. "Ms. Carmack, we're finished here so we can take you to the hospital. I'm hoping to get an update on Mr. Redmond's condition for the report."

She nodded. "Thank you. He drove us here tonight, so I have no way of getting there outside of calling a ride share service."

"The back seat of a police cruiser might not be ideal, but we will get you there."

She followed him to the car, and once inside, she rested her head on the back seat. What was she going to tell Jamie when she saw her? How could she explain what had happened? How her brother had saved Vivi but put himself in danger? And how would Jamie respond to her when this was all her fault?

The ride to the hospital didn't take very long, and Vivi was soon running through the emergency room doors. A glance around the waiting room revealed that Jamie had beat her there. The younger woman approached her and put her arms around her in a quick hug. Jamie then stepped back and looked her over. "Are you okay?"

Vivi nodded, then burst into tears.

Vivi opened her eyes to find herself sprawled over an upholstered bench. She sat up and recognized Jamie sleeping in a nearby chair. Vivi touched her arm to rouse her. "The doctor hasn't come out to give us an update on Brian yet, has he?"

Jamie grimaced. "It's been hours since they said they were going to take him for an MRI, CT, whatever it was they said." She closed her eyes and rubbed them. "I didn't mean to fall asleep, but it's so warm in here."

Vivi grabbed the neckline of her blouse and tried to fan herself. "I know what you mean."

"Family of Brian Redmond," a woman in a white lab coat called.

Jamie stood. When Vivi didn't move, Jamie asked, "Aren't you coming with me?"

"I'm not family."

Jamie linked her arm through hers and raised her to her feet. "Please. I don't think I can face this on my own."

The doctor motioned for them to follow her through the maze of examination rooms. Finally, she stopped in front of one. "The good news is that the trauma is minimal."

Vivi flinched. "Trauma? So what's the bad news?" Ugh, this was all her fault. He'd gotten hurt trying to save her, after all.

"Brian hit his head pretty hard, and he's got a concussion, but it could have been a lot worse. So, there is no bad news."

Jamie and Vivi looked at each other. Vivi didn't think this seemed possible. They had to have missed something because a man couldn't get hit by a car and be fine. He'd have broken bones at least. "I'm sorry. I don't understand what you're saying."

The doctor faced her. "He's going to have one heck of a headache for a few days, and we'll be keeping him at least overnight, if not longer, for observation. But he's going to be just fine."

Vivi broke into tears as Jamie swallowed several times. The doctor stepped back to let them go ahead of her. "He looks worse than he is, so don't let that worry you."

They stepped into the room. Brian lay unconscious on the bed with what looked like a hundred wires and tubes connected to various parts of him. A machine beeped beside him, monitoring his vitals. Jamie ran to his side and took his hand in hers. Vivi went to the other side and stared at him.

He looked so pale, whiter than the sheets he lay upon. She stared at his hand and eventually took it in hers. When she squeezed, he didn't wake up or squeeze back.

"Why isn't he awake yet?" Jamie asked the doctor.

"With head trauma like this, his brain is conserving energy to heal itself."

"He's in a coma?"

"No, just sleeping. Which is the best thing for him right now." A nurse entered the room and said something to the doctor, who nodded. "There's a room opening up in a short while, so we'll be moving him upstairs at that time. You both can go home and get some sleep and return later."

"When will he wake up?" Vivi asked the doctor.

"Could be anytime."

"Then I'm staying until he does."

Jamie gave a firm nod. "Me, too."

"I'll inform you when he gets moved upstairs, then."

Jamie looked back to Brian. "Can we stay in here until you move him?"

"Medical staff will be coming in and out checking his vitals. It's best if you stay out of the way in the waiting room until we're ready."

She and Jamie returned to the waiting room and the uncomfortable plastic chairs.

Vivi held Jamie's gaze. "I'm so sorry about all of this."

"You're not to blame."

"But he got hurt trying to save me. How is this not my fault?"

Jamie reached over and took her hand, squeezing it. "I understand where you're coming from, but please don't go there. The person to blame in this situation is the driver who hit him. Not you."

Vivi held onto Jamie's hand. "I feel guilty all the same. It should have been me in that hospital bed, not him."

Jamie fell silent while Vivi stewed over her responsibility in the accident. She'd been looking at him and not the cars in the parking lot. She'd been so focused on him that the car coming at them hadn't even been on her radar.

But it had been on Brian's. He'd even nudged her closer to the side where the car couldn't have reached her. He'd saved her, for which she was grateful.

And yet she was so full of guilt that she could almost taste it every time she swallowed.

She realized Jamie had been talking and tried to focus. "Sorry, I was just thinking."

"My mom's on a flight up here. I told her that I'd call her and my dad once we had updates, but she insisted that getting here sooner was more important."

"What about your dad?"

"He may be retired from the military, but he's still working and couldn't get the time off on such short notice."

"It's good that your mom can be here, though."

Jamie settled into the chair. "We could be here awhile, so I'm going to grab a quick nap."

That sounded like a good plan, but Vivi couldn't shake the image of Brian in the hospital bed.

CHAPTER ELEVEN

HIS HEAD THROBBED. He thought about opening his eyes but was afraid of what he would find once he did. Eventually, curiosity won out. He raised an eyelid and spied Jamie asleep in a chair next to the bed. "James."

Her head popped up. "You're awake."

He nodded slowly and glanced around the room. Where was he? Looked like a hospital. But what in the world had been done to his head that made it hurt so bad? "What happened?"

"You don't remember?"

The car. Distracted driver. Heading toward Vivi. Shielding her with his body. "I think I do."

He closed his eyes for what felt like a minute, maybe two. When he opened them again, Jamie was gone and Vivi sat in the chair. He smiled. "Hey, you."

"Hey, yourself."

He tried to shift a little to ease the tension in his muscles. "Jamie?"

"She went home to take a shower and change. You've been asleep for a few hours."

"Sorry."

"Don't apologize. You've been through a lot." She reached over and took his hand in hers. "I don't know how to thank you for saving me last night."

"It's okay."

"No, it's not okay. It was incredible, and I'll never be able to repay you."

"Don't need to."

A wave of fatigue hit him, and he closed his eyes once more. When he opened them again, Vivi was gone, but a nurse was there taking his vitals. "How are you doing, Brian?"

"Thirsty."

"I'll get you some water." She took the blood pressure cuff off his arm. "Your blood pressure is a little high, but that's probably due to the concussion. What's your pain level?"

He frowned as he thought it over. "Four maybe?"

She noted that on the tablet as he asked, "I have a concussion? How did that happen?"

"Probably when you saved your girlfriend." She peered at him. "Do you remember what happened?"

He tried to recall. "There was a car." He nodded. "That's right. Distracted driver heading right toward us."

"You pushed your girlfriend out of the way and got hit instead. The doctors are saying it's a miracle you got out of it virtually unscathed. Only a bump on the head and a concussion."

He put his hands to his temples. "That's why I have this headache."

"I can get you something for that."

"Where's Vivi and Jamie?"

The nurse glanced up from the tablet and looked at the empty chair beside his bed. "They'll be back soon. I think they went downstairs to the cafeteria to get something to eat."

"What time is it?"

"Just after noon on Sunday. If you're hungry, you can use the phone to call down for a tray." She placed the bedside table with the phone closer to his side. "I'll be back in a little bit to switch out your saline IV and give you some antibiotics. Do you need anything else?"

"Just Vivi."

The nurse gave him a smile. "I'm sure she'll be back shortly."

After she left the room, he closed his eyes. He didn't mean to keep falling asleep, but he couldn't control whether he stayed awake or not. This time when he opened his eyes, Vivi had returned but she was standing against the wall, watching him sleep. He gave her a smile and patted the bed beside him. "Come here."

She approached the bed, but he could see the hesitation in her eyes. Maybe seeing him like this scared her. "I'm glad you're here, but…"

She frowned at him. "But?"

"You should go home. Get some rest."

She shook her head. "I slept in the waiting room for a bit. I'm fine."

"No, you're probably exhausted and for good reason. Did you get any sleep last night?"

Her eyes started to glisten, and he watched a single tear make a wet track down her cheek. "I'm sorry. I didn't mean to make you cry. I take it back."

She shook her head. "It's okay. I am tired. But I shouldn't complain. Not when you're here and hurt."

He tried to sit up further but winced in pain. Vivi rushed to his side. "What is it? What can I do?"

"Nothing." He shut his eyes, then opened them quickly so he wouldn't fall back asleep. "I love having you here, but you should go home for a little while. Besides, you have to have dinner with your mom tonight. Tell her that you're going to be bringing me over soon."

Vivi took his hand in hers and kissed it. "I wish I could make this up to you."

"You don't have to." He reached up with his free hand to touch her cheek. "Go home. And I'll see you tomorrow?"

She nodded, then carefully leaned over to give him a quick peck on the mouth. He smiled. "A kiss from you is the best medicine."

"I'll see you tomorrow after school gets out."

"Great. Love you."

She hurried to leave the room. He could tell by the way her shoulders shook that she was crying as she did. Jamie entered the room shortly after. "Is Vivian okay? She looked upset when she left."

"I saw. Maybe it's just all the emotion of what's happened. I told her to come see me tomorrow. She usually has dinner with her mom on Sundays. I told her to go do that."

Jamie shot him a look and collapsed in the chair beside the bed. "What am I going to do with you? You don't kick out the woman you love when she's scared to be here in the first place. And she blames herself for what happened, in the second. She needs kindness right now. Lots of it."

"It's not Vivi's fault I'm here."

"No kidding. You couldn't have gotten out of the way of that car in time?" She shook her head. "Mom had a few choice words to say about that."

"You spoke to Mom?"

"You missed out on quite a bit while you were sleeping. She's on her way up here from Florida. Dad wanted to come, too, but he's tied up at work. I have to pick her up later tonight when her flight gets in. I guess she had several layovers since this was so last minute."

He tried to clear his mind, focus. "This medication is messing with my head. All I want to do is close my eyes, but when I do time passes and I can't keep track of what's going on."

"What's going on is you're going to be laid up for a while. You'll probably get out of here by tomorrow or Tuesday at the latest. Mom's planning on moving in and taking care of you until you can manage on your own. And that means you're off work for a while, too."

Brian frowned. "No, that's not going to work. I've got things I have to do. You know my schedule. There are a lot of projects that are at crucial stages, and I need to be there to oversee them."

"You're going to have to learn to work from home and delegate because that's what's about to happen. The mayor insists on it, in fact."

Brian groaned and laid his head back on the pillow. "I just wanted to protect her. I didn't think this would happen."

"Because you weren't thinking." She stood and slugged his shoulder.

"Hey!"

"You didn't get hurt there, so don't even try that, mister." She ran a hand through her short hair. "Do you even understand what you've put us through?"

"I did the right thing."

"But do you know what it was like to get the call from the police that you had been hurt? To wait for hours until the doctor came out to tell us you were going to be okay?"

"James, I couldn't let Vivi get hurt. I just couldn't."

"I know. I know." She collapsed back into the chair beside his bed. "It's just that you're my big brother and I love you, you noble do-gooding jerk."

He gave her a smile. "I love you, too, brat."

VIVI DRAGGED THE fork through the mashed potato crust of the shepherd's pie her mother had made for dinner. She'd lost her appetite. Her mom cleared her throat, and Vivi looked up at her. "Sorry. I guess I'm not hungry."

"And you're pretty quiet, too."

"Got a lot on my mind."

Her mom took another bite and watched her. "Something you want to share with me? Like maybe about that bruise I can see on your wrist?"

Vivi's hand went to her opposite wrist, which she'd used to brace herself when falling as Brian pushed her out of harm's way. "There was an accident last night. A car hit Brian and almost hit me, if not for Brian's quick thinking."

Her mother dropped her fork on to her plate, and she rose to her feet, crossing to where Vivi sat. She put her hand on her forehead and then touched her face and arms as if checking for any more bruises or any broken bones. "You've been here over an hour. When were you going to tell me about this? Were you going to tell me at all?"

"I was eventually." She took her mom's hands in hers to stop her from checking her out. "I'm okay, Mom. You don't have to probe me any more."

"And Brian?"

Vivi tried to keep the tears from falling down her cheeks. "He's hurt. He's going to be okay, but it'll be a while before he recovers."

Her mom sat in the chair beside her. "I'm so sorry, sweetheart. I know how much you care about him."

"It's all my fault. It should be me in that hospital bed, not him."

"It was an accident. You can't control those any more than you can control the spinning of the world on its axis."

But she could have shielded him just as he had protected her last night. She knew this year would bring its troubles. "I should have broken up with him for good and not let him sweet talk me into staying together. Then this wouldn't have happened."

"Maybe. But what about the fact that he was there to protect you? What does that tell you? I should be thanking him for saving you."

Vivi wiped her face with her napkin. "I was supposed to ask you tonight if he could accompany me to a Sunday dinner soon. But now, I don't know. I'm not sure I should be inviting him to do anything with me."

"Is that really what you want? Or what he

wants? The guy saves you, and you're going to break up with him?"

"I think it would be better for him if I do."

"Better for him? Or for you?"

Vivi frowned at her mother. "I'm trying to save him just like he did for me. To protect him from the danger that could happen if we keep seeing each other."

Her mother's mouth was set in a tight line, and she didn't say anything for a long moment. When she did, her voice was low, and she knew her mom spoke from experience. "You listen to me, young lady. If you were to break up with an honorable man like Brian, it would be the worst mistake of your life."

"Then it wouldn't be the first time I messed up. And probably not the last."

Vivi held out a large spoonful of stewed prunes. "Just give it a try."

Brian wrinkled his nose. "Why? The car didn't kill me, so you're going to by feeding me that?" He shook his head. "I'd rather starve. Couldn't you have brought me some contraband? Potato chips or a burger or something?"

"I'm not a strict rule follower like Cecily

is, but I know that eating a burger is probably not what's best for you right now."

"And prunes are?"

"There's some fruit cocktail on the tray. Would you rather eat that?"

He shook his head. "Read my lips. Potato chips. Burger. Pizza." He closed his eyes and gave a soft smile. "Mmm. Pizza. That's the ticket."

The door to the hospital room opened, and a short woman entered with a tote bag under one arm. She stopped short at the sight of Vivi sitting on the hospital bed next to Brian. "I didn't know you had company, son."

So, this was Brian's mother. Vivi slid off the bed and approached the woman, her hand extended. "Mrs. Redmond, it's nice to finally meet you in person."

Mrs. Redmond looked at Vivi's hand then shook her head and grabbed her into a tight hug. "Don't mind me, but in this family we're huggers, sweetie." She released Vivi, then looked at the food tray next to Brian. "How do they expect you to heal when they feed you that stuff? You need something that will stick to your bones. Hearty meals, not clear broth and fruit cups." She started to unpack the tote bag, bringing out several plastic tubs. "I didn't have the time to make you my Belgian beef stew, so I'll have to whip that up for you another day. But I was able to throw together some spaghetti and meatballs."

Brian rubbed his hands together. "One of my favorites." He looked at Vivi. "I've always loved my mom's spaghetti sauce."

His mom smiled at him, reaching out a hand to caress his cheek. "And I love making it for you." She handed a plastic container and fork to Vivi. "Here. Give him this."

Vivi took her seat beside Brian once again, then removed the lid from the container. Several large meatballs sat in a nest of noodles. She took the fork and the plastic container and handed them to Brian, who smacked his lips. "I bet they're your best ever, Mom."

Mrs. Redmond smiled at him, then started to fuss with the blankets covering his legs. "Because I always put in my special ingredient."

Vivi looked at the meatballs. "Basil? Garlic?"

Brian smiled. "She always puts love in every dish she makes for our family."

"And my food will heal you quicker than anything these doctors can do." Seemingly satisfied that he was properly covered and that Vivi was looking after him, she took a seat in a second chair that had been added to the room. "Did the nurse say when you'll be able to go home?"

Brian shook his head and swallowed his bite before answering, "They are talking about later tonight hopefully. They want to run one more CT scan to make sure everything is all right. They've been trying to get me in for a while this afternoon, but they're backed up."

Vivi frowned. "A CT scan?"

"Checking my brain, I guess." He gave her a grin. "Probably making sure I still have one."

"That's not funny. This is serious." She dropped her gaze to the floor. Hadn't he trusted her with the information? Didn't he think she could handle that he wasn't out of the woods? Because she could. "I feel so bad about all of this."

Brian reached out and touched her hand,

rubbing his fingers across it until she looked up at him. "It's not your fault."

"You wouldn't be here if it wasn't for me." She looked into the depths of those hazel eyes and wished again that she had met him at a different time in her life. Then he wouldn't be here in this hospital. "So, it is my fault."

"You've got to stop thinking like that." He put a piece of meatball on the fork and held it out to her. "And you've got to try this. My mom's meatballs really are the best."

She knew he was wrong. Knew that all of this could be traced back to her. She took the bite and chewed it slowly. "Very good."

"I told you."

"Just get better soon."

He winked at her. "I'm working on it."

THE HOSPITAL RELEASED Brian into his mother's care later that evening. The faint scent of bleach in the air meant she'd probably been cleaning. Although when she'd found the time since arriving the night before, he didn't know. But then, that was his mom. A real dynamo with endless energy.

His mom brought him one of the pillows

from his bedroom and placed it behind his back as he settled in the recliner. "How does that feel?"

"I'm fine, Mom."

"Oh, I forgot the extra blanket."

She turned as if to leave the room again, but he called, "I don't need another blanket. Actually, I'm a little warm." She walked to the thermostat and adjusted it. "Mom, could you just sit down for a minute? I'm fine. Really."

She took a seat on the sofa and clasped her hands together, one of her feet tapping on the soft carpet beneath. "Are you hungry? I could fix you something. What time is it? It's almost seven. I know you ate the spaghetti earlier, but I could make you a quick dinner."

"Mom, I love you but it's too much already and we've only been home for a little over an hour."

"I just want to make you comfortable."

"I know you do, but I'm fine. Really."

"Do you need some pain medication? What's your pain level?"

"A two. I'm fine."

She sighed and shifted farther back into the couch cushions. Then she darted up and searched for the television remote before handing it to him. "In case you want to watch something."

He peered at her, sensing something was off. "What's going on?"

His mom shook her head. "Nothing."

He narrowed his eyes at her. "You're nervous. Why are you so nervous?"

"A mother doesn't like to see her child in pain. She does everything she can to make it better. So please let me do something for you."

Brian could see her struggling to find some way, however small, to make him more comfortable. "You know, I'm not hungry enough for a big dinner, but I could use a snack. A healthy one, maybe?"

She smiled as if relieved to finally be of use. "I bought some apples. I could slice one for you."

"With peanut butter?"

She nodded and left the room. He adjusted the blanket over his sore knee. His mom had given him a pillow to place under it to take the pressure off keeping it straight out. His cell phone rang, and he reached over to answer it. "Hey, Vivi."

"Hey, your sister called to let me know they released you from the hospital and you're back home."

He smiled at the sound of her voice. "They did. And yes, I am."

"The CT results came back normal?"

"Yes. Finally. You're welcome to stop by tomorrow if you'd like."

"You probably need the time to rest. But I'll call you tomorrow night." She hung up the phone before he could respond.

His mom returned from the kitchen and gave him a plate with apple slices and a healthy dollop of peanut butter. She'd also found a small knife with a ceramic handle that he didn't even know he owned. It was the perfect size for the task. "Thank you, Mom."

"Who was that on the phone?"

"Vivi. She's going to call tomorrow once I've had a chance to settle in."

His mom sniffed, then started to search for the television remote, which lay in plain sight on the coffee table. She grabbed it and turned on the television. "Do you mind if I watch my stories?"

He'd known his mom to watch soap operas his whole life. They'd be on when he came home from school no matter what state or country his dad was stationed in. She loved her stories and had found a way to enjoy them no matter what language they were broadcast in. She took a seat on the sofa and changed the channel to bring up the on-demand programs before turning to him. "You don't mind, do you?"

"It will feel like old times when I stayed home sick from school."

She grinned and increased the volume. He took a slice of apple, spread it with some peanut butter, then took a bite. Vivi's call replayed in his mind. She'd sounded distracted, but then she had seen him a few hours earlier and probably had a million things to do before she could finish her day. On the other hand, she'd been distracted since the accident. Maybe he'd ask his mom for advice.

On the first commercial break, he broached the subject. "So, what do you think about Vivi?"

His mom focused on him, and said, "She's a nice girl." She turned back to the television, though her program hadn't resumed.

He frowned at her words. Of course, Vivi was nice, but she was so much more. Was his mom keeping something from him? "You don't like her?"

"I didn't say that."

"But you didn't say that you did." He slid his plate to the side. "Do you like Vivi?"

"You like her. That's enough for me."

"Mom, I more than like her. I'm in love with her, and I plan on marrying her one day if she'll have me." His mom's mouth puckered into a tight knot that he knew meant she disapproved. "Why don't you like her?"

"Brian, you've had a rough day and you should probably get more rest. We can talk about your girlfriend later."

"I feel fine, so there's no reason we can't discuss this now."

Her program came back on, and he knew that trying to talk to her while it was on would be pointless. The next commercial break, he asked, "What's wrong with Vivi?"

"There's nothing wrong with her. I just don't think she's the right woman for you."

"How could you know that she would be wrong for me? You've only met her this afternoon."

His mom stared at him, mouth open, before she shook her head. "Because she doesn't love you. And I don't know if she'll ever love you like you want her to."

His mom didn't know what she was talking about. She didn't know Vivi like he did. "I know she's cautious when it comes to relationships, but I told her that I'm willing to go as slowly as she wants until she's ready to get serious."

"Maybe I'm wrong about her. I hope I am. But I have a feeling that she's going to break your heart. I only want what's best for you."

"Vivi is what's best, Mom. I know she is. She just needs time."

"I hope you're right."

He did, too.

VIVI HAD FOUND excuses to avoid going to see Brian the last couple of days, but she was now running out of them. Time for a bit of courage, she told herself, as she pulled to the curb in front of his house. She stared up at it, trying to will herself to get out of her car and go inside. The sheer curtains moved in the front window, and she figured someone had noticed she was here. Taking a deep breath, she reminded herself to not do anything hurtful or rash. Even if she had been thinking of nothing else but breaking up with him since the accident, she couldn't do it. Not when he was still recovering and not after everything that had happened.

No, it would be better to wait. Once he was completely healed and she could tell him how she felt. How much she cared for him and always wanted the best for him, and how that wasn't her.

She took her time walking up the sidewalk to the front porch and stood on the steps for a minute before ringing the bell. Brian's mom answered the door, her smile tight and looking forced. "Mrs. Redmond. It's good to see you again."

"Vivi." She swung the front door wider and ushered her inside. "Brian has been expecting you."

She could hear the censure in his mother's words as if he'd been waiting for days for her to come see him. Maybe he had. Her heart seemed to beat harder in her chest to a rhythm of my fault, my fault, my fault.

The figure sitting in the recliner stirred

as she walked around to take a seat on the sofa. "Hey."

Brian smiled, his eyes soft and still a little sleepy. He reached out for her, and she put her hand in his. He brought it up to his mouth and kissed it softly. "You made it."

She took her hand back, the kiss still moist on her finger. "I did." She pulled a small bag out of her purse and handed it to him. "I brought you a little get-well-soon gift."

He took the bag of candy from her. "You remembered these are my favorite."

"They're *our* favorite. But you like the red ones and I prefer the blue."

"Right."

She put her hands together in her lap, searching for something to say. "Um, you look pretty good."

"Thanks. I'm feeling pretty good. I talked to Josh earlier, and I'll be returning to the office next week."

"So soon? Are you sure that's wise?"

"I can only do so much from my laptop here, and it's critical that I return to the office."

Mrs. Redmond entered the room. "Your

health is much more important than your job."

Vivi had to agree with her. "What would a few more days hurt?"

"The doctor cleared me to go back to work. And I feel fine." He turned to his mom. "I really am."

She waved off his words. "Can I get you something to drink, Vivi? Some hot tea maybe? The temperatures are supposed to drop even more later tonight."

Vivi found herself nodding. "Tea would be wonderful."

"Honey? Lemon?"

"A little honey, please."

Mrs. Redmond asked Brian, "You want some more water?"

"Any more and I'll float out of the house. I'm fine, Mom."

Mrs. Redmond gave a nod and left the room. Brian turned to Vivi, shaking his head. "I love the woman, but she needs to go home to my dad soon."

"She loves you. That's why she fusses over you."

"I know, but I don't need fussing anymore. I'm fine on my own. But she worries."

"We all worry." Seems like that's all Vivi had done since Saturday night. Worry about whether Brian was going to be okay. Worry about what might happen now with their relationship. Worry that she was going to make a huge mistake.

Brian reached over and took her hand in his. "I'm fine."

She looked at her hand in his. "Brian…"

Mrs. Redmond re-entered the living room and handed Vivi a mug with steam rising from it. "Your tea, dear."

Vivi let go of Brian's hand to put hers around the warm mug. "Thank you."

Mrs. Redmond turned to leave. "I've got to keep moving. There are a thousand and one things that need doing around here."

Brian smiled at Vivi. "Now, where were we?"

"You said we had something to discuss." She racked her brain. What would he want to talk about?

"The booklet. Where are we on that?"

She cocked her head to the side to look at him. "That's what you want to talk about? The book?" She shook her head. "That's not important right now. What's important is that you get better."

"I told you. I'm fine." His words came out with a little heat behind them.

"We can talk about the book later."

"No, let's discuss it now. The timeline…?"

"If anything, we're ahead of schedule. I only have a few stories that need to be edited, and we're still on time to meet the deadline for the printers."

"Good."

She looked at him, weighing her words. "Brian, we need to talk about something else. Like about what happened last Saturday and what that means for us."

He winced. "I know. I'm being a coward and trying to put it off."

"I don't remember you ever being afraid of talking about us."

He scooted to the edge of the recliner and looked into her eyes. His eyes seemed full of pain. Maybe regret? She put her mug of tea on a coaster on the coffee table in front of her. He swallowed, and she found herself doing the same. He sighed and closed his eyes. "There's no easy way to say this, but I think we need to take a break."

"You think we need to step away from the relationship?" Although she'd been thinking the same thing, it hurt a little to find out he'd been the first to say it. "I know why I think we should, but why do you?"

He opened his eyes. "We can't give each other what we really need right now."

"I want to make you happy, but I don't think I can."

"You can't love me like I want you to."

"I'm sorry."

He reached out a hand to her. "Don't apologize. It's not your fault."

"But I feel like it is. I want to be what you need, but I can't, even though I've tried."

"I know."

"This doesn't mean that I don't like you, Brian. But I…"

"It's okay."

She took a deep breath and tried to keep her emotions in check. It wouldn't help him to cry, even though that's all she could think about. "It doesn't feel okay."

"I'd like us to be friends after a little while. If we can."

She gave him a smile that she didn't feel. "I'd like that."

"Me, too."

She took another deep breath. "I know this is the right thing for the both of us, so why does it hurt so bad?"

"We both wanted this to be something more. It's as if we have to let that expectation go. And in time, we can find something else."

"I guess."

Vivi stood and grabbed her purse and coat that she'd laid on the sofa beside her. "I guess I should go, then."

"We can discuss the booklet next week in my office. I'll have my assistant call you to set up a time that's convenient."

She nodded and stared at him, not wanting to leave because once she left, it really would be over between them. She stepped in and gave him a quick hug, but he held on to her tightly for a long moment before letting her go.

"Goodbye, then."

"Until next week."

THE FRONT DOOR slammed shut, and Brian closed his eyes at the sound of it. His mom entered the living room. "Where did Vivi go? I thought you might invite her to dinner." She looked at his face and frowned. "What happened?"

"She had to leave." He took his time getting out of the recliner and standing up. "I'll be right back. I just want to get something from my bedroom."

He took his time moving down the short hall to the bedroom, then shut himself inside and walked to the dresser. Looking at his reflection in the mirror above the dresser, he wasn't sure who he was staring at. His heart still beat, though. His lungs still breathed in air.

Even if he wished they didn't.

He leaned forward and rested his forehead against the cool surface of the mirror. Disappointment inside him grew. He'd really believed that Vivi had been his future. Been so sure that they would share a life together. And now…how did he let that go?

A knock on the door caught his attention. "I'll be out in a moment, Mom."

"It's Jamie."

He took a few deep breaths before opening the door. "Mom sent you down here to make sure I was okay?"

"More like Vivi."

He winced at the sound of her name. "She called you?"

"She was crying so hard that I could barely understand her. Good thing I was on my way here already." She put a hand on his shoulder. "Are you okay?"

"I'm fine."

Jamie kept her voice low as she entered the bedroom and shut the door behind her. "Who broke up with who?"

"Does it really matter? It's done." He held up his hands as if to say he had no idea. "I guess it was inevitable. She knew it wouldn't last between us, and I guess I should have believed her every single time she tried to tell me."

He opened the bedroom door. "Nothing else to say."

He walked back into the living room and took his usual perch in the recliner. Jamie took a seat beside him on the sofa where Vivi had recently sat. He pointed at her. "Don't look at me like that."

"I'm not looking like anything."

"It looks a lot like pity and something else. Maybe a little anger there?"

"Why shouldn't I be angry? She's kicking you when you're already down."

"She didn't kick me. We let each other go."

Jamie didn't say anything but settled back on to the sofa. After a while, she cleared her throat and said, "Mom invited me to stay for dinner. And I intend on taking home leftover meatloaf for sandwiches, so you better not eat it all."

"I just lost the love of my life. I'm recovering from a concussion. So I think I'm entitled to a few extra slices of Mom's meatloaf."

"As long as she's not making her oh rotten potatoes to go with it."

"They're called au gratin."

"I said what I said."

Brian gave her a smile even though he didn't feel it. "I'll be fine, James. Really. You don't have to worry."

"Who says I'm worried? I thought it was pity and anger."

"You're deflecting with humor. It's your go-to response."

"Have you told Mom that you guys broke up?"

"It just happened so not yet. Maybe when it's not so raw."

Jamie reached out and took her hand in his. "Whatever you need, just ask."

Vivi stood in the middle of a barn, a yoga mat at her feet. When the instructor called for them to do downward dog, she grimaced as a baby goat climbed on top of her back. The extra weight made her sag, and she had to fight to bring herself back into alignment. She glanced over at Cec, who had a goat nibbling on a strand of hair that had fallen out of her ponytail.

When Cec had suggested they try a session of goat yoga held at a farm about a half hour north of Thora, Vivi had thought it would be kind of cool. And it would get the breakup off her mind for at least an hour. But now that they were surrounded by goats of all sizes and smells, she had doubts.

Because Brian was never far from her thoughts.

She thought he would have liked to try goat yoga. That he would have the best stories to tell later about the woman in the striped leggings who kept making kissing noises to the goats, but they stayed away from her. Or the guy who wore bright orange from head to foot and grunted with every pose.

"And now down to the child pose."

Vivi lowered herself to her belly, trying to keep the baby goat on her back. By the time she had reached the mat, the goat had jumped off her and ran to go jump on someone else.

Cec turned her head to look at her, blowing air to discourage her goat from chewing her hair any more. "Please tell me we're almost finished here."

Since there were no clocks in the barn, she wasn't aware of what time it was. "Your guess is as good as mine."

"No talking please, ladies."

Cec rolled her eyes, and they dropped the conversation.

After the class finished, Vivi rolled her mat and placed it under her arm. She walked to the side of the barn where she had left her coat and purse before class. Cec joined her. "I'm not sure if I want to sign up for a second class. Do you?"

"It was different. And kind of fun."

"But is it worth coming back a second time?"

Vivi wrinkled her nose. "Maybe not."

Once they got into Cec's car, she turned to Vivi. "I could go for a hot chocolate. I heard that a pop-up shop opened up in that huge retail space off Floral. Evidently, it's a kind of hot chocolate bar. What do you say?"

"And consume all the calories we just worked off?" Vivi paused, then nodded. "Sounds like a great idea."

The hot chocolate bar boasted twenty different toppings and flavors for their drinks. Cec chose a sea salt caramel while Vivi decided to try the s'mores flavor with extra marshmallows. They strolled past the different booths, window shopping as they sipped.

Cec fingered a beaded purse in one place, then focused on Vivi. "I'm going to bring it up if you won't."

The marshmallows seemed to congeal in the pit of her belly. "There's nothing to talk about."

"Really? Because I've been careful not to mention the dark circles under your eyes. Or how your eyes looked red when I picked you up this morning as if you'd just been crying."

"And yet you have mentioned it."

"How are you doing?" Cec put a hand on Vivi's arm. "And I mean, how are you really doing?"

"I don't recall bugging you about your feelings when Tom left you."

"That's because that's all I talked about for about a week after it happened. You haven't said a single word except to say that you and Brian broke up."

Vivi swallowed and glanced away. She didn't want to cry in public. Didn't want anyone to see how miserable she'd been. She closed her eyes and took a deep breath before facing Cec again. "It's fine. I'm fine."

"Liar."

"I'm trying to be fine. Is that better?"

"At least it's closer to the truth."

"I know the decision to break up was mutual, but it doesn't mean it hurts any less."

"Because you really cared for him."

"Of course I did." She sipped her hot chocolate, which didn't seem as sweet now. "But I should have known that the curse would have its way with me."

"This has nothing to do with bad luck and more to do with two stubborn people who are afraid."

"Brian isn't afraid."

"Please. He was terrified that you'd leave him, so he left first and made it seem like you had come to a mutual decision."

"But I was going to break up with him. I was going to wait until he was fully healed, so he wasn't wrong about that."

"Okay, so maybe it was a mutual decision, but that doesn't mean he's not hurting, too. And maybe starting to regret this choice."

Vivi stopped walking and looked at her friend, hoping she might be right. "Do you really think so?"

Cec put her arm around Vivi's shoulders and got her to start strolling again. "I'm pretty sure I'm right about that. I mean, aren't you regretting what you said?"

Vivi nodded, blinking away the tears that she had grown weary of. "You're right."

"What can I do to help you?"

"I made this mess. I'll figure it out alone."

"How about you come over for dinner tonight? I made clam chowder in the slow cooker, and Pops said he'll make his famous melt-in-your-mouth biscuits to go with it."

The idea of eating anything made her

stomach revolt. She placed a hand on her belly. "I don't need food."

"I also have a bottle of that wine you enjoyed at the faculty Christmas party last year."

"Alcohol isn't going to fix this." Although it might make looking at her pitiful life a little easier, it would only delay the inevitable.

"So, what will?"

"Time." Vivi looked down into Cec's face and gave a half-hearted shrug. "It's going to take me some time, but I'll be okay eventually."

"But for now?"

A tear escaped the corner of her eye, and she took a shuddering breath. "I just want to be alone. You understand?"

"No."

Vivi frowned at her response. "What do you mean 'no'?"

"Did you let me wallow when Tom left me? Did you leave me alone? No. You came over and helped me pack and moved me into your place. If I didn't have Pops to watch over, I'd move you in over there and mother you and help you get back on your feet. But instead, I'll be by your side and hold you up when you need me to and sit in silence when you need that more. You understand?"

Vivi felt the beginning of a smile on her face, and she reached over and grabbed Cec into a tight hug. "I don't deserve you as my best friend."

"And I don't deserve you. But we're stuck with each other."

Cec rubbed Vivi's back, then released her. "So, dinner tonight?"

"I don't think I could eat."

"So, you can sit there and watch Pops and I eat some of the best clam chowder you could ever have. And if you change your mind, I'll let you try a little."

"I won't be very good company."

"I don't expect you to be."

Cec nodded at a few neighbors who greeted her, then turned back to Vivi. "Be there at five thirty."

It didn't sound like Vivi had much of a choice.

CHAPTER TWELVE

A COUPLE OF DAYS PASSED, and Brian felt a lot stronger. He'd even been able to return to the office. His first visitor was Mrs. Vincenza, who had packed a lunch for them to share. "You didn't need to do this," he said, waving to the tubs of food around them.

"You've fed me enough meals. Besides, you're the one who needs an extra hand right now." She pushed the tub of chicken salad from the local deli closer to him. "Put another scoop on your plate. You need the extra protein."

He obeyed her and took a small bite of it. "My mom's been visiting from Florida to help take care of me, so I've been eating pretty good."

"And she went home yesterday, so we need to make sure you are taken care of."

He frowned at her words. Did everyone know his business? "How did you know she went home?"

"It's a small town. I hear things." Mrs. Vincenza looked at him over the edge of her glasses. "I also heard you and that sweet teacher from the high school broke up. Such nonsense. You two were good together. What were you thinking?"

Brian groaned. He didn't want to talk about Vivi. Didn't want to think about her, despite the fact that she was always on his mind. He missed her a lot. "She's not up for discussion."

"Because you still love her."

"Because there's nothing to talk about anymore." He took a large bite of chicken salad and chewed it slowly so he wouldn't have to speak.

"You know I have a granddaughter who's close to your age. I could set something up between you two if you're interested." She searched through her handbag until she found a picture of a girl that had been taken years before when she was probably still in high school. "She's never been married. No kids. Has a good job at a lawyer's office and owns her own condo."

"I'm not interested in dating anyone right now."

"Well, the offer still stands if you change your mind. It will only take a phone call. I'm sure she'd be willing to go out with someone like you."

"I don't think I'll be dating anyone for a while." He couldn't even think about another woman besides Vivi.

A knock on the office door announced his assistant Mallory's arrival. "Uh, Brian. There's someone here to see you. She had called for an appointment, but I forgot to put it in your calendar."

"I'm still meeting with Mrs. Vincenza."

"I could ask her to come back later, but this afternoon you have that meeting with the city council regarding the final plans for refurbishing the park."

Mrs. Vincenza perked up. "Is it a young woman? Is she a good person? Attractive looking?" She elbowed Brian in the side, and he winced at the force such an elderly woman could muster.

Brian's heart lurched inside his chest. "The deadline for the senior project is coming up, isn't it? It's Vivi, right?"

The assistant nodded once, and Mrs. Vincenza looked between them, seeming a tad too excited. Brian plucked up a napkin and wiped off his mouth. "Thank you for lunch today, Mrs. Vincenza, but I should take this meeting."

"Are you going to try to win her back?"

"We can meet again next week at our usual time. And I'll be the one bringing lunch for our meeting."

Mrs. Vincenza nodded and gathered up the leftovers, putting them in the large tote bag she'd brought with her. "Of course. And you'll give me all the details of what follows."

Mrs. Vincenza took her time putting everything away, glancing at the door as if waiting to see what would happen when Vivi entered the room. Mallory ushered Mrs. Vincenza out, and she gaped as Vivi moved past her into the office. The last thing Brian saw before Vivi sat down was Mrs. Vincenza staring at them, then giving him a wink. Brian turned back to look at Vivi. "We're still on schedule, aren't we?"

"Your assistant told me this was your first week back in the office, so I imagine things have been a little chaotic. She also explained that she forgot to put our appointment on your calendar. I didn't mean to interrupt like this."

"You're not interrupting at all, Vivi. I'm glad to see you." When her head jerked up at his words, he cleared his throat. "So where are we on getting the stories to the editor?"

Vivi sat staring at him for a moment. "All the stories have been submitted to the editor, and she'll have them to the printer by the end of this month. That puts us on schedule to have the booklets ready for the fundraiser in July." She paused. "You're looking better than the last time I saw you."

He wished he could say the same for her. But her skin was pale and she had dark circles underneath her eyes, which seemed to indicate she wasn't sleeping. He wanted to ask her how she'd been but kept the question to himself.

Silence fell between them and stretched past the awkward point until the air filled with unspoken tension.

Why aren't you sleeping? Do you miss me as much as I miss you? Have you changed your mind about me? About us?

Vivi glanced at her bag and coat. "I guess that's all we need to discuss?" She rose to her feet and grabbed her things. "Maybe it's better if we communicate through text and emails going forward. There's really no need to meet in person, is there?"

"Is that what you want?" Every inch of him wanted her to change her mind. To say "no." He got to his feet, trying to prepare himself for her reply.

She shook her head, but said, "Yes."

So she had wanted to see him as much as he needed to see her. But he didn't call her on it. Instead, he nodded and returned the lie. "I agree."

"Sorry, again, to have barged in here and wasted your time." She turned and strode out of the room.

He slumped back into his chair. Jamie appeared in the doorway. "I spotted Vivi as I was walking in. How awkward was that?"

"She wants to only communicate electronically going forward. Texts. Emails."

Jamie took the chair that Vivi had vacated. "She really wants that? And what about you?"

"Whether either of us truly wants it or not, it's what we'll do."

Then he leaned over his desk to grab the file

with the next problem that needed his attention, and wished that he could get over Vivi.

VIVI SAT NEXT to her mom in the doctor's waiting room, flipping through a magazine but not really paying attention to the pictures or articles. All she could think of since she'd gotten her mom's call about the appointment was what the doctor might say. The thought of it being bad news brought tears to her eyes.

She glanced over at her mom and took her hand. Her mom turned to her and tried to smile, but she seemed just as frightened about the appointment.

"Whatever it is, Mom, we'll fight this together."

Her mom squeezed her hand. "Thanks, baby."

Time seemed to move backward as they sat and waited for the nurse to call her mom's name. Finally, the nurse stood in the doorway and said, "Constance Carmack."

Her mom took a deep breath, then she and her mother both stood and followed the nurse down a series of hallways until they reached an examination room. Connie took a seat on the paper-covered table while the nurse took her vitals and made notes on her tablet. She gave them both a smile. "The doctor will be with you in a moment."

Vivi took a seat in a plastic-molded chair next to a window and glanced outside. It had been sunny when they had arrived, but clouds had formed and made the sky gloomy and foreboding. "Do you think we're going to get more snow?" she asked her mom. "It looks like we might."

"I don't care about the weather right now. I just want the doctor to come in and tell me what's wrong and then we can deal with it. Hopefully it's not as bad as I've been imagining."

Vivi got out of the chair and walked toward her mom. "I haven't slept all week since you called about today."

Her mom took her hand. "I'm so glad you could arrange the time off to come with me."

"Of course, I did. You're the only mom I've got." They both laughed at that.

Dr. Edwards arrived. "Ah, Mrs. Carmack, you brought your daughter with you. Good." He held out his hand to Vivi. "It's Viola?"

"Vivian."

"Right. I remember the faces, but the names often escape me."

He took a seat on a small, wheeled stool and read from the tablet in his hands. Vivi held on to her mom, rubbing her arm with her free hand. Her mom cleared her throat. "Be straight with me. What is it we're facing? Cancer? Heart disease?"

Dr. Edwards looked up and blinked at her. "No, no, nothing like that. You've developed type two diabetes."

Vivi frowned. "Mom's diabetic? Is it serious?"

"Yes, but very treatable with a good diet and regular exercise. We can start you on certain medications to help your blood sugar numbers improve. And given your family history of high blood pressure, it's important that we make these lifestyle changes right away."

Vivi plopped down in the chair as the doctor talked about reducing carbs and sugars in her mom's diet and boosting her intake of vegetables and lean proteins. Vivi held up a hand. "Wait. My mom's not dying?"

"If this were to go untreated, yes, she could. But with proper self-care and management, your mom can expect to live a long time."

He started to talk about how Connie could introduce more movement in her day. Something about counting steps and… Vivi tried to understand what he was saying. Her mom wasn't going to die? She'd been losing sleep imagining the loss and how she was going to cope. She'd cried and bargained in order to save her mom.

The doctor finished giving Connie his pep talk, handed her several pamphlets on diet and exercise and wrote a quick prescription to be started immediately. Vivi felt as if she couldn't breathe. He asked, "Do you have any questions, Mrs. Carmack?"

Her mom looked stunned but shook her head. Vivi shrugged. "Not right now, I guess."

"I know this is a lot to take in, so we'll meet in about a month to see where your numbers are and any improvement that we can see. Sound good?"

He handed her mom the prescription. "You both seem shocked. But I assure you, with this new direction and family support, we will see a change for the better. You're going to be fine."

When he left the room, Vivi burst into tears. Connie slid off the exam table and approached her. "Sweetie, what is it?"

"I thought you were dying."

"I'm not. This is good news. So why are you crying?"

"I spent hours worrying about something that isn't going to happen. Planning for the worst possible outcome. And for what?"

Her mom frowned at her. "I thought you would be happy."

"I am." Vivi was genuinely grateful that was all that was troubling her mother. "I'm relieved that it's not as bad as I thought it would be. But…" She wiped her face with her hands before her mom passed her a tissue from the box on the counter. "Have I been doing this with everything? Expecting the worst?"

"Are you just realizing that now?"

"Grandma died. Shelly moved away. You and Dad got divorced. The accident. The broken engagement. They were horrible things that happened."

"And you survived them. I'd even go as far as to say that you grew stronger because of them. Or maybe that should be in spite of them." Her mom put a hand on her shoulder. "Sweetie, I know you think that this seven-year cycle brings bad luck your way, but things just happen when they do."

"Brian tried to show me the same thing."

"Sounds like you've fallen for a very wise man."

Vivi looked up at her mom. "I haven't, though. I told you we broke up."

"A wise woman would realize that a man like Brian doesn't come around every day. And that if she really wanted to, she could repair the relationship. But the question is, are you willing to do the work it could take?"

BRIAN RUBBED HIS forehead and tried to focus on the papers before him. Since the accident, he'd found it increasingly difficult to concentrate on things for extended periods of time. Unfortunately for him, much of his job required reading lengthy proposals, contracts and budgets. He picked up the phone and dialed his assistant's extension. "Can you bring me some aspirin? This park commission's report is giving me a headache."

"On its way."

He returned to the screen and squinted his

eyes to continue reading but found it futile. He pushed away from the desk and rested his head on the back of his desk chair.

"Here."

That wasn't Jamie's voice. He opened his eyes to find Vivi standing there with a glass of water and two tablets in her palm. "I heard you need these."

He blinked as if half expecting her to disappear. He'd imagined her here often enough that it wouldn't be impossible for her to be a mirage. He reached out a hand and touched her shoulder. "You're here."

"I'm here."

He took the aspirin from her and popped them in his mouth before chasing them with a few gulps of water. Once he'd swallowed the medication, he set the glass on his desk. "What are you doing here? We don't have another meeting scheduled."

"No, we don't."

"And the last we spoke, you wanted to keep our communication to texts and emails." He looked into her eyes, trying to figure out if anything had changed. She did look a little different. More rested, perhaps. And there was something else. Peace?

She took a seat on the edge of his desk. "I was hoping you'd be willing to have dinner with me tonight."

His heart beat a little faster at her invitation, but he told himself not to appear too eager. "And why would I do that?"

"I think we need to talk."

Her eyes looked bright, as if she had a secret she was trying desperately to hold on to. But that didn't mean anything. Couldn't mean anything. "I think we said all there is to say. So if you're looking for some kind of closure…"

"What if I'm asking for a second chance? What if I realized I made a mistake and I want to make things right between us?"

"Actually, it would be your fifth chance. Or is it your sixth? I'm not sure we should do this, Vivi. It hasn't ended well for us so far."

His headache was only intensifying. "I'm sorry, I don't have the energy to discuss this with you right now, Vivi."

"So meet me for dinner. We can talk about it then—"

The office door opened, and Josh entered. "Oh, uh, Brian, I was just wanting to ask you about those budget figures."

He could feel Vivi's gaze on him, longed to ask where she wanted to eat tonight, but he wouldn't give in only to end up wondering how long it would be until things fell apart for them again. He couldn't do that to her or to himself.

"Vivian, I think it's time for you to leave."

She glanced from him to Josh and then back to him, before she closed the door behind her.

Josh spoke first. "I've always thought you were smart, but it looks like you've really done it this time."

"Don't, Josh. I can't argue with you both about this."

"Then don't argue. But at least hear what she has to say."

"I'm hurting, in more ways than one. I'm not sure—"

"You can be strong while also being kind and listen to her."

Brian brought the notepad he'd been scribbling on closer to him. "I'll have those figures for you before the meeting. I can't ask the committee to reschedule again."

"It's nice that the team has been so understanding toward you. I wish more people were like that."

Brian rolled his eyes and concentrated on the report.

VIVI ACCEPTED THE tissue that Cec held out to her. "He said no. I don't know what to do now, Cec."

"Can you blame the guy? You broke his heart." Cec stepped around her coffee table and slipped an arm around Vivi's shoulder.

"But to not even give me a chance to explain, to tell him what's different…" She dabbed at her eyes. "I'm not sure what comes next. He's never going to listen to what I have to say."

"So find a way to make him listen to you," Pops said.

Cec and Vivi turned to Pops, who opened his eyes. He was napping on the recliner. "What? It's not like I can sleep through your chattering." He set the recliner to rocking slightly. "The way I see it is, if he won't listen to you, you'll have to find the means to make it so that he has to hear you."

"Like a microphone?" Cec asked.

"That's one option. But he can still walk

away from that." Pops chuckled and gave a soft smile. "I remember this one time Gladys and I were fighting like cats and dogs. Both of us talking so loud and over each other's words that we couldn't hear what the other was saying. Then she turns on her heel and leaves the room. I was stunned. How could she just walk out in the middle of that?"

They waited several minutes for him to continue. Finally, Vivi asked, "So then what happened?"

Pops held up a finger. "Ah. You just figured out what Gladys did. That there's a lot that can be said when you don't say anything at all. I finally paid attention to what was concerning her and we sorted it out."

"So I'm supposed to say nothing? Wait for him to come to me and ask what it was that I have to tell him?" Vivi shook her head. "What if he doesn't want to know?"

"That's a risk you take."

Cec winced. "No, I think Pops's first idea of getting him to a place where he has to listen to you is better. Are there any elevators around here that we can trap you two together in? Or what about getting snowed in at a remote cabin?"

"You've been watching too many movies lately. Let's be realistic here."

"Maybe you haven't been watching enough. What you have with Brian is special, right?"

Vivi dabbed at her eyes again. "Worth fighting for, or at least, I think so." She crumpled the tissue in her hand and shrugged. "What if I can't make it work, though? What if I do run away again? I wouldn't do that to him another time, would I?"

"Those are the wrong questions. The only one that matters is, do you love him? Is that why you want to talk to him so much? Or is that you just want to be loved by him? Which isn't fair to either of you," Pops said. "That's what you have to figure out first."

He peered at her, as did Cec. Vivi sniffled, then blew her nose. "What if I do love him?"

Cec huffed and threw her hands in the air. "Pops is right. Answer the question. Do you love him?"

Vivi took a deep breath and thought about their words. Sure, she liked Brian. Admired him, even. But did she love him? She cared a lot for him. But love?

She thought of that night when she had waited for news on his condition after the accident. The thought of losing him had felt like a part of her would be lost, too.

She blinked and nodded slowly. She felt like that, felt that kind of pain because… because she loved him.

She loved him.

And while it was scary to think that things could happen to separate them, that he might not be able to love her anymore, she realized her love for him would never change. Because it had always been there despite her fears.

And it always would be. Curse or no curse, she would love him anyway.

She got to her feet and gave a short nod. "I have to find a way for him to hear me because I do love him."

Pops whooped and clapped, then turned to Cec. "This is better than those schmaltzy movies you've made me watch. Now, let's put our heads together and get this thing figured out."

BRIAN STOOD IN the renovated retail space and double-checked his phone for the message from his assistant. Mallory had said a new business owner was interested in opening a booth but wanted to check out the space first, as well as talk particulars. Usually, he would meet with new vendors in the office, but this person had insisted on meeting at the pop-up shop.

He glanced at his phone again. Booth number twenty-nine was near the back of the space, if he remembered correctly. With a new vendor in that spot, the occupation rate would be over 80 percent, which he had set as a goal at the beginning of the year. Business was good, and this would mean more revenue, more dollars being spent in Thora. A special thing for the community.

He gave a wave to Alyssa, a beekeeper, who ran a booth that sold candles made from beeswax. The last he'd heard, she would be expanding into a larger retail space in the summer since business was going so well.

He arrived at booth twenty-nine, but frowned. This space was supposed to be empty. Instead, it appeared to be staged for business already. Rocks had been attached into the shape of a heart on a canvas. In the middle of it, scrolled in bright red paint it read, "I love you, Brian."

He walked to the canvas and placed a

hand on it. A voice behind him said, "Some-one once told me that a rock store wouldn't work. But I thought I might give it a try."

Brian turned to see Vivi standing there, her hands behind her back. She gazed at him without faltering.

Brian frowned. "What is this? Did my assistant set me up?"

"She didn't know it was me. And I only want to talk."

"Is there something for us to talk about, Vivi? I'm not sure…" He began to leave, and she didn't say anything. Just stood there, her attention on him and only him. It didn't feel right to take another step away. "What did you want to say?"

"I've been so wrong, and you were right."

He felt a faint smile play on his lips. "That's a good way to start the conversation. Go on."

"You tried to tell me that it didn't matter what happened this year so long as we could face it together. And I thought that I had to keep you at a distance to protect you. To keep you from getting hurt."

"Vivi…"

She took a deep breath and looked into his eyes. "The thing is… I was only protecting myself. Protecting my own heart." She wrung her hands together. "I've been hurt so badly, and I wanted to keep from hurting again. Only, I discovered that I ache when I'm not with you. It hurts more to be apart than it ever did worrying about it when we were together."

He didn't know what to say, so he stayed silent. His heart ached as tears landed on her cheeks. Finally, she asked, "Is there any way that you could forgive me? Give us one more chance?"

"I don't know…"

"I love you and I know that you're going to need some time to get there, too, but I'm willing to wait."

He felt his mouth moving, but no words came out. Clearing his throat, he managed to say, "I'm sorry, you what?"

"It's like the sign says. I love you, Brian. And I hope that you still love me. Would you give me another chance to prove it?"

His heart seemed to have stopped, and he took a deep breath as if that would restart it. "You love me?"

She smiled. "I can't seem to help it, no matter how hard I try."

He smiled back.

"Even though this is the absolute worst time to fall in love, it doesn't matter. Because you're the best man I know. I don't think I've ever met someone who is so compassionate, kind and…"

"Nice?" He winced at the description. "You think I'm nice."

"I know you are. And that's exactly the kind of man I want." She looked down at their hands now joined together. "Are you still sure about us?"

He stroked her cheek with his free hand and looked deeply into Vivi's eyes. "The moment I bumped into you at that New Year's Eve party, I knew you were the one for me. You're beautiful, smart and passionate. And I recognized that together we would make a great team."

"So does that mean…"

"That we're going to try this for the sixth time?" He laughed and wiped her tears away. "But we'd better get it right this time because, after all, seven doesn't seem to be a very lucky number for you."

He rested his forehead against hers. "I don't think I could bear losing you again."

"I'm in this for good."

He stroked her cheek again, then kissed her softly at first, then pulled her in closer to deepen the embrace.

"What did he say?" he heard someone shout from the other side of the booth.

Vivi giggled and pointed. "My cohorts in this plan to win you back." She leaned away and yelled back, "He said yes!"

Several whoops and shouts filled the air. Brian's laugh joined Vivi's until he silenced them both with another kiss.

VIVI GRASPED THE first copy of the book and ran a hand over the title. *Moments in Thora's History.* Hard to believe that after all the work, she now held the proof of it in her hands. She opened the booklet to the table of contents and let her finger drift down the list of names of those who'd contributed. The cooperative senior citizens, as well as her top-notch students, who had all graduated and were now heading off to college, each intent on making their own mark on the world.

Brian came up behind her and rested his chin on her shoulder. "Pretty amazing, huh?"

"I can't believe it's finally here. And that we made the deadline for the fundraiser."

"Pre-sales are booming. We might have to order a second printing to meet demand."

She placed the book on his desk and smiled at him. "Now, is the business portion of our evening over?"

He gave a nod. "I'd say so. Unless you wanted to start planning for next year's book."

"No, I'd prefer to move to the date portion of our evening. Did you place our order at the diner?"

"I did."

"And I hope you don't mind taking me on a picnic now that it's warmer outside. At least we won't be shivering as we slurp soup."

"Hey, I thought you said it was fun."

"I believe my words were that it was *different*."

"And different is good?"

"When it comes to you, different is great." She put her arms around his neck and clasped her hands together. "I can't believe we're here. Together."

He drew her closer. "Exactly. Despite a car accident."

"And you breaking up with me."

"I believe that was mutual. And then me trying to stay away from you and failing."

"Then there was that horrible bout of food poisoning we both had."

Brian paled. "Yeah, that was bad. And then that fight you started."

"I started that fight?"

"Okay, we started?" He shook his head. "It doesn't matter though, does it? We made it to the summer and only have six more months to face before the new year. We're going to make it."

Vivi smiled. "You know, I believe we will. Because no matter what else the remainder of this year throws at us, we'll be able to face it."

"Together."

Her heart was full. "Nowhere else I'd rather be."

* * * * *

Get 3 FREE REWARDS!

We'll send you 2 FREE Books plus a FREE Mystery Gift.

FREE
Value Over
$20

Both the **Love Inspired**® and **Love Inspired**® Suspense series feature compelling
novels filled with inspirational romance, faith, forgiveness and hope.

Get 3 FREE REWARDS!

We'll send you 2 FREE Books plus a FREE Mystery Gift.

FREE
Value Over
$20

Both the **Harlequin® Special Edition** and **Harlequin® Heartwarming™** series feature compelling novels filled with stories of love and strength where the bonds of friendship, family and community unite.

YES! Please send me 2 FREE novels from the Harlequin Special Edition or Harlequin Heartwarming series and my FREE Gift (gift is worth about $10 retail). After receiving them, if I don't wish to receive any more books, I can return the shipping statement marked "cancel." If I don't cancel, I will receive 6 brand-new Harlequin Special Edition books every month and be billed just $5.49 each in the U.S. or $6.24 each in Canada, a savings of at least 12% off the cover price, or 4 brand-new Harlequin Heartwarming Larger-Print books every month and be billed just $6.24 each in the U.S. or $6.74 each in Canada, a savings of at least 19% off the cover price. It's quite a bargain! Shipping and handling is just 50¢ per book in the U.S. and $1.25 per book in Canada.* I understand that accepting the 2 free books and gift places me under no obligation to buy anything. I can always return a shipment and cancel at any time by calling the number below. The free books and gift are mine to keep no matter what I decide.

Choose one: ☐ **Harlequin Special Edition** (235/335 BPA GRMK) ☐ **Harlequin Heartwarming Larger-Print** (161/361 BPA GRMK) ☐ **Or Try Both!** (235/335 & 161/361 BPA GRPZ)

Name (please print)

Address   Apt. #

City   State/Province   Zip/Postal Code

Email: Please check this box ☐ if you would like to receive newsletters and promotional emails from Harlequin Enterprises ULC and its affiliates. You can unsubscribe anytime.

Mail to the **Harlequin Reader Service:**
IN U.S.A.: P.O. Box 1341, Buffalo, NY 14240-8531
IN CANADA: P.O. Box 603, Fort Erie, Ontario L2A 5X3

Want to try 2 free books from another series! Call 1-800-873-8635 or visit www.ReaderService.com.

*Terms and prices subject to change without notice. Prices do not include sales taxes, which will be charged (if applicable) based on your state or country of residence. Canadian residents will be charged applicable taxes. Offer not valid in Quebec. This offer is limited to one order per household. Books received may not be as shown. Not valid for current subscribers to the Harlequin Special Edition or Harlequin Heartwarming series. All orders subject to approval. Credit or debit balances in a customer's account(s) may be offset by any other outstanding balance owed by or to the customer. Please allow 4 to 6 weeks for delivery. Offer available while quantities last.

Your Privacy—Your information is being collected by Harlequin Enterprises ULC, operating as Harlequin Reader Service. For a complete summary of the information we collect, how we use this information and to whom it is disclosed, please visit our privacy notice located at corporate.harlequin.com/privacy-notice. From time to time we may also exchange your personal information with reputable third parties. If you wish to opt out of this sharing of your personal information, please visit readerservice.com/consumerschoice or call 1-800-873-8635. **Notice to California Residents**—Under California law, you have specific rights to control and access your data. For more information on these rights and how to exercise them, visit corporate.harlequin.com/california-privacy.

HSEHW23

THE NORA ROBERTS COLLECTION

40% OFF!

Get to the heart of happily-ever-after in these Nora Roberts classics! Immerse yourself in the beauty of love by picking up this incredible collection written by, legendary author, Nora Roberts!

YES! Please send me the **Nora Roberts Collection**. Each book in this collection is 40% off the retail price! There are a total of 4 shipments in this collection. The shipments are yours for the low, members-only discount price of $23.96 U.S./$31.16 CDN. each, plus $1.99 U.S./$4.99 CDN. for shipping and handling. If I do not cancel, I will continue to receive four books a month for three more months. I'll pay just $23.96 U.S./$31.16 CDN., plus $1.99 U.S./$4.99 CDN. for shipping and handling per shipment.* I can always return a shipment and cancel at any time.

☐ 274 2595   ☐ 474 2595

Name (please print)

Address   Apt. #

City   State/Province   Zip/Postal Code

> **Mail to the Harlequin Reader Service:**
> **IN U.S.A.:** P.O. Box 1341, Buffalo, NY 14240-8531
> **IN CANADA:** P.O. Box 603, Fort Erie, Ontario L2A 5X3

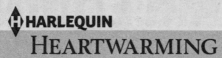
#487 THEIR SURPRISE ISLAND WEDDING

Hawaiian Reunions • by Anna J. Stewart

Workaholic Marella Benoit doesn't know how to have fun, even at her sister's Hawaiian wedding! Thankfully surfer Keane Harper can help. He'll show Marella how to embrace the magic of the islands—but will she embrace his feelings for her?

#488 A SWEET MONTANA CHRISTMAS

The Cowgirls of Larkspur Valley • by Jeannie Watt

Getting jilted before her wedding is bad enough, but now Maddie Kincaid is unexpectedly spending the holidays on a guest ranch with bronc rider Sean Arteaga. 'Tis the season to start over—maybe even with Sean by her side...

#489 HER COWBOY'S PROMISE

The Fortunes of Prospect • by Cheryl Harper

The history at the Majestic Prospect Lodge isn't limited to just the building—Jordan and Clay have a past, and now they're working together to restore the lodge's former glory. But it'll take more than that to mend their hearts...

#490 THE COWBOY AND THE COACH

Love, Oregon • by Anna Grace

Violet Fareas is more than ready for her new job coaching high school football. But convincing the community that she's capable—and trying to resist Ash Wallace, the father of her star player—is a whole new ball game!

HWCNM0823

HARLEQUIN
PLUS

Try the best multimedia subscription service for romance readers like you!

Read, Watch and Play.

Experience the easiest way to get the romance content you crave.

Start your **FREE TRIAL** at
<u>www.harlequinplus.com/freetrial</u>.